# THE GIRL IN APARTMENT 9

## A.J. RIVERS

*The Girl in Apartment 9*
Copyright © 2022 by A.J. Rivers

All rights reserved. Without limiting the rights under copyright reserved above, no part of this publication may be reproduced, stored in or introduced into retrieval system, or transmitted, in any form, or by any means (electronic, mechanical, photocopying, recording, or otherwise) without the prior written permission of both the copyright owner and the above publisher of this book.

This is a work of fiction. Names, characters, places, brands, media, and incidents are either the products of the author's imagination or are used fictitiously. The author acknowledges the trademarked status and trademark owners of various products referenced in this work of fiction, which have been used without permission. The publication/use of these trademarks is not authorized, associated with, or sponsored by the trademark owners.

# PROLOGUE

*There used to be light ahead of me.*
*When I thought about the future... there was one.*
*I wanted to do things. I wanted to be things.*
*And I believed I could.*
*That's not there anymore.*
*The light is gone.*
*Sometimes I wonder if it was really ever there to begin with. Maybe it was nothing but an illusion.*
*M says I'm right.*
*The light, the aspirations, the beliefs. They were there only because I was told they were.*
*I believed what I was told to believe.*

SHE DIDN'T KNOW IF ANYONE WAS LISTENING. SHE TOLD HERSELF she didn't care. This wasn't for them. Not really. It was for her. This was her way of having a voice. Outside of this space, she was silenced. Even when she did speak, it was nothing more than a recording. She opened her mouth and relied on words already spoken to tumble out. Her mind gathered them back up—polished them, recycled them, broke phrases apart and stitched others together. Readied them to fall out again. They were all the same.

When she spoke, it was in stale, reused words. When she laughed, it felt like sawdust.

None of it meant anything.

It was only when she was here, the only light in the dark apartment coming from the glow of the computer screen, that she felt like she was saying new words. When she opened her mouth, fresh, cold words of reality and truth flowed out. She didn't laugh.

She was doing it for herself. To give herself that chance to speak. But she wasn't alone in the world, as much as she felt like she was. If she'd really been doing it only for herself, she wouldn't post the videos. She could create them and put them in a folder on her computer, hide them away where no one else would ever know they existed. She could revisit them when she wanted to hear them, if she ever did. And if she really never wanted them heard, she would simply erase them.

Instead, she sent them into the world. She released those videos to where anyone climbing through the circuitry hell of the blackened corners of the internet could find them and immerse themselves in her fog.

She didn't care if anyone was listening. Not that she didn't care if she was speaking into nothingness, but that she didn't care if there was someone on the other end, playing voyeur as she bared everything inside her. Maybe if someone did happen to stumble upon her, it was because they needed to. Like the tendrils of fate had wrapped themselves around their hands and forced them to watch. They needed to hear what she had to say. After all, that was how she had been found—right when she needed to be the most.

*All my life, I was told I was going places. I was going to be somebody.*

*It never occurred to me to wonder why I wasn't already.*

*Wasn't I somebody just by merit of being alive? Of existing? Of thinking and breathing and living and taking up space in this world?*

*It's only recently that I realized maybe that's the point. Those things don't make me somebody. I was taking up space, but that was all I was doing. And it's still all I'm doing.*

*It's getting harder to pull myself out of the darkness even for a few minutes at a time. The longer I keep trying to walk forward, the more I find myself getting dragged into the past. I can't let go of it. Or maybe it can't let go of me. It dug its claws into me, and I've learned that the more I struggle to try to get free of it, the deeper the claws sink. I'm helpless to do anything but hang from them.*

*So many times, I've been told to always look for the light at the end of the tunnel. From the first time I felt myself sinking into depression, that was the image that was given to me to keep me going forward. The doctor, my family, my friends, my teachers... they all told me there was a light. I just had to keep moving toward it and I would get through.*

*And for a long time, that light was there because they said it was there. I could see it because I felt like I had to. If all of them were saying it was there, it had to be. If I didn't see it, that meant there was something wrong with me, or that there wasn't any point in anything I was doing or had done. It meant there wasn't any point in everything I'd gotten through. I'd survived. I'd gotten to the point where I could look at myself in the mirror again. I was still there, and it didn't mean anything.*

*So, I told myself there was a light ahead of me. I repeated it enough so I could see it for myself. All I needed to do was keep moving toward it and eventually, I would get there.*

*There were even times when I thought I was getting close. Life was better. I could breathe. I even let myself think for a while there that I'd gotten to that elusive place. I was somebody.*

Her shoulders tightened with those words. It was hard to say them, and heat washed over her cheeks and down her chest when they came out of her mouth. If there was anyone out there watching, they wouldn't know about that reaction. With her back to the camera, she stayed anonymous. Outside of this place, she had no voice. Here, she had no face.

She wondered how many people knew both halves of her—the one with no voice and the one with no face—but didn't put them together. They saw her smile like a puppet, heard her recycled words and her sawdust laugh. They thought she was perfect.

Then they stepped out of the sunlight. They pulled back the covers and burrowed inside. Here they saw the shadows on her back and the heave of her shoulders, heard her honest words and no laughter. And still, they thought she was perfect.

In both places, she was what they needed, but it was getting harder to ever feel like *she* was what she needed. That anything was what she needed. Time was running out.

*I know better now.*

*That was all just another illusion. I've never been more afraid than when I started to see the truth about myself. Those crippling moments brought me* back to the tragedy and how helpless I felt after. The guilt crushed me both times. The first time, for my family. The second time, for me.

The light I thought I was getting close to started to get farther away. The tunnel kept getting longer. It didn't matter how far I went, how hard I tried, how much I stuffed everything down and pretended I wasn't going through what I was, I never got closer. Then it just started to fade.

I tried to hold onto it. If you're listening and you care, I want you to know that. I didn't just let it go. I fought. Some days, I'm still fighting. M tells me I don't have to fight. I'm worth more than fighting. I'm worth more than putting myself through this. When I hear that, I believe it. I wonder why I'm fighting when I can't even say what I'm fighting for.

Remember when I said I looked into the future and saw things? Wanting to do things and be things?

Now I can't even say that sentence because there's no end to it. Just starting it feels false. When I look into the... what? I don't know where to go from there because the word "future" doesn't mean anything to me anymore. I can't look ahead of myself and see a future. I don't see anything. It's only darkness.

I want to see it. I want to want things again.

But I'm coming to understand I never will. That's not for me. Maybe I can't see a future ahead of me because there isn't one. M says our hearts know what is waiting for us. When we envision what's ahead, and really listen, our hearts will tell us what is possible.

I'm starting to listen.

I don't know what else I can do. I've tried. I keep trying. But every time I close my eyes, I see them. I hear them talking to me. I feel them with me. They know I'm living on stolen time. I'm losing bits of myself because they should never have been there to begin with.

I'm like the light everyone around me sees. I'm what I am because it's what they say I am. I'm here, I exist, because they think I do. But the longer it goes on, the more obvious it is that I'm just taking up space. They can't keep willing me into being forever. Eventually, I have to become what I really am.

I'm afraid to find out what that is.

I'm doing the best I can. I just don't know how much longer I can keep trying. It keeps getting harder and I don't know how much more I can take, or how much more I can pretend.

More and more I know that M is the only one who really understands me, or even tries to. Thank you, my dearest friend, for being there for me and wanting what's best for me, even when it's not what you would want. I can't tell you how much I appreciate you. Always.

She reached behind her and ended the recording so her back stayed to the camera. Turning around, she made sure the footage was saved before turning off her computer. She'd deal with editing and posting it later. That was her usual routine. When she sat down to record, she rarely knew what she was going to say. There was just something aching right in the center of her chest, and she needed to get it out. She'd sit down at the computer and talk until the ache lessened. Then she'd walk away from it. Later she'd come back and use the distance to sift through what she'd said and get it ready to post.

She gathered pajamas and got in the shower. The hot water and smell of soap soothed her, but as she walked out of the bathroom, a sound at the front of the apartment made her muscles tense again. She was supposed to be alone.

There was another sound, something scraping across glass. The student apartment was far too small for sound to be lost before it got from the combination living and dining room to the bathroom positioned beside one bedroom and across the hall from hers. The sounds weren't carrying from another apartment or from the street. There was someone there.

She started to call out, but the hollow greeting stopped in her throat. Instead, she walked toward the sound. Turning the corner into the living room, she noticed something flickering. Before she could process what she was seeing, she felt someone step up behind her and a large hand clamp down over her mouth.

# CHAPTER ONE

*Now*

I STOP WITH A PAIR OF LEGGINGS HALFWAY TO THE SUITCASE OPEN on my bed, gripping the phone in my hand tightly.

"Miley Stanford?" I ask. "You knew her?"

"Yes," Angelo confirms. "I didn't want to say anything while you were here because I didn't want the others asking a lot of questions. I figured the less they know, the better, but then I got to thinking about it and I know you're trying to help."

My mind is spinning as I drop the leggings into the suitcase and sit down at the edge of the mattress. When I'd shown him and the other members of Salvador Marini's house staff the picture of the missing woman, I hadn't been expecting them to recognize her. Not really.

The woman he should have recognized was Serena. She was the one complicit in all the Emperor's plans; the one posing as a goddess to lure victims for him to destroy. Miley had disappeared long before that happened, long before the woman who had taken her identity had infiltrated the Emperor's inner circle while secretly working for Leviathan.

But now Serena is dead and there's no sign of Miley. Until now.

"The less they know about what?" I ask.

"What he did. Or what he might have done. What you told us really shook Louisa up, and I've never seen her shaken up. I don't want to add to any of it if I can help it. But I lost your number. I knew she had it, so I'm using her phone, but she can't hear me. I don't want to upset her."

I nod even though Angelo can't see me through the phone. "No, no. I get it. That makes sense. Are you willing to talk to me more about it?"

"Yes, if you think it might make a difference," he replies.

"Great," I say. "I'm actually getting ready to go out of town for a couple of days, but when I get back, I'll get in touch with you. Should I call Louisa's phone?"

"No. I'll give you mine," Angelo says.

I rush over to the nightstand to grab the pad and pen I keep in the drawer and jot down the number he gives me. I offer him my email address in return.

"If there's anything you want to tell me before I get back with you, go ahead and email me. Thank you for saying something. Any information you have could be really valuable."

We get off the phone and I look up as Sam comes into the bedroom with a basket of clean laundry.

"Any information who has?" he asks.

"That was Angelo—one of Marini's house staff. He was calling to say he recognized the picture I had when I went to interview them," I explain.

"He recognized her?" Sam asks.

He unceremoniously dumps the entire basket of clothes right into the middle of the bed, but I'm too distracted by the conversation I just had to even be aggravated by it.

"That's what he said. That he knew the girl in the picture and her name was Miley," I tell him.

"But that shouldn't be that much of a surprise, right? I mean, I know that you said Marini never brought her to his house so the household staff wouldn't know who she was, but maybe he did introduce her to Angelo, like at an event or something. He was supposedly really into her. At least for a little while before he murdered her," Sam points out.

"Yeah, can't forget that little detail," I say. "And you're right, that's not totally out of the realm of possibility. Serena did go to a lot of events with him, and Angelo might have crossed paths with her in some context. But I'm not even at that point yet."

"What do you mean?" Sam asks.

He's sifting through the laundry pulling out individual socks and seems to be making a pile of them in front of him rather than actually pairing them off to go into the suitcase.

"I showed them two pictures," I say. "Serena and Miley."

Sam's eyebrows raise at the revelation. He knows what I'm getting at.

"So, which Miley was he talking about? If it's Serena, that means Marini did introduce them and he thinks her name is Miley because of that."

"But if it's the actual Miley, this just got a lot more interesting," I complete his thought.

My mind goes to the necklace still wrapped in the corner of the handkerchief sitting on my desk. I know it belonged to Miley. What I need to know now is how it got to Myrtle Beach, hanging on a statue for me to find.

"Emma," Sam starts. I know that tone. It tells me this wouldn't be the moment for me to mention the socks. "You said you were done. You weren't going to mess with that case or anything else for Jonah anymore."

"I know," I say. "And trust me, I'd like nothing more in this world than to not ever think about Jonah again. It would be amazing to know I really don't have to deal with him anymore, that he's gone and out of my life. But I'm not there. Not yet."

"Why not?" he asks. "This doesn't have anything to do with you. The Bureau isn't handling the case. The police aren't involved. She isn't even officially recognized as a missing person."

"Doesn't that bother you?" I ask. "She didn't just stop existing when Serena took her place. Jonah superimposed reality. He took one human being and used her as a patch to cover up the hole left by another human being disappearing. Miley was a person all her own before she had anything to do with this whole situation, and wherever she is, she's still a person. The fact that no one knows what happened to her, and no one is even trying to figure it out, isn't okay."

"But why does that person have to be you?" Sam asks. "Don't you think you have enough on your plate right now?"

"And most of it is wrapped up in this. The police department's official investigation into Marini and his crimes might be closed, but until I know the names of every person he killed and can return them to their families, I'm not done. I want to know what he did and who helped him, and I want to make sure they suffer for it. I'm not going to pretend what happened to Dean didn't happen. Or that Eric didn't almost die. For all we know, there could still be people out there being tortured. Someone helped him, and until we find out who that was and stop them, this isn't over.

"Miley is a part of that. She and Serena are inextricably linked to each other, and to Marini. I still don't know what Miley has to do with him, but I can't just put her aside and keep pursuing everything else. If I'm going to finish this, I have to finish it all. This isn't about Jonah, Sam. It's about the victims. I'm not hunting him anymore. When I can take him down, I will. But it's not my focus."

The front door opens, and I hear Dean calling out to us.

"You're coming with us," Sam says.

It's not a question. I nod.

"Of course, I am. I told Angelo I'll get in touch with him when I get back." I lean back so I can shout more in the direction of the door. "We're up here. Just getting finished with packing." I straighten back up and start adding more to the suitcase. "I'm not going to miss the chance to celebrate Xavier coming home from prison."

"It was only a few weeks," Sam counters.

"In *federal prison*," I repeat. "For something he didn't do."

"No," Sam says, shaking his head. "For something he did do. He volunteered to go in there. That's all on him."

"And he got us invaluable information and made it out. He deserves a celebration. So, we're going to the beach," I shrug.

"He's going to bury me in the sand," Sam grumbles.

I nod. "Probably." I toss a few more things into the suitcase. "But if it gets to be too much for you, just go into the water to about your shoulder level."

"Is he a bee?" Sam asks.

"No, but he doesn't like being too forward with the ocean. He says it has the ability to pick him up and throw him out, so he doesn't go far enough in to offend it."

"Of course. How did I not know that?"

I zip up the filled suitcase and pick it up, patting Sam on the cheek and kissing him.

"I'm not sure. Come on. Bring your sock pile."

I make my way down the stairs to find that Dean has already broken into the bag of road trip snacks I packed, and Xavier is already wearing his swimsuit.

"It's a bit of a drive until we get there," I say. "Are you sure you want to be in your swimsuit for that long?"

"I don't like changing clothes in the middle of the day," Xavier says. "They don't get their full use. And this way I fit in with the locals."

I don't mention that the locals probably don't drive around in their swimsuits. He probably won't notice. To him, he'll be rolling like the beach bums.

# CHAPTER TWO

*Van*

**V**AN PULLED UP THE SEARCH HISTORY ON THE COMPUTER IN front of him and scanned through all the entries for the last several weeks. He thought about leaving a few of them in place, so maybe it wouldn't look so obvious, but ended up deleting them all. When he was finished, he tucked it back where he'd found it and slipped out, leaving the room behind him silent.

His phone rang in his pocket, and he scrambled to pull it out and answer it. The voice on the other end of the line was angry.

"Where the hell are you? You were supposed to be here fifteen minutes ago."

He hadn't realized how much time had passed. He'd been in there for far longer than he intended to be.

"I'm sorry. I had some car trouble earlier, but I'll be there as soon as I can."

"You better be. Next time you're not going to show up on time, you need to call."

The line went quiet. He remembered the way landline phones sounded when they were slammed down in old TV shows and movies. It was a much more satisfying sound than the faint click that came with someone hanging up at the end of a cell call. If it could really be described as a click at all. It was more like the reverse, a sudden absence of sound that was so defined it seemed to take on something audible of its own.

Van glanced around as he put his phone away and started along the cracked sidewalk that led to a narrow alley between the apartment buildings. He didn't think anyone had seen him there. He hadn't parked his car out front the way he usually did to make sure a neighbor peering out their front window or someone walking by wouldn't be able to track his movements that morning. He was expected somewhere else. To anyone who mattered, that was where he needed to be. Even if no one actually saw him there.

Being late was a major mistake. It meant it would be easy to figure out he wasn't where he said he was. He'd have to find a way to confirm his lie, to make it so that he could explain away the hiccup in his timeline. But he could manage that. He'd cover his paces and smooth out his schedule so no one would question him. It was the least of his worries right now.

What mattered was keeping them from finding out.

Lila was waiting for him when he pulled up. Her arms were crossed tight over her chest like she was cold despite the warm breeze that had just started waking up the blooming trees that lined the sidewalks. But Lila was always cold.

"I can't stay," he said before he even got to her. "I'm late already."

"I don't care. Did you tell her?"

Van felt his spine freeze. He nodded. There wasn't anything else to do.

"Of course."

Lila thawed just a little. There was even something close to a smile on her lips.

"Good. So, it's done then."

Van ran his tongue across lips that felt suddenly like sandpaper.

"It's done."

# CHAPTER THREE

I GET HOME FROM THE BEACH A FEW DAYS LATER THE SAME WAY I GET home any time I visit the beach: wishing I was still there. There's never enough time in the sand for me. I'm blissfully happy settling onto a blanket spread out under my classic rainbow beach umbrella and letting the day drift by on the salty air and sound of the waves.

And yet, I can't imagine picking up my life and moving to be closer to the beach. Sherwood is my home, and I know it always will be. I'm happy and comfortable here. This is where I feel closest to my family, where I fell in love with Sam, where I can still talk to people who knew my grandparents. People who thought I was just a normal grandchild who came to spend time with them occasionally rather than always being more or less on the run.

That doesn't make it easier to leave the beach. Those few days I got to spend there with Dean, Sam, and Xavier were some of the most fun I've had in a long time. They were the perfect way to get everything off my mind. Sam survived getting buried in the sand; Xavier briefly got his shoulders wet. I got time to sink down into the sand and let the stinging heat remind me of those kinds of hazy days from the past that meld together and take bits of each other to craft golden memories.

But life's waiting here. It's time to get back.

It's late enough in the day when we get back to Sherwood that Sam and I take a shower, finish up the picnic food from our cooler for dinner, and go right to bed. The next morning I'm up early, my mind already zeroed back in on the call from Angelo right before we left.

He didn't call or message me while I was gone. I try to tell myself I let him know I was going out of town and would get in touch with him when I was back, but there's still a little twinge of disappointment in the back of my mind. Part of me hoped to already know more by this point. And at the same time, there was that one key missing piece I had to have before I could even start sifting the meaning out of what he was going to tell me.

Which picture was he talking about?

I go back and forth with which one I think it is as I drive down to see him. I called him while I was brewing coffee, wanting to catch him before he went to work, and he let me know he had some free time later when he could meet. During that conversation, I wanted to ask him which picture he was talking about but stopped myself. I don't want to let on that there is any question about it until I'm right there and can gauge his reaction.

Angelo seems like a good guy, and I don't have anything overt to make me suspicious of him, but that's not enough. If this case has proven anything to me, it's that chameleons exist among us. People can easily look you in the eye and lie. They can move among others without hesitation or concern that someone will detect the way they shift and change to suit their current circumstances.

I'm a good reader of people. Observation and noticing details in chaos are skills that have carried me through many of my most complicated investigations. I'm finding that ability to be even more important recently as people around me become more adept at hiding behind the illusion they've created.

Angelo is waiting at the fountain in the park where he directed me. A nearby coffee cart smells incredible, and I wave at him as I walk directly over to it. He's already gripping a cup, so I buy one for myself along with a couple of pastries and bring them over.

"Hi, Angelo," I say as I make my way toward him. "Thank you for meeting with me."

"Absolutely," he nods. "I'm sorry for not telling you everything right from the beginning."

I look around and see a bench off to the side, away from the people clustered around the fountain enjoying the late spring weather. We cross to it and sit. He accepts the pastry I hold out to him but sets it on his thigh rather than eating it.

"I understand why you didn't want to say anything in front of the others. What matters is you're willing to talk to me about it now." I pause and he nods, so I set down my coffee, wipe crumbs from my fingertips, and take printouts of the two pictures from my bag. "Just for official confirmation, could you point out the picture you were talking about?"

I ask it casually, like it's just basic procedure rather than like I'm actually questioning him. Without hesitation, Angelo points to the image of the real Miley.

"Her," he confirms. "That's Miley."

I hear the breath catch in his chest for a second and he forces it out. He didn't just know of her. He hadn't just seen her a couple of times or been introduced to her in passing. Seeing the picture of her is affecting him in a way it only would if he actually knew her. She meant something to him.

"Okay. Perfect. What can you tell me about her? How did you know her?" I ask.

"You already know she's missing," Angelo says. "Or, at least, she hasn't been heard from in a long time."

I nod. "Yes."

The way he worded that strikes me, but I decide to put it aside and let him keep talking.

"I met her about a year before she disappeared. We were at a rock climbing event."

My reaction comes so fast, I don't have the time to conceal it. My face twists and my head pulls back in confusion.

"Rock climbing event?" I ask.

That's so far removed from anything I'd heard about Miley, and all the bits and pieces of her life I'd found hidden away in the house Serena took over. A picture had been painted of a spoiled, wealthy girl whose parents pried her from their home long after most people would be independent. She showed horses and favored expensive fashion. She clung close to the lifestyle her parents gave her and did little to break out of that mold. She certainly didn't strike me as the kind to strap herself into a harness and attempt to scale a wall.

"I belong to an outdoor adventure club—the Blue Ridge Backpackers. We meet up a couple of times a month to do things like rock climb, camp, kayak."

"So, this was outdoor rock climbing?" I ask.

The concept of Miley scrambling up an actual mountain is even more difficult to wrap my head around than her trying out a contained, regulated indoor course. Riding in dressage shows is the most athletic activity I got any indication of her participating in—unless swimming during lavish island vacations counted.

"Yes," Angelo says. He lets out the dry bits of a laugh that can't fully form. "The look on your face is accurate."

I shake my head slightly to reset my expression. "Sorry. I didn't mean to look like anything. I just… from what I know about her, that doesn't seem to really fit."

"It didn't. At least not at the beginning. That was actually what made me talk to her in the first place. The club had an open house, one of those events designed to get new people involved and let them try it out. Kind of a welcoming thing for newcomers. There were definitely a good number of people there who didn't seem to have any idea what they were doing, but Miley stood out from them.

"She looked completely out of place. I remember glancing over at her and thinking she looked like she'd shown up late to class on the first day of school, then realized she'd gone into the wrong classroom and was debating whether she should stay and try to blend in or figure out a subtle way to escape."

"Do you remember what she was wearing?" I ask. "I mean, was she actually there intentionally?"

"Yes," Angelo nods. "She was wearing all the right gear. And I mean all the right gear. Expensive stuff, the kind of newfangled state-of-the-art gear twenty-year veterans don't even have. This was a woman who knew how to shop. She'd decided she was going to participate in this activity and went ahead and bought everything she could find that went along with it. Clothes, shoes, all the fun accessories and toys. She was prepped to the nines and had absolutely no clue what she was doing.

"It was adorable, so I went to talk to her. She introduced herself and told me it felt totally crazy for her to be doing something like that, but she was excited. She asked if I was new, too, and I told her I wasn't, so I could help her if she wanted. We spent the rest of the event together, and by the end of it, she decided to join the club."

"You said she was adorable," I say. "Were you interested in her? As more than someone to crawl around on the sides of mountains with?"

This laugh was a little fuller than the last.

"Not at first," he tells me. "Don't get me wrong, she's beautiful, and it was adorable to see her decked out in her elaborate gear with a look somewhere between confusion and abject terror on her face. But that day I really was just approaching her as a member of the club. She obviously wanted to try, or at least she wanted to want to try, and I didn't want her to give up before she even took a chance."

"And she joined the club that day? So, I'm guessing she ended up being good at it?" I ask.

He chuckles, the sound softened with nostalgia. "Not particularly. She only got a couple of feet off the ground. But she enjoyed it and she said it made her feel free. I didn't know what she meant, but it sounded like something she needed."

"And you said you weren't interested in her at first. Does that mean you did end up becoming attracted to her? Did the two of you date?"

"No. After she joined the club, we started spending time together regularly. We had the events with the club, but she also wanted to meet up to try other things or practice what we were doing for the next event. She told me she'd never gone camping or kayaking or hiking. The normal types of things the club did were totally foreign to her, so she and I started doing them together. We got to be really close, and I started having feelings for her. But when I told Miley about them, she said she didn't feel the same way," Angelo says.

"Did that bother you?" I ask.

He shakes his head without hesitation. "No. I mean, obviously, it's a little disappointing any time you want to pursue something more with someone and it isn't reciprocated, but the feelings weren't overly strong. It wasn't like I was falling in love with her. I enjoyed her friendship and was happy to just keep that going."

That type of declaration would generally be cause to take note in a situation like this. Maybe not suspicion right off the bat, but certainly something to pay attention to. As much as we as people like to believe we've evolved and developed into a new version of the species, the truth is humans are still susceptible to the same kinds of impulses and triggers that we always have been. Rejection and unrequited love are two of the most common roots of attacks and murder. A man stating he had feelings for a woman who wasn't receptive to them is a red flag when that woman then goes missing.

But I believe Angelo. The way he's talking about Miley is definitely friendly, and even affectionate, but I don't sense any kind of resentment or pining. He seems sad because he misses his friend, not because she's the one who got away.

"Did she ever tell you about any guys she was interested in? Did she have a boyfriend, or someone she was even casually dating?" I ask.

The same kind of uncomfortable expression crosses his face as did when we were at Louisa's house. He looks uncertain, like he's holding something in and doesn't know if he wants to let it out. I don't push. I sit and sip my coffee, nibbling through my pastry until he's ready to speak. This is clearly hard for him, and I've learned pressuring someone who is voluntarily helping in an investigation is rarely really beneficial.

"I don't know his name," Angelo finally admits.

"Alright," I nod. "But there was somebody."

"Yes."

"Did she meet him through the club?"

"No. It was Marini's nephew."

# CHAPTER FOUR

"**H**IS NEPHEW?" SAM ASKS.

I nod, prying off my shoes and tossing them to the side of the front door. One of these days I'm going to be an adult who brings my shoes to my bedroom as soon as I take them off rather than just abandoning them wherever they fall when I walk through the door. Today is not that day.

"That's what Angelo said."

"I thought he didn't have any relatives," Sam muses.

He's sitting on the couch in the living room holding a piece of pizza halfway to his mouth. His phone is still resting on the arm beside him from where we were talking as I drove into town and walked up the sidewalk to our house. I lean over the arm and kiss his temple, then steal a bite of his pizza.

"That's what they told me," I shrug. "Well, actually what they told me was that he didn't have any children. I asked who was going to inherit his estate and all Louisa and the others could tell me was that he didn't have any children so they didn't know who would inherit it."

"But you haven't heard anything about a nephew coming to claim the property, or making a statement about his death, or anything?" he asks.

"No," I say. "But there could be a reason for that. I'll be right back."

I head into the kitchen to get my own plate of pizza and a drink. It's been a long time since that pastry and cup of coffee in the park, and my stomach is letting me know it does not approve of my unintentional foray into intermittent fasting.

"Way to leave me hanging," he calls.

"I'm just getting some pizza. I'll be there in just a second. Don't panic."

"You know you shouldn't say you'll be right back. Rules of horror," Sam says.

"Well, if there's an axe-wielding madman hiding in the refrigerator waiting to get me, should I offer him some pizza?" I ask.

"The one with the vegetables," he says. "The chunks of tomatoes are too big."

I load up a plate and carry it along with a cup of sweet tea from the refrigerator, which was predictably movie villain-free, into the living room.

"You know," I comment, dropping down onto the couch beside my husband, "if there's a killer getting ready to come after me because I declared I would be right back, the least you could do would be to offer him some of the good pizza as a distraction."

"Maybe he likes chunks of tomatoes on his pizza," Sam shrugs.

"No one likes chunks of tomatoes on their pizza, Sam. It's all a marketing ploy."

I bite down into the pepperoni, pineapple, and onion slice I picked up first.

"Fair enough. Anyway, I'm still hanging. What could be the reason that the nephew wouldn't be inheriting Marini's estate?" Sam asks.

"There are a couple of them. First, the staff wasn't exactly kept abreast of everything going on in Marini's life. He saw them as below him and wouldn't have introduced them to people who mattered to him, especially his family. Angelo only knows of the guy as his nephew because he was with Marini a lot and one day Angelo heard him introduce the guy as his nephew to somebody who came to the house. He didn't say his name, only that it was his nephew."

"That's strange," Sam notes.

"I thought so. But that's what brings us to why he wouldn't have come forward to claim the estate or even be a part of the aftermath of his death. You'd think a nephew would at least come forward to make a statement about the death, or want information from the police, or plan a funeral. Something. But no. And here's the reason: he's missing."

Sam stares at me silently for a few seconds. I stare back at him.

"Missing?" he finally asks.

"There it is." I take another bite of my pizza and chase it with tea. "Yes. Missing. At least, that's the best way Angelo can describe it, according to him. The supposed nephew used to hang around Marini's house all the time, but Angelo says he hasn't seen him in a couple of years."

"A couple of years?" Sam asks. "That timing sounds familiar."

"Doesn't it? Now, apparently there wasn't ever any verified relationship between the two of them, but Angelo said he brought Miley by the house a couple of times just very briefly and he noticed there seemed to be an attraction between the two of them. She even asked about him. Wanted to know everything Angelo did about the guy. Which, of course, was nothing."

"So, all he knew was that the two of them looked at each other and seemed interested? They never actually interacted?" Sam asks.

"Not as far as he knew. He didn't have any kind of personal information about the guy to give her. Not even his name, remember. And she never mentioned to him that she found out anything about him."

"That's not very much to go on."

"It's not. But since we have so little to go on we might actually have negative stuff to go on, I'm happy for anything. And you have to admit, it does seem interesting that the two of them disappeared at around the same time. Angelo said as soon as he couldn't get in touch with Miley anymore and didn't see the supposed nephew hanging around, the first thing that came to his mind was that they were together," I say.

"That's a big leap to make," Sam says.

"It is. They never even said hello to each other that Angelo witnessed, but he said that really wasn't all that unexpected. He didn't bring her to the house very much. That was heavily frowned upon by Marini. It was considered unprofessional to have any guests at the house, even if it was only for a few minutes while they were picking up a paycheck or even doing extra work he called them in to do. Angelo was also protective of Miley and didn't like the idea of her being around Marini."

"Why is that?" Sam asks. "You said they didn't know anything about his extracurricular activities."

"They didn't. But anybody near that man for long could sense that something was off about him. He was charming as hell, but that is very frequently a bad thing, especially when it comes packaged in a dude that is known among his staff for being rude, nasty, and even cruel. It seems like a reach for him to think the two of them were together, but at the same time, what else was he supposed to think?

"Apparently, there was enough of a vibe between them even just looking at each other, and with whatever Miley asked about him, that Angelo could tell there was a strong interest. It's not out of the realm of possibility that they were able to connect somehow away from Angelo and decided not to tell him about it. Whatever happened, it's an odd situation. But it also aligns with what I was already thinking. This was Marini's doing."

# CHAPTER FIVE

*Miley*
*One year before disappearance*

F ROM THE MOMENT SHE FIRST SAW HIM, SHE KNEW HE WOULD change her life. Nothing would ever be the same.

Angelo didn't want to bring her by the house where he worked. He didn't get into it with her, but she knew by the way he talked about his boss that they didn't get along. But he paid decently, and Angelo had close friends and family working for him as well, so he tried not to rock the boat. He didn't say it outright, but Miley got the feeling he was afraid that if he crossed his boss, the wealthy, powerful man would make sure Angelo never worked again.

The few times Angelo did talk about him, it was in an almost hushed tone, like he thought someone was going to report back about what he was saying. None of it intimidated Miley. She was accustomed to money and to the people who had it. Not that she told Angelo that. She didn't want him to know about her family or the way she grew up. What they had was nothing like what the man he called Boss Man had, of course. They didn't have quite that level of luxury in their lives. But it was still far more than what Angelo was used to.

And she didn't want him to know. She wanted to separate herself from it as much as she could. Her whole life, she'd let herself be defined by her parents and what they gave her, what they told her to be. For a long time, it didn't bother her. It didn't occur to her for it to. She never did without, and she always had what she wanted. So there were times when she wondered if she actually ever wanted anything, or if she just picked up on the cues around her to decide what she would aspire to.

Then there came that moment when her parents were gone and she had the feeling deep in the pit of her stomach that they wouldn't be coming back anytime soon, if at all. In that moment, she realized something incredible. She could decide.

Not just whether she wanted something, or what she wanted, or even if she wanted something at all.

She could decide who she was. She didn't have to continue to follow the path they laid out for her. She could find one of her own.

It wasn't that she resented her parents, or that she didn't appreciate everything they'd done for her. They'd given her a life so many would envy. The way they'd done it was on them. She'd promised herself when she was very young and coming to the realization that her parents weren't like the other adults she encountered that she would never judge them. Or at least that she would do her best not to. It wasn't her job to determine who they should be or what they should do with their lives.

And yet it didn't cross her mind that she should question them making those same decisions for her.

Until it did. And once it did, the world opened. She knew there would always be people who questioned her ability to live a life of her choosing, away from the control and the guidance of her parents. They would always wonder if she could make the right decisions. But that was just the thing. Miley didn't need to make the right decisions.

After a lifetime of having everything written out for her, everything planned and proscribed, every detail right down to her identity crafted in a way that held her captive even as it promised to give her the world, she was more than ready to make some mistakes. They could keep thinking anything they wanted to about her. They could think she was still desperate to cling to her parents, or that she was floating along with no purpose, just continuing to let them draw her along like on a string.

What really mattered was that she knew she was venturing out. The old cliché talked about spreading her wings, and she'd never really thought about it before, but that was exactly what this felt like. It was like there were parts of her body, muscles and bones and veins pumping with blood, that she never knew she had. And she was finally discovering how to use them.

Angelo had been a huge part of that. He didn't question her. He had no expectations of her. He didn't belittle her or make her feel like she wasn't good enough, even when she most certainly wasn't good enough. He let her try what she wanted to try and fail if she was going to, then decide whether she wanted to try it again or just move on to something else. It was refreshing and empowering, as much as she'd come to hate that word. If she was ever going to use it, it should be for something like this.

She was getting used to the life she was living. But then Angelo told her they needed to go by the Boss Man's house to pick up something he'd forgotten. He didn't want to bring her. He warned her not to try to be friendly if Boss Man was there. He wouldn't greet her, and very well could make some disparaging comment. Just let it roll over her, knowing it wasn't actually personal. He hated everyone. Even the people he purported to like.

They were only going to be there for a minute, but that was long enough for her to see the man with piercing blue eyes and dark hair that brushed the back of his collar. He didn't get anywhere near her. She saw him only from across the room. But their eyes met and something inside her clicked into place.

The stare lasted only a second, but it lingered with her. Like she could look in the mirror and see a veil of blue over her own brown eyes.

Angelo ushered her out of the house at the same time the man walked deeper into it. Part of her went with him.

Another piece went two weeks later when they went to the house again and she caught another glimpse. By now Angelo had told her he knew nothing about the man. Not his name or what he did when he followed Boss Man around all day. He didn't even know when he would be there and when he wouldn't. That didn't stop the little piece of her from following after him.

A month passed. And then another. She didn't go back to the house, but she didn't stop thinking about him. Maybe it was those thoughts that drew him to her, or maybe it was the little pieces of her that were guiding him, but however it happened, Miley felt like she was breathing for the first time when she turned around and saw piercing blue eyes and dark hair. She'd noticed his eyes when she first saw him. Then his mouth. She noticed his mouth again now. There was a smile on it, and she wanted to know what it tasted like.

"It's you," he said.

She'd come to the farmer's market that morning because there was nowhere else for her to be. She'd come for summer berries and greens. She left with him.

Jason called Boss Man Mr. Marini and had just as little interest in talking about him as Angelo did. He admitted he knew Angelo's name. He actually knew the names of everyone who worked there in the house, and in the office, and everywhere else Mr. Marini needed people to do his bidding. He just never said them. The only names he said were Mr. Marini's and his own. Usually not even his own.

She asked what he did for Mr. Marini and Jason told her whatever he needed to.

And with that, the conversation was closed. He didn't offer anything else. Miley didn't ask. It didn't matter. As far as she was concerned, none of that existed when they were together. They were in a bubble together, and she didn't want anything to come into it.

The first time she saw him, she knew her life was going to change. She just didn't know how much.

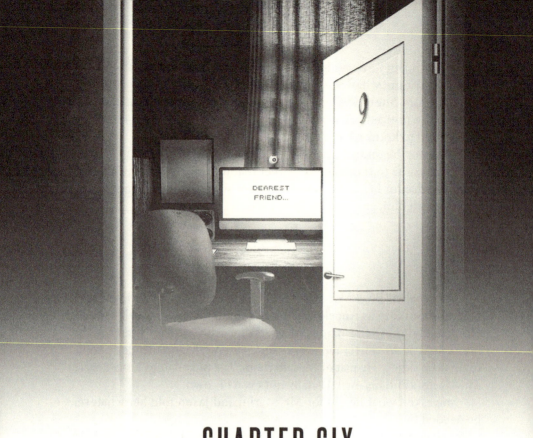

# CHAPTER SIX

*Now*

T HE NEXT DAY SAM HEADS INTO WORK TO ENSURE THE PEOPLE OF Sherwood are properly served and protected while I spend the morning on a mission through the aisles of the grocery store. The next hour is spent measuring, mixing, and pouring before finally several layers of cake are in the oven. While they bake, I sit at the kitchen table with my sketch pad and pencil working on a design.

This isn't just a flagrant display of domesticity with some revisiting of my artistic roots sprinkled in for good measure. Tonight is Game Night with Janet and Paul, and I've been tasked with making a cake for the festivities. This isn't the first time I've made a game-themed cake for our gathering with the neighbor couple from across the street. The Clue board confection from a few years ago is still infamous, preserved for posterity in a picture framed on the wall above the table where we spread out our board games.

Today's cake is to celebrate our return to Game Night after several weeks of having to skip them due to Janet being sick. I've run back and forth across the street with food to leave on the porch and sent countless waves through the window as she watched me jog by each morning, check the mail, or just sit on the porch enjoying the spring weather. Those days have become few and far between as I've waded through the constantly thickening swamp of cases I'm working through, but I take them when I can.

I was excited when they called us up to let us know Janet was feeling up to a game showdown tonight, with her one request being a themed cake. Now I'm trying to come up with the perfect theme. I don't want to do another Clue board. Because I've already done it, but also because it's still my nemesis in toy form. I don't need another edible reminder that the FBI agent can't ever figure out who killed that damn Mr. Body with the candlestick in the parlor.

The cake is cooling on the counter, and I just hit upon an idea when I get a text. My fingers covered in the modeling chocolate I'm using to make Monopoly player icons that will mingle with other game pieces on the imagined ultimate game board, I carefully navigate opening the screen on my phone to check the message.

It's a response from Xavier. I've been waiting for him to reveal to us how Jonah escaped ever since we had to blow his cover and pull him out of prison. He said he was 'pretty sure' he'd figured it out, which translated from Xavier means he knows down to the smallest detail, but then never filled us in. Finally, this morning while standing in line at the grocery store, I sent him a message asking if he was ready to tell me.

**Xavier:** *I have to confirm it.*

Both the brevity and the content of the message are a bit concerning to me. Xavier is usually more effusive than that, but being straight to the point can just mean there's too much else going on in his head for him to squeeze a lot of other words through. It's that content part that's really getting to me.

How does he plan on "confirming" it?

I can only hope it means Dean is helping him with an investigation.

Sam gets home just in time to take a fast shower and head across the street. They have the front door standing open before we even get to the end of their sidewalk. With the longer days stretching out toward summer, the sun isn't all the way down yet, but the glow of lights from inside their house still looks warm and welcoming. By the time we get onto the porch and I'm hugging Janet, I can smell that she's been cooking.

The long table is set up against the wall in the den, heavily laden with enough snacks for at least three times as many people, and the stack of games on the corner of the table waiting to be sorted through brings a smile to my face. It's nice when things feel normal for a little while.

"What are we playing tonight?" Paul asks.

"Since tonight is celebrating Janet, I say we let her choose," Sam suggests.

She smiles and I feel a little heaviness in my chest. Though she's looking a lot better than she has, she's still pale and looks tired.

"Well, we did get a game from our son for Christmas that we haven't tried yet. Want to give that a whirl?" she asks.

We all agree, and she goes to the stack to pull out a box still in its shrink-wrapping. The game is based on a haunted house and has a long list of infuriatingly complicated and sometimes seemingly contradictory rules for players moving throughout the house represented by the board, haunting each other with the ghosts and collecting enchanted objects. Which means it sounds like a fun evening.

A couple of hours into laughing our way through trying to follow the rules, Paul's phone rings in his pocket. He pulls it out, looking like he's planning on just ignoring it, but when he looks at the screen, he pauses.

"Sorry, I actually need to take this. Be right back."

He gets up from the table and walks out of the room as he answers.

"Perfect opportunity for a snack break," I say, getting up from the table and heading back to the food table.

"How is everything going?" Janet asks as I sit back down. "I feel like I haven't talked to you in ages. You must have a million new stories for me. I saw all that stuff on the news about the deadly sins murders. That's a disturbing case."

She shudders slightly, but I know she wants me to share every detail. Some people watch true crime shows on TV. Janet talks to me. I can't tell her everything, of course, but she loves when I give her the recaps of my cases. I'm filling her in when Paul comes back. He looks confused and concerned, but he stuffs the phone back in his pocket and takes his seat.

"Alright, where were we? Sam, I think you had the headless knight chasing after Janet in the dungeon," he says.

Janet reaches over and rests her hand on her husband's arm. It's one of those gestures between people who have been married for decades that have come to mean more to me now that I'm married. I'm still firmly planted in the newlywed stage with only a little more than a year behind me, but I can see how much more that simple touch means than just her getting his attention.

"Honey, is everything okay?" she asks. "Who was that on the phone?"

They never talk about it, but both of them are still haunted by terrible memories from years ago when their granddaughter was one of the victims in the case that brought me back to Sherwood. The little girl fortunately survived, but the days of not knowing what happened to her and if they were ever going to see her again took an understandably massive toll. I know they've both hoped one day they'll be able to fully put it behind them and forget, but I know they never will.

"I'm not totally sure. That was Joe." He looks across the table at Sam and me, realizing we won't know who he's talking about. "A good friend of mine from college, Joe Corrigan. We've been trying to get together for a few months now and he was supposed to drive down here for a visit tomorrow, but he just called to say he isn't going to be able to make it. He's having to deal with an emergency on campus."

"Campus?" I ask.

Paul nods. "He's President over at Baxter. He didn't give me any details about what was going on, he just said he has to stay there and handle the situation."

"I hope everything is alright," Janet says.

"He sounded like it was causing him some stress, but hopefully it's just something aggravating but minor and it will all get resolved quickly. I was looking forward to seeing him."

"I know you were. I'm sorry, honey. I'm sure it's just a controversy with one of the teachers like has been all over the news recently. It's not the easiest environment out there for…" she hesitates, "well, anyone, really."

Paul chuckles. "You're right about that. Hopefully, that's all it is. Now, how much cheating went on while I was on my call?"

# CHAPTER SEVEN

*Angela*

"When was the last time you saw her?"

Angela stormed through the small living space of Apartment 9 with heat rising up the back of her neck, stinging in the follicles of the tiny hairs that never cooperated with her no matter what she tried to do with them. The tiny hairs that she noticed her daughter shared with her the moment she was born.

An edge of accusation sharpened the words, making them more aggressive than a simple question. It was because she'd already heard the answer. She just wanted it to be different.

"Friday morning," Jasmine said. The girl shifted uncomfortably. She wouldn't make eye contact, like she hated that she was even saying the words. Like she was ashamed of them coming out of her mouth. "Around ten, I guess."

"She should have been in class."

"It was canceled. She got an email before she got up. I don't know if she went to class that afternoon."

Angela eyed her, making her shift more. "You have that class together."

"I didn't go. I went out of town for the weekend with my boyfriend," Jasmine said. "We wanted to get a head start, so we left right after I had breakfast. Sydney was here. She was sitting in the living room writing in her notebook." She pointed at the couch as if they would be able to envision her sitting there. "It looked like she was studying for something."

"And she didn't say anything? She didn't tell you she was planning on going anywhere?"

Jasmine shook her head. "No. I told her I would be back Sunday. I had a test, so I couldn't skip the day. She didn't say anything about not being here or that she had any plans for the weekend. I got the impression she was just going to be studying. I know she has a couple of big projects that are due soon and she's been working on them a lot."

"And you didn't notice when she wasn't here when you got back?"

The door to the apartment opened again and Wesley came toward them with long strides. His face was etched with the same worry and frustration. They were already behind. All this had happened, and no one told them. No one even knew.

"The apartment manager couldn't tell me anything. She didn't know Sydney wasn't here. All she could say was this isn't one of the apartments that causes her trouble, so she doesn't think about it much," he said.

"She means she doesn't think about Sydney much," Angela snapped.

"What is she supposed to do? Come by every day with milk and cookies and ask how her classes are going? Require a check-in call when she gets home?" Wesley demanded. "That's not her job, Angie."

"She's here to take care of things like broken appliances, not..."

His voice trailed off and the heat on the back of Angela's neck turned into a stinging burn on her cheeks as anger flooded her. She preferred it to the fear that had started to form deep in her stomach when Jasmine called to ask if Sydney was with them. She wasn't. She hadn't been home since the holidays.

"Not broken people?" she said, her voice a low, accusatory hiss.

"That's not what I was going to say," Wesley responded, his voice dropping to scrape across hers.

Angela stared at him for a moment. She wanted to love him in that moment. She wanted to be able to look at him and see comfort and strength, not a dry, jagged canyon that seemed to get wider even as she watched. When there was nothing to soothe it, she turned back to Jasmine.

"Why didn't you notice she wasn't here until this morning?"

"It was late when I got back, and I went right to bed. When I got up the next day, her room was closed. I figured she had already left since she's usually gone early. I had a study group yesterday after class and then I went out, and when I got back, her room was still closed. I know how hard she's been working, so I didn't know if she was at the library or sleeping and I didn't want to disturb her. This morning I needed to ask her for some notes from our class and I knocked on her door. She didn't answer," Jasmine explained.

"So, what you're telling me is you didn't bother to check on her even though you hadn't heard a single word from her or seen her in four days," Angela said.

"I called her," Jasmine replied, trying to argue but not gaining any ground. "And I texted her."

"But she didn't respond, and you didn't think it might be important to check on her," Angela pressed.

It wasn't a question. She wasn't gauging the roommate's reaction or trying to draw anything out of her. She already knew. The girl who had lived with her daughter for two years, who shared classes and jeans and went through the flu with her, who she'd brought home for Thanksgiving and made a Christmas card, didn't even notice when Sydney disappeared.

# CHAPTER EIGHT

I T TOOK SOME CONVINCING, BUT ANGELO FINALLY RELENTED TO ME talking to Louisa about the man he knew as Marini's nephew. I promised him I wouldn't talk to her about Miley. At least not right now. At some point, I might have to. If I can't piece the details together, that might be the route I have to take. But for now, I'll keep his secret.

"Yes," she finally admitted when I asked her, telling her the same thing Angelo told me about overhearing Marini introduce the man to someone visiting the house. "I remember who he's talking about."

She's uncomfortable. I can see that she doesn't want to be talking about this. Her eyes flicker back and forth even though it's just the two of us in the room, and it seems like her voice has gone down a little, like she's trying to keep someone from hearing her. But at least we're making some progress. I'll take whatever she has to offer.

"What do you remember about him?" I ask. "Did you hear him introduce him that way?"

"I heard him," she says. "I don't know who he was talking to. We rarely knew who was coming to the house or why. We were just told that he was expecting someone and that we weren't to get in the way. He'd give us instructions for how to make the house look and if there was specific food he wanted, but that was it. If they were ever in the same room as us, he acted like we were invisible."

She looks understandably angry. I can't imagine working in that kind of environment, being treated like a lesser being. I'm sure a lot of people would judge her and ask why she didn't just leave when he was as awful to her and the others as he was. But I can also tell by the look in her eyes whenever she talks about it that she had no other choice. She couldn't just walk away.

"Did you know anything else about him? His name or why he was around a lot? Why he stopped coming around?" I ask.

Louisa shakes her head. "No. I do remember thinking it was strange that he was around so much. He was young and attractive. He seemed nice. Not that we ever spoke, but you know how you can have that feeling about someone? I guess that's not something I should say now, should I?"

"What do you mean?" I already know, in some ways, what she means. But I want to hear the way she puts it together.

"Since he died, I've heard so many people talk about what a fantastic guy Salvador Marini was. That he was so charming and kind and generous. No one said a single bad word about him. Except for those of us who actually interacted with him from day to day."

"That happens when people die. Especially when it's tragic or unexpected. It is interesting that those people just choose to ignore the reality that he died the day he was turning himself in to the authorities for some pretty horrific crimes," I reply. "Of course, the details of what he did weren't released to the public. But I've read plenty of articles about him and his death. Nearly all of them mention that he was preparing to serve what was likely to be an extremely long prison sentence."

"He was charming enough for people to ignore that," she says.

"He was manipulative enough for it," I point out.

She nods. "And that's what I mean. The other man didn't seem like that. There were a couple of times when he was around that he looked right at us and smiled. He even said hello to me once or twice. I know that doesn't sound like much and I am probably pathetic for even clinging to that, but in that household, around Marini, that meant something."

"I know it did," I tell her. "I don't think you're pathetic for feeling that way at all. Trust me, I'm in no position to judge. One day, we'll sit down for some coffee, and I'll tell you some stories."

Louisa smiles, but it only gets to part of her eyes. She looks down at her lap and takes a breath.

"You said this guy could be important?" she asks. "His nephew?"

"He could be," I nod. "He seemed to spend a considerable amount of time with Marini, which means he might have known more about him. He could also be his only family, which means he would be the one who would inherit his estate and have access to things like security deposit boxes that could contain really valuable information. The fact that no one has heard from him in a couple of years, though, is problematic."

She makes a sound like someone who has walked through a spiderweb and gets up from the table to get a glass of water. Swallowing it down in a long gulp, she leans both hands against the counter and takes a breath.

"This is really eerie," she says.

"Why do you say that?"

She shakes her head, rocking back and forth for a second before turning and coming back to the table.

"I know he's dead. I do. It's not like I think that this is all some elaborate plan involving him faking his own death and going underground."

"Maybe not as crazy as you'd think," I mutter.

"This is going to make me sound completely insane, but I actually called the funeral home myself to make sure they cremated him. I know the man is dead. But there's always this feeling. I can't really explain it. It's like even though he's dead, he could still take me out. It's particularly haunting now that I know what he did, but he promised if any of us ever crossed him, we would pay."

That statement sends a shiver down my spine. The threat wasn't slight or casual. It wasn't just something Salvador said to scare the people working for him or make himself sound intimidating or powerful. That was the Emperor speaking, telling them his full intentions without hesitation.

"Did you ever know of anyone who crossed him?" I ask.

"There were never any heads on stakes in the backyard or anything, if that's what you're asking. But it was what came to mind as soon as I realized his nephew wasn't coming around anymore. When he didn't show up for a few weeks and I noticed Marini wasn't saying anything about him, I got worried. I didn't know what he could have done, but he suddenly wasn't around anymore, and I couldn't help but think it was because something happened to him."

Louisa's extremely disturbing revelation is still with me when I'm home sitting at my desk scrolling through search results on my computer. She wasn't able to give me any more information about the actual identity of the man who was supposedly Marini's nephew, but what she could tell me makes it even more important for me to figure out who he was and what happened to him.

I hope Angelo's instinct was right. Nothing would make me happier in this situation than to think Miley and this man simply ran off together. It's obvious Miley didn't tell Angelo everything about herself, and that she was trying to break free of what her parents, and likely everyone else in her life, thought of her. As aggressive and demanding as Marini was to everyone around him, it's not out of the realm of reality to think he wouldn't tolerate his nephew getting involved with someone who was friends with a member of his staff, and may have even been threatening toward her.

It's a warming, happy thought that maybe the two of them just decided they didn't want to deal with their lives anymore and just wanted to be together, so they picked up, ran off, and started over without anything. They just cut ties with anything and everything behind them and created something totally new with just each other.

But it's taking far too much effort to hang onto that as plausible. I want it to be. I really want to believe they are out in the world somewhere, maybe living off of money they siphoned off Marini. Typically, I'm not the kind to celebrate the idea of breaking the law, but knowing what I do about Marini, I would happily look the other way if I knew the two of them were funneling money from the ultra-wealthy, disgusting man to fund their life together.

I know it's not true. I don't know what happened to them, but it isn't good.

Now I need to find someone who can help me figure it out. I just don't know who that person is.

I've been scouring through everything I could find to see if I can identify his nephew, or anyone else who might be able to tell me who he is. There are plenty of people who have business connections or even proclaim a personal relationship with him, but it isn't like I can just start calling everybody up and seeing which one of them might be able to tell me about the guy who used to hang out with Marini all the time but has since disappeared.

At least not yet. I'll give it a little longer and then we'll see where I am with that plan.

Finally, I see something that might save me from the cold calls. A lawyer named Nathan Klein.

Of course, I would expect a businessman like Marini to have a lawyer. Most likely a team of them. This one in particular seems to be more than just a corporate lawyer or someone who consulted with Marini occasionally. His name appears in guest lists, panels, and acknowledgments for a long list of events, as well as in more than one role within the company.

I get his contact information and call the listed number, but only get a recording. On it, Klein curtly announces to callers that the easiest way to get in touch with him is through email. The message cuts off and I look at the phone in a moment of confusion. It seems odd to have a listed phone number and then not answer it and tell people to email. Usually, people don't want to get more emails and ask to be called. But with as much as he clearly works, I guess there is the possibility everything keeps him so busy it's difficult to be able to have protracted phone calls. It would be easier for him to just read emails, sift through the information, and decide how to handle them effectively rather than dealing with someone rambling.

I'd much rather be able to just speak directly to Nathan Klein, but that's clearly not an option right now, so I open up an email and try to distill the situation down to the most direct message possible. I make sure to tell him I understand confidentiality could limit what he's able to tell me, but I'd appreciate as much information as possible. I give him my contact information and sign off, hoping I'll hear back from him soon.

## CHAPTER NINE

Sam appears at the door to my office right as I'm closing my computer.

"Hey," I say. "I didn't hear you come in."

"Trying to keep me from seeing your illicit emails to your boyfriend?" he cracks.

"Absolutely," I say, standing up and bending back to stretch the long hours of sitting out of my muscles. "But there are some non-illicit ones to him you can read if you want to."

"What are they about?" Sam asks.

"Mostly play-by-play reviews of cooking competition shows and neighborhood gossip. Some philosophy."

I wrap my arms around his waist and smile up at him.

"Meh, I'll pass," Sam says. "You know I can't stand philosophy."

I grin and give him a kiss before patting him on the chest and heading into the kitchen. I'd intended on starting dinner a while ago and had even pulled out a recipe and a few ingredients but got sidetracked by my search and never did anything with them.

"Make dinner with me," I tell him. "I'll tell you all about my conversation with Louisa."

As we cook alongside each other, I fill Sam in on what I learned from Louisa, and then from traipsing through everything I could find about Marini.

"I'd think you would have had some contact with his lawyer by now," he says, dumping a couple of handfuls of chopped onions into the pan on the stove. "Wouldn't he have been a part of the investigation? Or there during the interrogation? Or at least have said something after his death?"

"I thought about that, too," I say. "I can understand why he wasn't there during the investigation or interrogation. From what I understand, he's a corporate lawyer, not criminal. So, he wouldn't be the one Marini called when he needed a lawyer during his showdown with the police. He did have a lawyer then, but it was a different one. But it does strike me as odd that Klein didn't come forward after Marini's death. They've worked together for a long time and Marini apparently thought enough of him to have him fulfill various capacities in his company. I'd think he would have at least wanted to know what was going on."

"Even if not for his own personal reasons because they knew each other, wouldn't he be responsible for handling things after his death?" Sam muses. "That would require some cooperation with the investigation."

"As far as I can tell, he would be the one to do things like distribute the estate, manage any trusts, handle all the business contracts in the fallout of Marini's death, so, yes, he should have been involved. But I didn't hear anything about him."

"Interesting."

"I thought so."

My phone rings and I go back into the office to answer it. A couple of minutes later, I'm back with Sam, a whole new set of questions and confusion swirling around in my head.

"What did Dean say?"

I frown. "How did you know it was Dean?"

"Every time he calls with a big update on a case for you, you come back with a look on your face. I could tell right away it was either him or Xavier, and since I didn't overhear you negotiating the transfer of a few dozen jars of sourdough starters into our pantry, it had to be him."

I shrug. "Xavier's missed them ever since being away. He doesn't want to part with them for now. Anyway, I asked Dean to look into some possible hints I found about Marini. I thought it was strange there was nothing about his family and thought maybe he'd done something to cover it up. It turns out, he did. He started using his grandfather's last name when he was in his early twenties. But Dean was able to find records of his life before then, including his family. And guess what he found out?"

"That he's an only child?" Sam suggests.

"Not quite. He only has one sibling. A sister who doesn't have any children."

"So, no nephew."

"No nephew."

"Maybe he was using it colloquially," Sam offers. "The guy was a family friend or someone he was close to, and he grew up thinking of Marini as an uncle, so that's why he called him nephew."

I make an incredulous sound. "I mean, I guess that's possible, in the way that things like that do exist in the world with normal people who have normal feelings and relationships. But this is Salvador Marini we're talking about. He doesn't strike me as the type to be colloquial. Or particularly affectionate. I can't really imagine anyone wanting an Uncle Emperor."

"That's true," he admits.

"I'm just hoping the lawyer will be able to explain it."

Sam looks like he's about to say something but is cut off by the sound of the doorbell. We look at each other with slightly raised eyebrows as if both of us are waiting for the other to admit to inviting someone over and forgetting about it. When neither cops to it, Sam finishes chopping the mushrooms in front of him, tosses them into the pan with the onions, and goes to answer.

I'm expecting him to accept some mail put in a neighbor's mailbox, or to shoo away a kid from the high school selling nuts for the band fundraiser. The shelf in the pantry stacked high with canisters of various flavors and mixes proves he has not done the latter as often as he perhaps he should be. Instead, I hear Paul's voice.

"Hi, Sam. I'm sorry to come over here right at dinner time like this, but I need to talk to Emma."

I walk into the living room and see Paul looking upset and on edge. He crosses toward me as I come in.

"Hey, Paul," I greet him with a tentative smile.

"Emma, I'm sorry for showing up like this. I didn't mean to interrupt your dinner," he says.

I shake my head to dismiss that concern. "We're just cooking. Don't worry about it. What's going on?"

"Why don't you come in and sit down," Sam says. "Can I get you something to drink?"

"No, I'm okay," Paul replies as we go over to sit on the couch and loveseat. "I just talked to my friend Joe again. I called to check in with him and make sure everything was going alright. It's not. It turns out the emergency he said he needed to handle is a missing student."

"A missing student?" I ask.

He nods. "A girl disappeared from campus over the weekend and he's really worried. He's trying to manage the family while also handling campus and how everyone is reacting, trying to keep the other students safe while figuring out if there's anyone who knows anything and isn't saying. As you can imagine, it's causing him a lot of stress and he doesn't know what to do. He's never dealt with something like this before. Baxter isn't exactly known for being a wild school."

"What exactly happened?" I ask. "How much do they know?"

"Well, that's the other part of it." Paul shifts his weight on his legs, back and forth, looking down at the phone in his hands. "He, um, he said he can't really share too many details with me. But I told him my good friend and neighbor is an FBI agent…"

He gives me a meaningful look and my breath hitches. I hate when people do this. I hate when people think they can bring their personal problems to me just because of my profession. I'm good at what I do, and I love doing it, but I'm not a private investigator. I'm not someone you can just come to to get your cat out of a tree. I'm busy enough as it is with all the cases already on my plate.

But a memory bubbles up into my mind that I can't just ignore. I know what it's like to be worried about a college student disappearing. One of my best friends did, back when I was in school. She didn't show up for lunch one day, and then never came back. I was so worried about her. Nobody believed me at the time. They all thought she just left school without a word. But it wouldn't be for another thirteen years before the truth of her disappearance was finally revealed.

If there is a girl missing, I owe it to Julia to try to find her.

I reach a hand out and Paul places his phone in my hand. Joe's contact information is already pulled up, so all I have to do is press the call button.

I'm greeted with a professional sounding but otherwise unremarkable voice on the other end. "Hello?"

"Joe Corrigan? This is Agent Emma Griffin with the FBI."

"Agent Griffin," he replies. "Paul has told me about you. Are you calling about..." he trails off as if he doesn't know how to say it.

"Your situation?" I offer.

"Yes," he replies. "Thank you so much."

"Before we begin, Mr. Corrigan, you should know that I can't necessarily open a Bureau investigation for this yet. I'll do what I can, but that may not be much. Would you mind telling me any of the information you have on the missing student?"

"Yes, of course. Her name is Sydney Parker. She's coming to the end of her junior year. Apparently a very good student, involved in mentoring other students, very determined and driven toward her goals. Her parents say she didn't socialize a lot because she spent her time studying. She lives in a student apartment with her roommate."

"Roommate's name?"

"Jasmine McGee," he tells me. "They've lived in the same place for the last two years and were friends before that. The roommate says she left the apartment Friday morning and came back Sunday, then noticed that she hadn't seen or heard from Sydney on Tuesday morning."

"Tuesday morning?" I ask. "That seems like a long time to just not realize her friend is not around."

"Apparently they have different schedules and it's not all that unusual for them to not see each other for a couple of days," Joe explains. "Sydney has been really pushing herself and Jasmine just figured she was at the library or sleeping."

"Were there any signs that something happened to her? Indications of struggle in the apartment? Strange messages on her phone? Anything?" I ask.

"The apartment looked exactly like it did when Jasmine left Friday. Nothing was out of place. The police haven't found her phone to look through it."

"So you have already called the police? Is there an issue with their investigation?"

Joe pauses for a minute. "Sydney's parents called the police as soon as they found out she was missing. But they're of the opinion that the investigation is stalling. And because she's over eighteen, the police aren't taking a very aggressive approach, which is frustrating them. The family doesn't want to become a media spectacle, so they're trying to keep the investigation as quiet as they can. I was hoping if you helped, it might get things moving faster."

"As I said, there may not be much that I can do in a situation like this. This is really outside of the Bureau's purview. Unfortunately, she is technically an adult under the law. Teenagers are still learning, but they're old enough to get sent off to college and live on their own, they are old enough to make their own decisions about where they go and what they do. Parents don't like that, but it's the way things are.

"Police tend to take a more cautious approach to missing college students, but they are still very aware that most of them just needed space and time, changed their minds about school, had a bad breakup, any number of things, and took some time away. From the information you told me, there isn't really anything to indicate this is anything other than that."

"But what if it is?" Joe asks. "What if something did happen to her? Wouldn't it be helpful to start an FBI investigation now?"

"The Bureau doesn't open investigations just because an adult isn't where other people think they should be," I tell him. "There are very specific guidelines about when the FBI will start or get involved in investigating a missing adult. Clear signs of foul play, the person being last seen on federal property, if the person is or is closely related to certain people, such as government officials. Right now, this doesn't seem like any of those. It's more of a case for a private investigator."

Joe lets out a sigh on the other end of the line and Paul does right there with him. The disappointment is obvious in Paul's expression. I didn't mean to sound harsh or dismissive, but I also don't want to get his hopes up. Paul is just trying to be helpful, but I can't offer official FBI involvement.

"Oh," Joe says softly. "I guess that makes sense. I just don't want anyone to be in any danger. And I don't want to cause a panic that would make all our students flee the campus."

"I can look into it," I say. I quickly clarify to make sure he doesn't get too hopeful. "This isn't an official investigation. I can't go into this in my formal capacity. But I'm willing to look into it more and see if I can offer any guidance. I'm sure the police are putting together an investigation according to their protocols, and I don't want to step on their toes, but I'm willing to go over the details and see if anything comes to mind."

"Thank you, Agent Griffin," Joe says, exhaling a relieved sigh.

"Go ahead and send me any information you have, contact details for the family, anything like that. We'll see what we can do."

We hang up and the atmosphere in the room seems to take on a new electric charge.

Paul's face brightens. "Thank you, Emma. I really appreciate it."

Sam and I walk him to the door and as I close the door after watching Paul cross the street back to his house, my husband comes up behind me to give me a hug.

"You're a good woman," he whispers into my hair. "You just made him feel so much better."

"I just hope it's nothing."

## CHAPTER TEN

"She's pretty," Bellamy comments.

I've shared my screen with her so she can see what I've brought up about Sydney Parker during our video call. I nod.

"Yeah," I say. "I can't believe how young she looks."

"She *is* young, Emma. She's only nineteen."

"I know, but when I was nineteen, I already felt like the world was sitting on my shoulders," I counter. "I was on my own and dealing with a world that was falling apart around me. Looking at her, I just can't imagine someone that young going through that. I didn't feel that young. I don't think I ever did."

"Did you find out anything else about her?" she asks.

"Not really. I haven't delved much into the info the school president gave me. For right now, I'm trying to find out as much as I can from what's publicly available. I'm honestly hoping she's just going to show back up and had run off with some guy or had gotten overwhelmed by school and just taken a break," I say.

"But it could have been something bad?"

I sigh. "Of course. What happened with Julia isn't far from my mind. She was held captive for years by a deranged professor."

"You have to admit that was a pretty unusual case, though," Bellamy counters. "How likely would it be that we deal with two of these in such short a time?"

"Not very likely," I admit. "I'm trying not to jump immediately to foul play. For all we know, maybe she just needed some time to get away."

"I remember a girl in the dorm who did that back when we were in college. She was the most scheduled, organized person I have ever encountered. From the first day I met her, every time she came to mind the first thing I thought about was the binder she carried around with little color-coded sticky notes and tabs for everything. Her planner was her life. She woke up at exactly the same time every day, went and took a shower, walked to the dining hall for breakfast, went to class, stopped by the library for exactly forty-five minutes, then went to the next class. That was what her entire life was like.

"One night I was in the lounge waiting for a study group and her roommate came down all worried because she wasn't in the room like she always was. We asked around and found out she hadn't been to classes and missed her weekly afternoon coffee with one of her former professors."

"I don't remember that," I frown.

"It didn't really get out a lot," Bellamy shrugs. "She wasn't exactly the most well-known girl on campus, and her parents lived really far away. By the time anybody got in touch with them late the next day, she'd shown back up. It turned out she woke up that morning, took her shower, walked to the dining hall for breakfast, headed for class, and just kept walking. She'd just snapped under all the pressure.

"She kind of came to a couple of hours later sitting on a bus still holding the croissant she'd brought out of the dining hall with her. She had no idea how she'd gotten on the bus or where, and didn't know where she was. She got off at the next stop and it happened to be near a hotel, so she decided she needed some time, checked in for the night, and just disconnected."

"It didn't occur to her to tell anybody where she was or what was going on?" I raise an eyebrow.

"Apparently not."

"Well, it would be fantastic if that was what was going on here. I've been going through everything that's out there right now, which isn't very much. They're not doing interviews and have been trying to keep the media out of it, so there's very limited information. I have what Joe Corrigan told me, but, again, it's not a whole lot. For the most part, it seems like a basic college girl who decided to take some time to herself."

"For the most part?"

I let out a sigh. "Yeah. I mean, there are a couple of things that are a little odd. Nothing totally bizarre, but a couple of details that stand out to me. Like, her phone is nowhere to be found, but according to the roommate, it doesn't look like anything else was missing. So wherever she is, she has her phone, but no clothes or anything else.

"And I'm still having trouble with the roommate's explanation of not noticing she was missing. These girls didn't just get put together in a dorm room randomly. They've been friends since high school and have been living in this apartment together for two years. They even have a class together. Jasmine said she called Sydney and sent her a couple of texts but didn't get a response. Yet, when she got home, she didn't knock on her bedroom door to make sure she was okay.

"I get that Sydney's a really intense student and has a lot going on for her academically, but it doesn't make sense to me that her friend would just ignore the fact that she hadn't heard from or seen her in several days. I don't know what their apartment looks like, but I'm assuming it's not sprawling. Their bedrooms can't be but so far away from each other. It just seems off to me that she would go about her life, eat, get ready for bed, sleep, get up, get ready, everything right there a few steps away from her friend's bedroom, and not at least knock on the door."

"That does seem strange," Bellamy agrees. "But maybe Sydney told her not to disturb her. If she's really concentrating on a project, she could want to just be left totally alone. Jasmine could have taken that literally, but now not want to admit it because it sounds irresponsible."

"I guess." Combing my fingers back through my hair, I sit back in my chair. "Really all I have left to do at this point is look through whatever social media of hers I can find and see if there are any suspicious comments or anything. That seems like something they would have already done, but maybe something will jump out at me that they missed."

Bebe pops up behind Bellamy and holds up a doll to show me. I smile at her and wave. She's getting so big, it's hard to believe. Eric and Bellamy have started talking about getting married, but no plans have solidified yet. I don't know if they will ever actually go through with it. Bellamy enjoys dreaming up ideas for the wedding too much. She figures once they get married, she won't be able to plan the wedding anymore.

Her current plan is to perfect her own wedding plans, get married, and then become a wedding planner. She hasn't returned to full-time work since Bebe was born, so she has the time. It would make her the only person I can imagine who would consider consulting with the FBI a good side hustle.

After getting off the phone with Bellamy, I scan through everything I've found about Sydney Parker again, waiting for something to have some sort of meaning. When nothing does, I decide to call Joe Corrigan again, just to see if there's anything more he can give me.

By the time I get off the call, I don't have a lot more information than I already did. So far it's turned up nothing new since last night. Nothing suggests Sydney was in any danger. I don't like the fact that no one knows where she is. That never sits well with me. But Jasmine's story is twisting in the back of my mind, telling me there's more to what she knows than she's actually saying.

I won't be surprised if it comes out in the next day or two that her roommate knows exactly where Sydney is and has just been covering for her, but it's gotten out of control.

# CHAPTER ELEVEN

*Wesley*

"YOU HAVE TO BE KIDDING ME. I'M HER FATHER. THAT DOESN'T count for anything?"

Wesley paced back and forth across the cramped hotel room until it felt like the carpet was going to give way beneath him. His fingers felt tight from gripping his phone hard next to his head and his jaw ached from how hard his teeth ground into each other as he spoke.

"She's nineteen years old!"

There were still words coming through the phone when he smashed the button to end the call, but he didn't care what they were. They weren't going to help. He'd heard everything they had to say, had gone over the same thing with every person he was transferred to over the last two hours. It wasn't going to change.

Angela stepped out of the bathroom, her hair hanging wet down to her shoulders and her eyes red. She pulled the towel wrapped around her tighter as she moved around him toward the suitcase open on the foot of one of the beds. She never brought clothes into the bathroom with her when she took a shower. She didn't like the steam making them damp and would rather give her skin a chance to dry a little before putting clothes on.

He used to think it was adorable, especially when it was cold. She'd come out of the bathroom on the tips of her toes and rush to the dresser or the closet, barely skimming the floor, making little squeaking sounds as the chill of the room cooled the water on her skin. When it was warm, he'd wait for her and grab hold of the corner of the towel, trying to yank it off as she passed by.

Now she pulled it closer and rarely looked at him when she went by.

"They won't give me her phone records," he said.

Angela stopped digging through the suitcase to look at him.

"You requested her phone records?" she asked.

He couldn't interpret the emotion behind the question, whether it was surprise or anger.

"Of course, I did. I want to know where the hell she is. But the company wouldn't give them to me. I gave them her phone number, her social security number, birthday, everything. But they said they can't share that information with me, even though I'm her father."

"She pays for her own phone," Angela pointed out.

"And who thought that was a good idea?" he snapped.

Angela drew in a breath. When she did that, he could almost hear the voice of her therapist echoing in the back of his mind. *Take a step back. Take a moment. Take a breath. Take back control.*

She used to hold Angela's hands and repeat those words over and over in a slow, methodical voice until they lost all meaning. And yet somehow, they meant everything to Angela.

"She needs some independence, Wesley. We talked about this. Before she came to school, we agreed it isn't going to do any good to coddle her. That she needs to have some space and figure out life for herself. You are the one who told me that. You're the one who said we shouldn't be hovering over her all the time."

"Don't put all this on me," Wesley fired back angrily. "Don't act like you're the perfect mother and everything that's happened is my fault."

"Who encouraged her to move into the apartment rather than staying in a dorm? If she had been in the dorm—"

"Stop," he snapped. "You're not going to blame this on me."

"Where is she?" Angela asked angrily.

"Why are you asking me that? I'm doing everything I can to find her, and all you can do is throw accusations around."

"I didn't accuse you of anything."

She grabbed a handful of clothes and started back toward the bathroom. Wesley snatched his keys from the nightstand and made his way to the door.

"Don't bother. I'm leaving."

"Where are you going?" she asked.

"To the police station. The phone company won't give me any information about her account or send the records of her texts and calls. The only way they'll release them is with a court order, so that's what I'm going to get."

# CHAPTER TWELVE

"It's on the grounds of an abandoned school," Dean tells me. "The building itself isn't there anymore, but the land hasn't been used for anything else in decades. The only reason anyone noticed it was because a couple of kids went out there with high hopes and dreams of making their very own meth lab and one of them noticed the access hatch."

I put down the picture in my hand and pick up another of the stack he brought me. The huge, dusty columns in the image are imposing and formidable—and nearly identical to the ones we found Eric fighting for his life under.

"And who says kids these days have no aspiration?" I chuckle. "I'm guessing since I'm looking at pictures of this right now, they decided to leave all this behind the hatch?"

"Well, one of them opened it, but they lost their nerve when they saw how dark it was down there and that it smelled horrible. They ended up calling the police, who went in. A buddy of mine from the service happens to be in that department and knew I've been looking into a similar case. He decided to bring me in and show me what they found to see if I thought they could be linked."

"It definitely looks familiar," I note. "But there aren't any pictures of anything beyond just this one big space and the tunnel."

"There is a bit of an argument over the ownership of the land and access rights," Dean explains. "Technically a land developer bought the whole plot a couple of years after the school shut down. Apparently, there were plans for some sort of neighborhood development and a park, but it never materialized. A couple of times it looked like it was going to turn into something, but the contract fell through, or things started up, only to stop pretty soon thereafter."

"Not the most uncommon thing," I say.

"Not at all. Especially these days," Dean replies. "Companies get these big ideas and have all the hope in the world, but the funding capital falls through, trends in the market change. Sometimes it's even as simple as a permit or zoning doesn't work out the way they wanted it to. There are tons of lots that were brought up in hopes of creating the next shiny mega-mart or cookie-cutter neighborhood, but nothing happens."

"Or like that one we saw where they started building up the neighborhood, but stopped, so all that ended up being there was roads and streetlamps and driveways to nothing," Xavier adds. He pauses, then shudders. "Driveways should go to something."

"Agreed," I nod. "Alright, so the problem is there's a private owner of the land, so technically they have the right to build a subterranean building that smells like death, and nobody can say anything about it?"

"Essentially," Dean says. "If the land was still owned by the state like it was when it was a school, the police will be able to go in and investigate as much as they want. Because somebody owns it now, they have to get permission before they can do a full investigation."

"And they haven't been able to find this mysterious landowner?" I intuit.

"It's not like that," Dean says. "There's no actual mystery. They know exactly who owns the land. And, no, it was not Salvador Marini, as much as that would add an appropriate little wrinkle to this story. Though, admittedly, it would be a terrible cover for him. It really is just an investor who thought the area would be a good possibility for a new neighborhood, but who hasn't done anything with it. Problem now is getting in touch with the man—he's apparently out of the country looking at other investments and hasn't been very responsive. The police haven't been able to get in touch with him and figure out what's going on."

"Figure out what's going on, like they genuinely do think that maybe he bought the piece of land, pretended he was going to put a neighborhood on it, then wandered out into the woods and built an underground lair that looks suspiciously like an arena?" I ask.

"I'm not sure the thought process has gone quite that deep yet, but... yes," he shrugs. "My buddy promised he would keep me up to date since I know about this case. He might even bring me in to help with the investigation. Of course, I'd take you along with me for the ride."

"Well, you know me, always up for a murder-focused road trip." I pick up another of the pictures and shake my head in disbelief. "Shit. This looks exactly like the two we've already identified. This is definitely another of the Emperor's sick little homes away from home." A breath streams out of me as I turn to another picture. "How many more of these does he have? And how many people has he kept in them?"

"And how many of them are still there?" Dean asks.

"Why is she so sad?" Xavier asks.

I sift through the pictures again and shake my head.

"Xavier, there aren't any people in the pictures," I say. "Who are you talking about?"

"Not in those pictures," he explains. "Her."

I realize he's looking at my computer where it's sitting on the coffee table. I'd been looking at a new article about Sydney's disappearance when he and Dean got here a little while ago. They were already on their way to investigate an area for one of Dean's new cases that's not too far from here, so they decided to come by and tell me about the new development in the Emperor case in person.

"Who is that?" Dean asks, turning the computer towards himself. "Wait, is that the girl who went missing from the college a couple days ago? I saw something about that online."

"Sydney Parker," I tell him. "Her parents have been trying to keep the story out of the news, but apparently some eager journalist wannabe from campus caught on and just had to write about it, and a few outlets picked it up."

"How do you know about it?" Dean asks.

"The president of the college is a good friend of my neighbor Paul. I was at Paul's house the other night and he got a call saying there was an emergency at the campus and his friend needed to handle it. Then Paul gave my info to his friend. He was hoping I'd get the Bureau involved in the investigation," I explain.

"Don't you hate that?" Dean asks.

"I do, but remember Julia? My friend from college who disappeared without a trace?"

Dean nods. "And you just couldn't help yourself but talk to him, huh?"

"I had to. I don't want to just brush off the possibility that something could have happened, no matter how unlikely it is. So I told Joe, the college president, that I'd at least look into it."

"It seems like a bit of a jump to get the FBI involved when a college-aged girl doesn't show up for a couple of days," Dean points out.

"I explained that to him," I say. "But he's worried and he says that the campus is getting tense. They don't want it to escalate and have the students panicking or anything. So, I agreed to look over the details on an unofficial basis. Just to see what's going on and possibly give some guidance. They've already contacted police, but she's an adult so they are taking a pretty conservative approach to searching for her right now. In the meantime, I said I could look into it."

Dean looks off into the distance, the way he does when considering all the facts of a case. "What do you think about it?"

"I think that it's never a good thing when somebody is out of contact with everybody they know for a few days, especially when they are young and it's hard to pin down exactly when they were last seen. But that's not necessarily an emergency. As far as anybody knows, nothing is out of place at the apartment except for her cell phone. There's no indication of a struggle or any violence inside the apartment. She didn't have a car on campus, so nobody's looking for that.

"She has no police record at all, not even a traffic ticket or underage drinking. Her parents told Corrigan she has never been a troublemaker. But sometimes those are the very people who need time away the most. They are the ones who have pushed themselves to the limit and need the break. I don't really know what to think exactly, but it doesn't seem like there's anything right this second that is worth panicking over. So, I don't want to cause her parents to panic."

"She's not okay," Xavier says.

"What do you mean?" Dean asks. "How do you know that?"

"Here," Xavier says, touching the picture of her. "She's not okay here. Look at her eyes. She looks like she's melting."

The description strikes me. I look at the picture again, wanting to see what he does.

"She looks happy to me," Dean shrugs.

"She's smiling," Xavier says, "but it's because she has to. The smile doesn't belong to that moment. Whenever this picture was taken, she's not smiling then. It's an old smile. She's been holding onto it, keeping it in the back of her mind like it's been hanging in a closet. It stays there until she needs it, then she takes it out and puts it on. It makes her blend in, but it doesn't protect her. She's still dissolving."

# CHAPTER THIRTEEN

TWO DAYS LATER, IT IS STILL NOT THE DAY FOR ME TO PUT MY SHOES away in my bedroom when I take them off. This time they are high heels, and they tip over onto the carpet with a far less satisfying sound than my boots. I shrug off my suit jacket and head into the laundry room where I happen to know my favorite pajamas have just gone through the dry cycle. I'm in the downstairs shower when the door opens.

"I didn't even get a hi, honey, I'm home," Sam calls in through the billow of steam. "I was standing there in the kitchen, cheese sandwiches grilling to gourmet perfection, and there was no acknowledgment."

"I'm sorry," I say, sticking my head out from behind the curtain to look at him. "I've just been really distracted today. There's a lot going on in my head."

"But I thought you finished that smuggling case today," he frowns.

"I did," I say. He looks at me with expectation and I throw one hand up in the air. "Yay."

"There's the excitement," he grins. "What's going on?" The scream of the smoke alarm makes him look over his shoulder. "I think dinner is ready."

I let out a short laugh. "Sounds like it. Let me finish showering and I'll be in there."

He rushes out of the room, and I close the curtain to finish up. When I'm in my comfortable clothes, my wet hair bundled up on my head, and my feet happily rewarded for a long day in high heels with a pair of thick socks, I head into the kitchen. Sam has set out dinner and has a cup of mint tea waiting for me.

"I figured you didn't need any extra riling up, so I went with tea instead of coffee," he says.

"Probably a good choice." I kiss him. "How was your day?"

"Pretty much the same as always. I did have to go explain to Mrs. Basil that putting her cat up in the tree in her front yard is not justification for calling the fire department. Twice. In the same day," he says.

"She really wants to be swept off her feet by a firefighter," I shrug. "I blame romance novels. I've seen that woman at the annual library book sale. She wipes that section out. And I've never seen her return one of them or sell them at her yard sale or anything. She must hoard them. I just imagine entire rooms in her house overflowing with old school bodice-rippers."

"I'm guessing you think that's a bad thing?" he asks.

"No," I reply. "At least not from a reading entertainment perspective. Maybe not as great for an eighty-nine-year-old woman who has taken to climbing out on her roof to put her obese cat in a tree in hopes of wooing a firefighter the age of her great-grandsons."

"Is that how she does it?" he asks, plopping a fairly charred grilled cheese sandwich on my plate and sliding a bowl of tomato soup over to me.

"Yep," I say. "I saw her try it last week. Fortunately—or unfortunately depending on how you want to look at it—the cat scrambled out of the branches, back up onto the roof, and into the window. I guess she perfected it today."

"I've got to give it to her, she's spry for her age," Sam admits. "Alright, now that we've gotten my day out of the way, tell me what you're so distracted about. I thought you'd be really happy that case was finally over with. You've been complaining about it for weeks."

"I am glad it's over with. I just can't stop thinking about Sydney Parker. You know, that missing girl."

"I thought you said you weren't trying to jump to the worst conclusions immediately."

"I know. And I am trying. I just can't stop thinking about Julia."

"But there's still no evidence anything happened to her, right?"

"I don't know. And I still don't know if there actually is anything to worry about, but something Xavier said really got me thinking," I say.

"What did he say?" Sam asks.

I tell him about Xavier looking at the picture and the way he described her.

"When I spoke with Joe, he had nothing but good things to say about Sydney. He said he hadn't had a lot of personal contact with her but described her as sweet and friendly when he had spoken with her. She's serious about her academics, but always friendly and positive. The people she's involved with on campus for her volunteering and student mentoring have always said she's a bright light for those she helps when they are reviewing her performance."

"What kind of student mentoring?" Sam asks. "Like tutoring?"

"No," I say. "She does mental health advocacy and peer support counseling. Apparently, she's very good at it."

"Mental health advocacy?" he raises an eyebrow. "Maybe she has some firsthand experience with it."

"That's what Xavier seems to think. And if that's the case, it could change everything about this. It makes me wonder what she could be dealing with, and if that could have anything to do with her disappearing. Either because she wanted to, or because maybe somebody else wanted her to."

"So, you think there's a possibility there is foul play involved?" Sam asks.

"I think it's worth looking into more. I have a couple of video conferences for work tomorrow, but afterward, I'm going to go up to Hinkley and look into everything a little more," I tell him. "Only for a couple days, but I'll get back as soon as I can."

"Sounds like I need to get in my sugar before you go then," he winks, leaning over for a kiss.

"Sounds like it."

My meetings the next day take longer than I expected them to, so I don't get on the road until after dinner. I've already let Joe Corrigan know I'm coming, and he said he'll have time to meet with me tomorrow.

Baxter College isn't too far away from Sherwood, but drives always seem longer when I get started at night. I'm about halfway there when my phone alerts me to a new email. Since I need gas anyway, I pull off and open the message while I'm filling the tank. A surge of hope shoots through me when I see the message is a response from Nathan Klein, but the feeling doesn't last. His response is stiff and tense, bordering on rude. He's clearly not pleased I'm asking questions about Salvador Marini, and dances around his willingness to give me any answers to them.

But it isn't so much what he says or how he says it that bothers me. It's what he doesn't say. Even though I blatantly asked about Marini's nephew, the lawyer didn't correct me. Now that I know Marini had no nephew, his lack of resistance puts me off. Obviously, Klein could just be choosing not to give me any information since he doesn't think I should be asking about it, but I would think a lawyer would be concerned about someone potentially faking a family relationship with his extremely wealthy client.

The new added layer is very odd, and it has me even more convinced that there is something very wrong about this whole situation.

But I don't have time to think about that right now. I'm here for Sydney, and I want to put all my focus and attention on her.

I go over everything I know about the case already, but there really isn't much. The only thing that's changed since I first heard about her disappearance is the content on her social media. There haven't been any new posts, but people are coming on to leave comments as the news of Sydney's ongoing missing status starts to spread.

It isn't a flood of comments. There's no overwhelming response or fake outpouring of concern the way that sometimes happens when strangers can't help themselves and need to get involved. Instead, I see people talking about how much she helped them. They mirror the comments Joe Corrigan made about how happy she always was.

The more they say it, the more I question it.

I follow a link to another platform where Sydney posted videos about her own mental health and the struggles she's faced. There's hope in all of them, a promise that going through these challenges doesn't have to define the lives of those struggling. It doesn't have to keep them from having the life they want. As I watch them, I can understand the high praise and admiration coming from Corrigan and the others. She speaks with openness and honesty, sharing who she is and welcoming people to know her, while offering to be there for anyone who needs it. I'm inspired by her, but I still find myself searching her face in the videos, looking at her eyes and her smile, wondering at what point Xavier would see her start to melt.

Xavier calls as I'm getting ready for bed.

"To your knowledge, is Jonah particularly flexible?"

"I imagine he'd have to be. Having so many complex, secret plans, he'd have to have contingencies for every situation. Plans within plans within plans. Especially his recent game of trying to bait me out; he's always got something secret in his back pocket to use just in case. So yeah, I would think so."

"No. His joints," Xavier says. "Specifically, his hips and shoulders."

"Oh." I don't know where he's going with the question, and I don't know if I really want to.

"As far as I know, he has a normal degree of flexibility for the average adult male," I say.

I cringe a little just saying that.

"And if you were to evaluate his ability to cling to something for a long period of time, perhaps while being subjected to varying extreme temperatures and a somewhat jostling and uneven terrain, would you say you think he would be able to hang on successfully?" Xavier asks.

I'm not sure if it would be more disturbing for him to be asking these questions about something he thinks has already happened, or that might happen.

"I don't really have a lot of experience with that particular element of his skillset, but I would think he would have just as good a chance of being able to hang on as anyone else," I say.

"That's what I figured. Can you put Sam on the phone? I want to ask his opinion."

"You're going to have to call him. I'm actually not at home. I came up to Baxter to look more into Sydney Parker's disappearance."

"Have you found out anything?"

"Not really, but I haven't talked to any of them yet. I've been trying to find out more about her as a person. What you were saying about her the other day really stuck with me," I tell him. "I found out that she has been suffering from mental illness for years, and she actually used to be an advocate and a mentor."

"Living with," Xavier corrects me.

"What?" I ask.

"Living with. She's been living with mental illness, Emma. Not suffering from it. She may have struggled, and she may even suffer sometimes, but just having a mental illness doesn't automatically mean a person spends their lives suffering. It doesn't define her. It's a part of her and something she likely has to acknowledge and find ways to cope with every day, but it's not who she is. It doesn't overshadow everything else that creates her.

"There is a prevalent fear and widely accepted prejudice that comes with mental illness. People hear that another person has depression, or anxiety, or bipolar disorder, and it becomes their label. From then on, it's the subtitle of their name. They can't escape it. They can't escape the way others look at them. So many will just dismiss a person because of it, assuming putting any attention or stock into them is like sitting and waiting for a timebomb to go off.

"But that's not what it is, Emma. She isn't dangerous or broken. She isn't destined for anything specific, or a lost cause. There's no reason to pity or condemn someone because of it. It's no different than someone who has allergies, or a heart defect, or hearing loss. They aren't the same things. They don't affect people the same way. It's just another element that makes them who they are. People with mental illness didn't cause those conditions, they aren't less because of them, and they learn to live with them in the same way that every person has to learn to live with the mind and body they were given.

"All of us have to overcome and adjust to cope and function in life. Some more than others. All in different ways. But when you put that blanket over her, you suffocate the rest of her being. The detail and clarity of every moment of her life are covered by the veil of suffering. Her grief and sadness are less authentic or worth acknowledgment because of that constant definition of pain. Her joy is less celebrated because it's inevitably temporary or others assume it's manufactured.

"Taking that away is like filling your hands with water from a spring rather than using a cup. It can be cold and intense, maybe even to the point of pain, but it's real. It's sweet and it's genuine and it's earned. No matter how she chooses to exist alongside her condition and cope with it in her daily life, don't assume Sydney is at its mercy."

It's a poignant reminder that I shouldn't need, especially after all I've been through with the very man speaking to me. But it still grounds me. It's still something I needed to hear. In some ways, he's really talking about himself. And it took me some time to see the true face of him, rather than simply the blanket that had been placed over him.

"You said she looked like she was melting, that she was dissolving away in that picture," I say.

"Like I said, she may be suffering. And in that picture, she was. But to say she suffers from her illness takes that from her. You don't see *her* in that picture, you see the illness. You need to see her, Emma. Everyone needs to remember to see her. Find out what is washing her away, not just what's making it harder for her to stay."

# CHAPTER FOURTEEN

*Jasmine*

J ASMINE LOOKED AT HER PHONE AGAIN FOR WHAT FELT LIKE THE thousandth time in the last few minutes. It hadn't rung. It hadn't chirped. There was nothing on the screen but the clock ticking, counting the minutes that were making her angrier with each passing one.

He was upstairs. She knew he was. But he wouldn't respond to her.

If she leaned back and looked at the rows of windows lining the tall building, she would be able to pinpoint which of them was his, but she wouldn't be able to see him in it. They were darkened, covered with a thick film to stop the glare of the sunlight and prevent people from the sidewalk from seeing inside.

The door was only a couple of steps away, but it didn't matter. She couldn't go inside. Anyone wanting access to the building had to prove they were authorized by swiping their school ID through the reader at the door, like getting into a hotel room. This meant only people who lived in the building, or those they were bringing with them, could get inside.

Jasmine was banking on being one of the latter. She only knew two people living in the building, which meant she was going to have to make herself into a guest.

She paced in short passes across the concrete patio in front of the door, waiting for someone to come out or go in. Finally, a hazy figure appeared through the tinted glass. She rushed to stand right near the door, making sure she was close enough to grab onto it as soon as it opened. Holding her ID in her hand was her camouflage, giving off the impression she was supposed to be there just like everyone else.

The guy coming out had shaggy hair falling over his eyes, earbuds stuffed in place, and a phone held up close to his face. He probably didn't even notice her snatch the edge of the door and pull it back so she could slip in behind him. The desk to the side of the entryway was manned by security guards later in the evening, but right now it was empty, meaning she could go right past without being questioned.

Tucking her ID away again, she didn't bother to wait for the elevator. Most of the students in the dorm only used the stairwell during the occasional fire drill when the elevators weren't an option, so it was empty as she climbed toward the fourth floor.

All along the hall, doors stood open, letting music, voices, and TV sounds pour out. His was one of them. No one paid attention to her as she stalked toward it, her hands tight at her sides. She didn't announce herself or knock when she walked inside. Van was sitting at the desk, hunched in front of his computer like he was studying. But Jasmine could see his computer screen over his shoulder. She could see Sydney's face.

He turned when her reflection appeared superimposed over Sydney's smile.

Jasmine's voice came out as a growl. "What did you do to her, Van?"

# CHAPTER FIFTEEN

Joe Corrigan and I planned to meet in his office first thing the next morning, and I get there several minutes early, prepared to have to wait for him to arrive for the day. But instead of directing me over to one of the chairs in a waiting area, the receptionist at the information desk playing gatekeeper over the pod of offices on the top floor of the administration building points me down the hall toward a big room.

"I think he's in there right now," she tells me.

I thank her and make my way to the room. Peering inside, I see a man right around Paul's age standing in front of the coffeemaker, staring at it like he hopes it will just spontaneously produce his cup of coffee without him having to do anything.

"Mr. Corrigan?" I start.

He looks up at me and I can see the effect of the last several days etched on his face. He looks tired and ragged, like he has been pushing himself and losing sleep.

"Yes," he says.

I take a couple of steps closer. "Agent Emma Griffin."

He takes the hand I extend to him and shakes it. Hearing my name seems to brighten him up just slightly.

"Yes. Agent Griffin. Thank you so much for coming. Please, call me Joe."

"You can call me Emma. Is there somewhere you'd like to talk?"

"We'll go to my office. Would you like some coffee?" he asks.

Extending the offer to me seems to remind him he needs to actually operate the machine, and he goes about brewing himself a cup, then one for me. I didn't ask for it and have already had some this morning, but I'm not going to turn it down. We augment our cups with the bottles of creamer stored in a refrigerator to the side and sugar from the counter. Mine is barely changed from its original state, but Joe seems to be more in line with Sam's philosophies about coffee. Either because he enjoys the flavor or he needs the added energy from the sweetness.

I follow him out of the lounge and down the hall to a heavy dark wood door bearing a plaque etched with his name. He opens the door and gestures to a seating area in the corner as he walks inside. We sit and I wait for him to take several sips of his coffee.

"I want to thank you again for coming out here. When Paul told me about his friendship with you, it really gave me some hope," Joe starts.

"I'm happy to help however I can, but I do want to reiterate that this is all unofficial..."

He nods in understanding before I can even finish my disclaimer.

"I know. Paul made sure I understood he didn't call in the FBI for me."

There's a slight smile on his lips and it looks like he's trying hard to be lighthearted, but the heaviness is pulling it down too much.

"I know we already talked about what was going on, but why don't you give me a quick recap from the beginning to make sure we're on the same page?"

"Tuesday afternoon, I got a phone call from Angela Parker informing me that she spoke with her daughter's roommate, Jasmine McGee, who let her know she hadn't seen or heard from Sydney Parker in several days. I met with Angela and her husband Wesley and found out they hadn't had contact with their daughter since the week before, but weren't overly concerned until they heard from Jasmine, who asked if she was home with them.

"They'd come to campus as soon as they could get here and went to Sydney's apartment. There were no signs of anything going wrong there. The door was locked. The windows were closed. There was nothing out of place, no blood, nothing broken. It looked like everything was exactly the way it was supposed to be. Except that Sydney wasn't there," he says.

"And you said her phone wasn't found there, correct?" I ask.

"Yes. Jasmine mentioned that Sydney's makeup was out on the counter in the bathroom and some of her textbooks were stacked in the middle of her bed. The only thing she noticed wasn't there is her phone. They've all called and texted multiple times. Jasmine reported that it rang during the weekend, then her voicemail inbox got full, then it went straight to that notification rather than ringing."

"So, she either turned it off on purpose, or it ran out of battery," I note. "Alright, and there haven't been any other reports of anything strange happening at or near her apartment complex? Any attacks, peeping toms, other students not being where they are supposed to be?"

"No," he says, shaking his head. "Things like this … they don't happen at Baxter. I know you told Paul this is a common thing, that girls go missing from college, but it's not common here."

"It's not just girls," I clarify. "People this age are just learning to be independent and have their own lives, and often that gets overwhelming. They have the option of just picking up and leaving when things get to be too much, so they do. The vast majority of the time, they are gone for a couple of days and then they come back."

"It's been more than a couple of days," he replies, starting to sound more emotional.

"I know," I tell him. "Which is why we need to look into it, but everyone needs to be honest and straightforward about it." He starts to protest, but I hurry to get in front of it. "I'm not saying you're not. I just want to put it out there that I know it can be uncomfortable talking about things that go wrong or that don't look great for a place you are very proud and protective of. I can tell this school means a lot to you, and I wouldn't want anyone to look badly on it, either, but it's critical for you to tell me about anything that could relate to this. Even if you don't think that it's connected, tell me."

Joe nods. "There have been a few incidents. Nothing like you hear about at the big universities or in the cities, but a couple of times there have been parties on campus that have gotten out of control. We've had fights and a few drunk driving issues. Some vandalism."

"How about sexual assault?" I ask.

His shoulders tense and the look on his face darkens. "There have been a few reports this year."

"What happened with the reports?" I ask. "Did the cases go to trial?"

"One did. Two others withdrew their complaints. The others were handled internally."

That is a sentence I never like to hear, especially when it comes to issues like this.

"What do you mean they were handled internally?" I ask.

"I spoke with the parties involved and the situations were brought in front of a conduct board," he explains.

"These aren't situations," I counter. "These are potential crimes, and they should be handled by law enforcement, not by a group of college administrators. How can you expect any student, female or not, to feel comfortable coming forward about something as sensitive and personal as rape or assault when they know they are going to have to talk about it in front of their peers, and those are the people who are going to determine what happens?"

"Conduct boards are common practice," he says, trying to defend the practice.

"I'm well aware," I say. "And if someone is caught cheating or plagiarizing, or they cause a disruption on campus, it's a perfectly fine approach. Sometimes even if it's something like vandalizing school property or fighting as long as it's not severe. But not sexual assault. These victims deserve respect, compassion, and discretion, and they're not going to get that from a group of students."

"These students are carefully selected from a pool of applicants that have to meet very strict criteria. They are mature, responsible, intelligent young adults who care about this school and the community of students," he says. "And they are supervised on the board by approved faculty members."

"That's all well and good, but they aren't police. They can't properly investigate allegations, nor can they dole out adequate consequences if it is found that the accusation was founded. To top it off, they are still students in the same school. The chances are far too high that they know the people involved, or are friends with people who do, which places far too much personal weight on the situations. Both for the alleged victim and the accused.

"Confidentiality doesn't exist on a college campus when it comes to the students. They will talk about what they hear, and they will come to their own conclusions, which can be devastating. And that goes for the potential victim and the accused. The accuser can face judgments about their behavior, where they were, who they've dated, and if they were really assaulted or if they just feel guilty for making a choice and now want to cover it up. They can become victimized all over again.

"For the accused, many times just having someone say something was done is enough to condemn them," I continue. "There can be no evidence, no corroborating witnesses, nothing at all to show that what the person is saying actually happened, and yet they are considered guilty and can be targeted. There've been cases where guys who have done absolutely nothing wrong were attacked and brutalized based purely on the fact that they were accused."

"That can happen no matter what," Joe replies. "Even if they go to the police and it's handled that way, people can find out and there can be consequences."

"Yes. But it's less likely when it's handled properly. And if something does happen, the police are already involved, so it can be dealt with more effectively." I realize we're spiraling away from the issue at hand and force myself to stop. "Were any of these reports from people who live near Sydney?"

"One of them lives in the same building," he says.

I nod. "Alright. That's something to follow up on. How about anything else? Reports of stalking, harassment, or physical attacks? Break-ins? Anything else that could be related to her disappearance?"

"No. Not recently. There were a few break-ins a couple of years ago. There was also an attack last year, but that was found to be random, and the attacker was arrested," he tells me.

"Okay. I'd like to see Sydney's apartment. Is that an option?"

# CHAPTER SIXTEEN

THE GIRL OPENING THE DOOR OF APARTMENT 9 LOOKS STARTLED when she sees the school president standing outside. She keeps the door partially closed, bracing it with her foot and holding onto the doorknob on the other side while leaning around it to look at us.

"Oh," she says, her eyes widening a little.

It's the reaction of a girl who didn't use the peephole. Either she is confident enough to never use it, which seems ill-advised considering the current state of her roommate, or she was expecting someone else.

"Hello, Jasmine," Joe starts. "This is Agent Griffin. She's agreed to help us find Sydney, and she'd like to look around the apartment."

There's no request. He's not asking her permission. He's informing her why we are here. It's a reminder that while this is her home, it is also a student apartment owned by the school, and the rules and policies that govern it are in control.

Jasmine nods and takes a step back to open the door. Her eyes flicker around the living room like she's doing an urgent check to make sure nothing is out that she wouldn't want us to see. I wonder if she's actually hiding something, or if Joe being there is just making her nervous. I've known people who automatically panic when they see a police officer anywhere near them, even if they are doing absolutely nothing wrong. She might be having that reaction. Or there might really be something she's hoping we don't notice, something that has to do with the person she was expecting behind the door.

"Hi, Jasmine," I say, offering her a small smile to try to calm her nerves. "Nice to meet you."

"You, too," she says. She hesitates. "Agent?"

I nod. "FBI."

Her hand goes to her heart, and she takes a step back. "FBI? What's going on? Did you find Sydney?"

The reaction strikes me as a bit strange, but I don't let on.

"No. There hasn't been anything new, as far as I know. I'm not here in an official capacity as an agent."

Her hand falls away from her chest and she looks at me with the suspicious narrowing of her eyes that is so specific to people this age. It's that expression of doubt rattling around in their brains, fostered and fueled by all the new information and rush of youthful confidence.

"Then what's this about?" she asks.

"Agent Griffin has agreed to use her considerable experience and knowledge to assist in the investigation," Joe explains. "She's offering her personal time to help find Sydney."

There's a slight warning hint in his voice and Jasmine silently submits.

"So, you were away for the weekend," I say, pushing the conversation forward.

"Yes," Jasmine nods, shifting her weight slightly. "I had plans with my boyfriend."

She sounds like she really doesn't want to be talking about this. I don't blame her. I wouldn't be eager to admit I'd ditched classes and went off on a second spring break the weekend my roommate vanished, either.

"And you left Friday morning."

"Yes."

"Did you try to get in touch with Sydney during the weekend?"

I already know she did. At least that she told the Parkers and Joe Corrigan when explaining the situation. But I want to hear it from her. I want to see how consistent everyone involved is when describing what happened.

"I called and texted her, but didn't hear anything back."

"Is that unusual for her?" I ask.

Jasmine shrugs noncommittally. "Usually she answers, but she was really busy with schoolwork, so I figured she was just taking the time I was away to really focus."

"But she doesn't do that most of the time?" I press. "I mean, even when she is really focused on her work, she usually answers the phone when you call, or at least texts you back?"

Jasmine nods. "Most of the time."

"So, what told you it wasn't important enough to check on her when you realized she wasn't getting back in touch with you?"

She looks surprised by the question, as if no one has asked her that from that angle.

"It wasn't that I didn't think it was important. I just figured she was busy. I got home, and everything looked the same," she says.

"But wasn't that enough to tell you that maybe something wasn't okay?"

"What do you mean?" she asks.

"Everything looked the same, right?"

She nods. "Right."

"Alright. Well," I take a couple of steps further into the apartment and gesture at the sofa. "I see a couple of throw pillows and a blanket on the couch, and the remote is sitting on the table. Were they like that when you got here?"

"No. I've used them since then."

"Before you used them, were they the way they were when you left on Friday?"

"Yes," she confirms.

"So, we're to believe that Sydney didn't touch anything in the living room for the entire weekend?" I ask. She opens her mouth to say something but stops. "And how about the kitchen? Were there any new leftovers in the refrigerator? Dishes drying by the sink? New trash? If she's so invested in her schoolwork she can't even sit down in the living room for four days, I can't imagine she's going to take the time to wash everything and put it away exactly where it was or take every bit of trash out."

"I didn't think about it," she says, her voice softer.

"That's okay," I tell her. "A lot of people would miss something like that. You don't know what to look for." I turn my attention over to Joe. "What did the police say when they searched the apartment?"

"There hasn't been a formal search," he admits.

That makes my eyes widen.

"Excuse me? They haven't searched the apartment?" I sputter. "I thought you said the police are involved. I know at the beginning they weren't doing any extensive investigating because Sydney is an adult, but she's been missing possibly a week at this point. Haven't they done anything else?"

"No," Jasmine says. "They came when we called and looked around. They didn't touch anything, and when they saw there wasn't any blood or anything that looked strange, they just took a statement from me and from her parents, said she would probably show back up, gave us each a business card to call in case anything else happened, and left. They haven't been back."

"Have they been in contact with you?" I ask Joe. "Or her parents?"

"I heard from them the day before yesterday," he says. "They were checking in to see if anyone heard from her and to let me know they were still aware of the situation."

"Aware of the situation?" I blink a couple of times. "Well, I'm sure that comforted the hell out of everyone."

"Why would they need to search the apartment?" Jasmine asks.

"The apartment should have been searched as soon as anyone realized she was gone. Checking the trash, looking in her room for notes, anything out of place, blood, hairs, anything that might not be immediately obvious, but could mean something. It's valuable to gather as much information as possible from the very beginning."

"You yourself said things like this just happen sometimes, and there was no reason to immediately assume something terrible happened," Joe says. "Now you think someone could have done this to her?"

The door to the apartment opens right as he's saying that, and two people I can only assume are Sydney's parents come in.

"What?" the woman asks, sounding shocked and upset. "What are you saying? You think someone took Sydney?"

"That's not what I was saying," Joe says, walking over to her.

"That's what it sounded like you were saying," she counters.

"Hi," I say, stepping up with an extended hand in hopes of diffusing the tension a bit. "Agent Emma Griffin. You must be Sydney's parents."

The agitated expression on the woman's face doesn't change. She leaves my hand unshaken in the air between us.

"I'm her mother. Agent? Are you with the FBI?"

My hand lowers as I nod.

"Emma Griffin, honey," the man behind her whispers. "She's the one we watched that show about."

Sydney's mother bristles slightly, but I can't tell if it's about me or the way he's speaking to her.

"Hi," I say, trying out the handshake with him. "Emma Griffin."

The man accepts it tightly, hanging on even after a few hard pumps.

"Wesley Parker. This is my wife, Angela."

"No one told us the FBI was getting involved," Angela frowns. "That means they know something. Something horrible has happened to Sydney. Why weren't we informed?"

She sounds almost frantic, but there's an edge to it, like she's offended not to have been kept up to date on every moment of the investigation.

"The FBI is not getting involved," I say, going for the full broken record trifecta. "I'm here in a personal capacity as a favor to a friend. A consultant. I'm here to help."

"Have you spoken with the police?" Wesley asks.

"Not yet, but I was planning on getting in contact with them today to offer my assistance," I admit. "Now, I can't promise you they will give me any access or allow me to participate in any capacity beyond what any private citizen could do. But I will work with them to the full extent, and I will do everything I can on my own as well. With your permission."

"What is it that you know about Sydney?" Angela asks suspiciously.

"Angie, she wants to help. Why are you being like that?" Wesley asks.

"She must know something. She wouldn't be here if she didn't. I don't want them hiding anything from me. This is my daughter we're talking about," she responds.

"I can assure you I am not hiding anything from you, and I don't intend to. I also don't know anything."

"Then why are you here?" she demands.

I take a look around the room and, with a sigh, finally decide to come clean.

"When I was in college, I had a friend who disappeared one day, too. She was supposed to meet me for lunch but she never did. And I did what little investigative work I could do, I tried to find her, but nobody believed me. I had to mount an investigation myself, but I was just a kid. I want to stress that I don't believe anything happened to your daughter as of now, but if there's even that remote possibility… I want to help."

"What happened to her?" Jasmine asks.

I glance over at her. They don't need to know the details. They don't need to know that we only found her after thirteen long years of isolation and torture by an abusive professor.

"We found her," I say vaguely. "Look. As of right now, all we know for sure is Sydney is not here at the apartment. There's no real reason to assume anything has happened other than that she left at some point Friday and hasn't returned. But I believe in being thorough. I've learned during my career to question everything, even myself. Making assumptions immediately in any situation can be really damaging to the investigation. We don't want to think we already know what happened and not pay attention to signs that tell us otherwise."

"You don't think she was taken?" Angela asks with a more cautiously calm tone.

"I don't think anything specific right now, other than the fact that if I was at the head of this investigation, the apartment would have been thoroughly checked much earlier. At this point, Jasmine has been living here for a few days, and things could have been moved or compromised. But you did say that you told the police about everything that was missing."

Wesley nods. "Not much is. Her phone isn't here, but just about everything else is. Her clothes, her makeup. Toiletries, computer, tablet, shoes. Nearly everything I would think a girl would want to have with her if she was going to be going away on purpose is still here."

"Just about everything else," I repeat. "Is there something else missing?"

Angela nods. "Her medication. I checked for it when I first got here. She takes antidepressants and antianxiety medication every day. But neither of them is here. I've been holding onto the hope that if she has those with her it means she really did leave on her own. Maybe she found something she really wanted to do and went off on her own for a little while, but she's coming back soon, so she's still taking care of herself."

"That's good. Thank you," I nod.

She looks over at her husband, who reaches for her hand. She takes it and I see a flicker of connection between them. The discomfort there at the beginning disappears briefly in the bond of their shared hope for their daughter. I'm glad to see that, but I also feel the need to temper their hope so they will stay focused.

It's not that I don't want them to have any optimism. Obviously, I want them to stay as positive as they can in what I can only imagine is a gut-wrenching situation. It's vitally important to hold onto hope when something like this happens. No hope leads to no motivation, to not even wanting to try, but too much hope can also have a similar effect. If Sydney's parents convince themselves that she is out there handling things on her own and could come back any time, they might back off the investigation.

    I don't want either to happen. Even if the girl did leave willingly, there has to be a reason. Something happened in her life that was significant enough to make her want to walk away from school, her family, her friends, and the people she helps and supports. That means something. Most importantly, she is still out there. And apparently without most of what she needs to survive. We need to find her. Or at least get in touch with her and make sure she's alright.

# CHAPTER SEVENTEEN

"Have you looked at her bank account to see if there has been any activity?" I ask.

"Yes," Angela confirms. "We're still listed on the account, so we were able to look at her statement. There were a couple of cash withdrawals before she was last seen, but not a huge amount. Less than three hundred dollars. Nothing else."

"Does she have a credit card or any other access to funds?" I ask.

"No. She just has her debit card. She worked through her junior and senior years in high school and both summers to save money to have while she was here. She has two scholarships for tuition and a meal allowance. We cover her rent and send her some money every month, but she also wanted to have her own savings so she could feel more independent. There's money in the account."

"Alright. That's something. She has a little bit of money, but definitely not enough to sustain her for long," I note.

"I reached out to the phone company to try to get her records so we could see who she called or texted, but they wouldn't provide it to us because Sydney isn't on our plan. She wanted to pay for that herself," Wesley says. "Maybe so we wouldn't be able to look at anything she was doing."

"She wanted to do it so she could work toward being independent," Angela corrects him. Any softness that might have briefly existed between them is gone just as quickly as it showed up. "I don't even think she would know about the phone company being able to send records of her calls and texts. Most people her age think once you delete something, it's gone forever."

"Have you contacted the police to ask them to request the records?" I ask.

"Yes," Wesley nods. "I went by the station this morning. They've assigned a detective to Sydney's case, and he said he would look into getting those for us."

"That's great," I say. "If we can find out who she was talking to and the kinds of messages she was getting and sending, it will tell us a lot about what was happening in her life leading up to her disappearance."

"The company can send you that?" Jasmine asks.

She sounds confused and surprised, the embodiment of the misled belief Angela mentioned.

"Yes," I say. "There are some pretty strict privacy laws that make it so they can only be released in very specific circumstances. But those records do exist. All the calls to and from the phone, transcripts of text messages sent and received, depending on the phone, some other data is accessible as well."

She swallows and nods. "That could be helpful."

"It definitely could. The important thing here is to trace Sydney's movements not only after the last time anyone had any contact with her, but also before. Things like this don't typically happen spontaneously. They have buildup and preparation, even if it isn't a lot. People who are planning on walking away from their lives, even temporarily, make plans. They look up where they want to go. They make reservations at hotels or buy tickets for a bus or a plane. They get money and supplies. They tell someone they are thinking about it. There's a trail. We just have to find it."

"You think she didn't leave for good reasons," Angela says.

"I don't know anything right now," I say. "But I think it's important to not put too much faith in any one theory. We need to stay open to all possibilities, and that could include that she left voluntarily, but because there was something going on in her life that she wanted to get away from."

"Like what?" Wesley asks.

"That's something that needs to be figured out. The three of you in this room know her the best. Something she said to one of you might be a hint. Or something you noticed about her. Has she been acting strangely recently? Any changes in her personality or her habits?"

"No," Angela says, shaking her head. "She seemed perfectly fine the last time I talked to her. Just like always."

"How about something going on in her life. Did anything major happen recently that might have upset her? Did she talk to any of you about dealing with anything difficult, or being upset by anything?"

"No," Wesley says. "She never really hid anything from us when she was younger. We were so close."

I notice Angela tighten up a bit again. The past tense stands out to me.

"You said when she was younger," I say. "So, she doesn't talk to you anymore?"

"She's becoming an adult," Angela says. "She doesn't confide in her father anymore."

"And you?" I ask.

"Yes," she nods, a slight stumble in her voice. "I mean, she would if there's anything to confide about. She always tells me about what was going on in her life, her classes, her volunteer position. She loves to gossip about the people around campus." Her face flushes like she realized what she said and wishes she hadn't said it. "Not maliciously. She doesn't say mean things about them or anything. She's just being playful."

"What do you mean?" I ask.

"Just telling me about the crazy outfits she sees, all the new trends. And there's a girl who walks past her every day who constantly changes her hair color and style. Sydney jokes it's her life's mission to find out if that girl is actually altering her hair, or if she just has a huge wardrobe of wigs."

She laughs a little, but there's pain in it.

"What about herself? Has she talked about any problems she's been having with anyone, or about feeling stressed? She has a lot on her plate, from what I understand."

"She puts a lot of effort into her schoolwork and works extremely hard toward her goals. She's always concerned about making sure she does her best, but I wouldn't say that she's stressed. Sydney handles things very well. She has coping mechanisms and manages that aspect of her life very carefully."

"And you can't think of anything that she's said or done that might be cause for concern?" I ask. "Or that might make you think she'd had enough and needed to get away?"

"Not at all," Wesley tells me. "As my wife said, we talk all the time. She calls home a few times a week, and usually, we put the call on speaker so we can all talk. The last time I talked with her was last Tuesday. She sounded just like her regular self. She was getting ready for finals and thinking about what she was going to do next semester. She was telling us about a few different programs and study abroad opportunities; I think she wanted to get a head start on applying to those."

"How about you, Jasmine?" I ask, looking over at the girl who seems to have faded into the background of the conversation. "You're her roommate. Have you noticed anything different about her, or has she confided in you about anything going on in her life? Anything you were concerned about?"

She starts shaking her head before I even stop talking. "No. It's like they said, she was just the same old Sydney the last time we talked. Other than being buried in books all the time." Her face goes red, and she makes a sound like she has something stuck in her throat. Her voice drops to a painful whisper. "I'm sorry. I didn't… I didn't mean…"

Angela crosses to Jasmine and wraps her arms around her in a gesture of affection that surprises me.

"It's alright, sweetheart. No one thought you meant anything by that." She leans away from the embrace and brushes Jasmine's hair away from her forehead. "We're going to find her. Everything is going to be alright."

"We need to identify when she was last seen and who she was with so we can create a better timeline of events. Once we can really pinpoint when Sydney disappeared, it will give us a more solid place to build off of," I say, not wanting to let the situation deteriorate into too much emotion. "Mr. and Mrs. Parker, I'd like your permission to speak with Sydney's professors and other people she had contact with. Would that be alright with you?"

They agree and Joe offers to send me her schedule and information about the teachers and other staff who had regular contact with Sydney. I thank them and we leave, but I can feel Jasmine's eyes on me as I close the door.

# CHAPTER EIGHTEEN

JOE WALKS WITH ME OUT OF THE APARTMENT AND WE MAKE OUR way back toward the main campus. It's only a few blocks, but the layout of the roads and the way the trees grow up around the sidewalks make it feel like we're going much farther.

"I want to thank you for your patience with Angela and Wesley," he starts.

"There's nothing to thank me for," I say.

"You're giving your time and energy to help find their missing daughter, and…"

I stop him.

"What matters is their missing daughter," I tell him. "That's it. They can be angry or suspicious or uncomfortable with me all they want, if that gives them one less thing they have to worry themselves about during all this. They're dealing with something unimaginable. I promise I have thick enough skin to absorb some of that so they have a direction to throw it." I think about the interaction for a few seconds before speaking again. "How well do you know the family?"

"The Parkers?" he asks, then shakes his head. "Not well. Not personally, anyway. Baxter isn't a huge school, but it's also not small enough for me to be on a close personal basis with all the families. I know of Sydney because of everything she does with the different student organizations, her academics, scholarships, but that's the extent of it. I've never had a long conversation with her, and I think I could probably count on one hand the number of times I've had any protracted interaction with her individually. But every student here is important to me, and I feel very responsible for them, so this has been very challenging for me."

"I understand that," I nod. "How about her parents? Have you interacted with them before this?"

"A couple of times. I know I met them during Orientation weekend before Sydney's freshman year, though I remember very little about the conversation. Then I had a longer talk with them at an awards ceremony her sophomore year. I've also had a few email exchanges and phone conversations over the last three years," he shrugs. "But I certainly wouldn't say we've developed a friendship."

"When you have had interactions with them before, were they as tense with each other as they were today?" I ask.

"I don't really remember," he admits. "If they were, it never stood out to me."

"And as far as you know, there isn't any particular conflict between Sydney and her parents?"

"Are you suggesting her parents might have had something to do with this?" he asks.

"I'm not suggesting anything. I'm just trying to get as clear a picture as I can," I clarify. "It's important to understand the dynamics of relationships in her life if we want to narrow it down to what may have made her want to leave. Her parents are going to be two of the most influential people in her life. Their relationship with each other, and how that translated to their relationship with her, could be a major piece in all of this."

What I don't tell him is the strange feeling I got from the way Sydney's parents talked about her. The shift between past and present tense was uncomfortable, though not totally unheard of. Some people naturally fall into discussing a person in the past tense when they aren't around, especially when there's a situation like this. But it's not generally the parents.

Usually, parents cling to the present tense, feeling like if they stop thinking of their child in the immediate moment, the child will slip away from them. Even though they know in the most logical part of their minds that they have no control over what's happening, they'll do anything they can to feel like they are helping, or at least that they aren't contributing to any more danger for their child. To the point that a simple word putting them in the past feels like it could be the very thing that ends it all.

But even if I put the tense shifts aside, they were so adamant about Sydney being fine and exactly how she always is, even pushing to make sure I understood she wasn't stressed. The thing is, she should be feeling stressed. It's normal and natural for a college student to feel stress toward the end of the semester, especially when trying to juggle a heavy course load and extracurricular activities. I don't believe for a second that Sydney never actually felt any stress or strain, no matter how she presented that to the world. Resilience is one thing. Immunity to stress and acting like everything is perfect is compensation.

Joe and I go our separate ways after he provides me with Sydney's schedule and directs me to the nearest professor's office. When I get there, the door is closed, but light coming from under it tells me there's a good chance the professor is there for office hours.

I knock and almost instantly a gruff, deep voice tells me to come inside. I step in and a heavyset man with hair that seems to have developed its own personality looks over his shoulder from where he's standing in front of a large whiteboard making notes. He looks surprised to not see one of his students, but not enough to stop what he's doing at this moment.

"Yes? What can I do for you?" he asks, already looking back at what he was writing and starting to work on it again.

"I'm Agent Griffin. Can I speak with you for just a minute?" I ask.

"Agent Griffin," he repeats. The usual tinge to the words that tells me the speaker has heard of me isn't there. "That sounds like law enforcement."

"Yes," I say. "I'm on campus looking into Sydney Parker's disappearance."

He pauses and puts the marker in his hand down on the little shelf at the bottom of the dry erase board bolted to the wall. Moving behind his desk, he uses one hand to pull his chair out so he can sit, and the other to gesture to a chair across from him.

"Arthur Boris," he says by way of introduction, extending his hand. "And you said your name is Agent… Griffith?"

"Griffin," I correct him. "Mythological bird-lion hybrid. Not small-town sheriff. Though, I am married to one of those. An actual sheriff, not a Griffith."

Arthur continues to stare at me, and I realize this is not a man for whom humor makes up an important segment of his life.

"You said you were here looking into Sydney's disappearance," he says, like he's guiding me back on topic. "Does that mean there's been a development?"

"No," I say. "I'm talking to as many people as possible to try to find out everything I can about her and her life, hoping it will help shed some light on where she could have gone."

"What would you like to know?" he asks.

"Anything you can tell me."

"Sydney's a great student. She's intelligent, driven, and eager to learn. The kind of student you wish you could have in every class. There were times when it felt like she and I were carrying the entire classroom discussion about a lecture."

"How has she been doing recently? Is she as engaged as she has been? Still performing well?" I ask.

"She has the highest grade in the class. I just graded a paper she turned in recently and it was exceptional," he says.

"Has she seemed happy?"

"Agent Griffin, I'm here to teach college students. What I care about is academic performance and development. I believe I'd notice if one of them came into the lecture hall distraught, but beyond that, I'm not really concerned with their happiness," he shrugs.

I give a single nod. "Understood. Well, thank you for your time."

I stand, but don't bother to shake his hand. Somehow, I don't think he would concern himself with that, either.

The next professor I visit teaches a massive section of hundreds of students with a few teaching assistants, so she is familiar with Sydney only in a basic way. The fact that she can pinpoint her at all in that sea of students speaks to Sydney being an impressive student, but that's as far as it goes with that teacher.

Things change when I notice on Sydney's schedule that her literature class should be just ending. I rush to get to the classroom before the professor leaves. Unlike the last professor's huge auditorium, this classroom is small, reminiscent of a high school, and has only a couple dozen students scattered throughout the desks. The time is officially up, but they are all still actively taking notes, some on computers and others in notebooks like I did.

I wait out in the hallway for a few more minutes before the class finally ends and the students stream out. When there's a break in the flow, I dip inside and approach the man at the front of the room. He looks a little bit rushed and breathless, like he lives his entire life trying to catch up. He starts stuffing a collection of things from the top of the podium and basic white banquet table set up beside it into a brown leather messenger bag, but his feet start moving toward the door before he's done, like the bottom half of his body has decided it's time to leave whether the top half is ready or not.

He manages to snag the last couple of things and nearly walks into me because he's looking down to put them in the bag.

"Oh," he says. "Hello. I'm sorry."

"It's fine. Are you Les Hall?"

"Yes," he says.

"My name is Emma Griffin. I'm looking into Sydney Parker's disappearance. Do you have a couple of minutes to talk with me?"

"If we can walk and talk," he says.

"Absolutely."

We head out of the classroom and his feet quickly pick up speed until I feel like one of those little old ladies who go to the mall far too early in the morning to take laps.

"It's just such a shame about Sydney. She's a really special girl."

"You have a good relationship with her?" I ask.

"She's taken several of my classes over the years, and I worked with her on an independent study course on depictions of mental health in classic literature," he tells me. "Her work was so compelling I encouraged her to compile it into a book for publication and asked her permission to develop it into a full lecture series."

"Wow. That's impressive," I say.

He leads me down a staircase at the back of the building and bursts through a door leading outside into a small courtyard.

"Very."

"Did you notice anything about her recently that seemed different?" I ask.

"Well, now that you mention it, yes, I did notice some changes in her. Nothing dramatic, I suppose, but enough. Sydney is a friendly, outgoing, energetic girl. She's always involved in something. Volunteering, tutoring, stuff like that. She's the kind that people say lights up a room. And that's the way she's been since the first time she came to one of my classes. Only, recently it seems like it's almost too much."

"What do you mean?" I frown.

We get to another building, and he pauses in front of it.

"Everything about her became bigger and more exaggerated. Smiling bigger. Laughing more and louder. Talking more. Gesturing. Everything is still *her*, but turned up brighter. And it seems like it came and went. Sometimes she could even turn it on and off on a whim." He looks up at the building and points to it. "I have to get to a meeting. Please let me know if there's any more help I can give you."

"I will. Thank you for your time."

He rushes into the building with intensity and urgency that reminds me of Xavier. I wonder if he saw something when he looked into Sydney's eyes that other people didn't see.

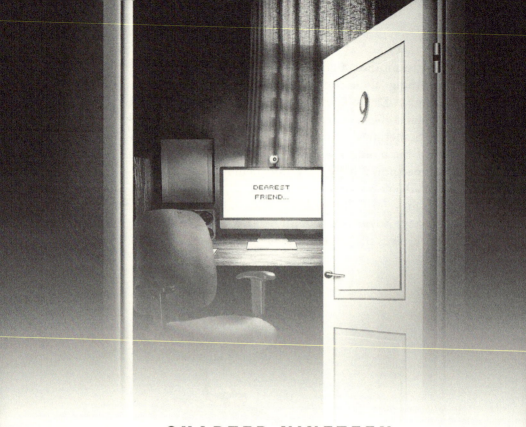

# CHAPTER NINETEEN

I FIND A TINY FOOD TRUCK OFF TO THE SIDE OF THE ROAD SELLING coffee and I get a cup. The caffeine from the cup that morning with Joe has worn off and I need to keep myself going. My phone rings in my pocket as I'm walking away, and I take a sip while pulling it out. It's Sam.

"Hey, babe," I say.

"Hey. How's everything going?"

"It's going. I met with Joe Corrigan this morning and got some more details about everything, then went to Sydney's apartment to look around. It turns out the police never even searched it. After she was reported missing, they glanced around, but they didn't actually do a search. And her roommate Jasmine has been living there since then."

"Where else would she be living?" Sam asks.

I sigh. "I know, but I just feel like they should have done more."

"But there's still no evidence of foul play, right? What else could they do?"

"I don't know," I admit. "But she's only nineteen. With everything going for her. The more I find out about her, the more I feel like there's something wrong about all this. I talked to her parents, her professors, and the head of the peer counseling program, and I feel like I'm getting competing ideas of who Sydney is, and what her life was like."

"What do you mean?"

"All the adults in her life except for one professor talked about how bubbly and bright and cheerful Sydney is. And that professor only said he didn't pay enough attention to his individual students to have that kind of evaluation of her. But her roommate didn't say anything like that. She was much more generic about describing her. Not that she was negative, and she did make it a point to say that she was happy and outgoing, but it was much more tempered. Her parents talked about how amazing she is and how she handles everything so beautifully. To hear them tell it, she's never stressed, doesn't get upset, never has anything bothering her."

"That seems a bit excessive," Sam observes.

"That's what I thought. This girl is in her third year of college, applying for major programs, and also grappling with mental health problems. She's going to be stressed. There are days when she's going to be upset. That's just part of being a person," I say.

"So, why did her parents feel it was necessary to pretend she doesn't?"

"Exactly," I nod. "I talked with her professors and one of them she apparently has a fairly close relationship with. She's taken a few classes from him and done an independent study, so they've spent more time together than she has with other professors. He told me that Sydney is exceptional, but lately, it seems like she's been almost over the top. Like she's exaggerating being happy and outgoing."

"That sounds like what you told me Xavier said about her," Sam notes.

"It does. Like she's trying to cover something up by seeming really positive and enthusiastic. And there was something off about her parents. I know that having a child missing can put a tremendous amount of strain on a relationship, but there were points where they almost seemed hostile toward each other. They both said that Sydney hasn't confided in them about anything going on in her life, and that they would know if something was wrong, but they were standing together, and we were in the room with Joe and Jasmine as well. I want to talk with them separately. It's possible she actually did talk to her mother about something, but she didn't want to admit to that in front of Sydney's father."

"Are you still planning on talking to the police today?" he asks.

"I'm heading there in just a minute," I tell him. "Apparently a detective has been assigned to the case. I don't know how they are going to react to me looking into things, so I want to be the one to approach them first."

"And see how much they'll tell you and gauge if you can direct them in how to investigate," Sam says with a hint of a smile behind his words.

"I'm not going to tell them how to investigate," I say. He makes a sound like he's not buying it. "I'm just here to offer my professional insights. That's it."

"Mhm. Well, since my lovely wife is out of town, I'll have no choice but to hunker down at Pearl's for the next several meals."

"Oh, that sounds like such a sacrifice you have to make," I say, rolling my eyes and smiling.

"Well, those hash browns aren't going to eat themselves. Someone has to do it."

"I'm sure Pearl is very appreciative of your service. Okay, I've got to call the police. Love you."

"Love you."

I use the business card Jasmine had from the responding officer to call the police department. They transfer me to the detective, Alyssa Bakker, but she's not in her office. I call the cell number provided on her voicemail and am quickly prompted to leave another message. I introduce myself, give her a brief overview, and ask her to call me back.

By this time, I'm far removed from breakfast and have missed the usual lunch hour by quite a bit. My stomach is rumbling, and I decide to go to the campus dining hall for dinner. I want to immerse myself in the campus and see it from Sydney's perspective as much as possible. I'm not sure what it will tell me, if anything, but I have nothing else to go on right now.

I brace myself for a dining experience like I had when I was in school, but this is nothing like that cramped, damp-feeling cafeteria. At the top of a spiraling staircase a bright, airy room spreads out on all sides. It's bustling with students visiting stations set up like tiny restaurants and milling around an impressive salad bar.

A payment station is set up at the top of the steps, and I pay before roaming through to explore my options. When I finally have a tray filled with what caught my eye, I head toward the booths and tables organized at the far end. I manage to snag a booth right next to one of the floor-to-ceiling curved windows and sit down, digging around in my bag to find the paperback I generally have on my person at all times.

Over time I've gotten more open to electronic books, but I'm never going to be the person who completely foregoes actual, tangible books. I open up to the last spot I remember reading and dig in. A few minutes later, out of the corner of my eye, I notice someone come up to the side of the table.

"Agent Griffin?"

I lower my book and see Jasmine.

"Hi, Jasmine."

"I'm sorry to interrupt your dinner," she says. "I just noticed you sitting here."

I shake my head. "No, it's fine. I'm just having a bit of a nostalgia moment. When I was in college, which feels like about a hundred years ago when I look at you guys, I used to sit in the dining hall and read for hours. Of course, it wasn't anything like this place. Everything smelled exactly alike, and it was really difficult to tell what you were eating. But they had a great cereal bar at breakfast, so that was a plus."

I don't mention to her that the sitting and reading for hours portion of my college experience came when I was still studying art. My transition over to studying criminal justice and preparing for the FBI Academy meant spending every available second studying and subsisting off whatever I could get into the library or out of a vending machine.

"Can I talk to you for a second?" she asks.

I gesture to the bench across the table from me. "Go ahead."

She sits and folds her hands on top of the table. She looks nervous and I give her a second to gather her thoughts.

"There's something I didn't mention when you were at the apartment earlier," she finally says.

"Alright," I nod.

Jasmine seems to grapple with choosing her words. "You should talk to her ex-boyfriend."

"Her ex?" I raise an eyebrow. "I didn't know she was dating anyone."

"They broke up pretty recently. He cheated on her," she tells me.

"How did Sydney react to that?"

"I mean, I guess how you would expect her to. She was angry and upset. But it wasn't anything extreme. I wouldn't say she was despondent or anything. She was just hurt and pissed about how it happened. But he wanted her back."

"He did?" I ask.

Jasmine nods. "He'd been calling and coming by. He was really trying to convince her that he knew he'd made a mistake and wanted to fix it, that he didn't want to be away from her anymore. But Sydney wasn't interested. She said she couldn't ever trust him again, and she wasn't going to lower herself by going back with someone who would cheat on her."

"Did he take the hint?" I ask.

"No. He kept pursuing her. She wasn't giving in, and it made him really angry. The last time I saw them talking, he seemed furious," she says.

"Why didn't you mention any of this when I was talking to you this morning? I asked if anything major had happened in her life recently," I say.

"I know. But I didn't want to get into the middle of anything. I didn't know if Sydney had told her parents about the breakup, and I didn't want to make everything more complicated for them. I figured it would be better if you looked into him first."

"Did you mention him to the police?" I ask.

She shakes her head. "They didn't ask."

"How can I get in touch with him?"

"His name is Van Oshanick. He lives in Murray Hall. I can give you his room number," she says.

"Can you call him and have him meet us here?" I ask.

"He's blocked me," Jasmine admits. "But I can give you his number. You might have better luck."

She takes a piece of paper out of the backpack she had slung on her shoulder when she came to the table. She writes down the details and hands the note over to me.

"Alright. Thank you for telling me this, Jasmine."

She nods, suddenly looking emotional. "Do you think she's okay?"

I choose my words carefully. "I think we need to find her."

# CHAPTER TWENTY

I hear back from Detective Bakker as I'm getting ready to take a shower at the hotel.

"I'm sorry to call you this late in the evening," she says. "It's been a busy day."

"It's fine. I can absolutely commiserate on the busy days," I say.

"From what I know about your career, I'd say that's an understatement," she replies with a slight laugh. "Your message said you wanted to know about the Sydney Parker case."

"Yes," I say. "The president of Baxter, Joe Corrigan, is an old friend of a friend of mine. When he found out about Sydney's disappearance, Paul suggested I look into the situation. So as a favor to him, I came down here to offer my assistance. But I want to assure you I'm not strapping on a cape and trying to take over. That's why I wanted to get in touch with you. I don't want to compromise any investigation you might have going already. I know Sydney's parents and roommate said there wasn't much police involvement as of yet, but I didn't know if you were just not disclosing all the details to them."

"Well, they are correct," Detective Bakker says. "There's very little we can do right now. There aren't any signs of foul play. There's nothing to indicate anything happened to her other than she just walked out of her apartment and decided not to go back. According to her parents, she has her phone and her medication, and she doesn't bring her medication with her everywhere she goes. This indicates to me that she intended on being away.

"We have a request in with the phone company to provide records of her calls and text messages, but that can take quite a bit of time to get. Until we have anything else, there's nothing we can do. Frankly—and I'm sure you can appreciate this considering the types of cases you have handled during your career—I am up to my eyeballs in cases and don't have the manpower available to pursue this when there's nothing to go on. Until there is something that we can work with…"

Her voice trails off. I understand what she's saying. As awful as it is and as frustrated as she sounds, it's an unfortunate reality of law enforcement. Sometimes there are too many cases at one time, and something has to give. Priority is given to the cases with the most information, or the strongest indication of serious danger. An adult going missing for a few days with no sign of anything suspicious beyond just the reality of the disappearance itself can't take precedence over a kidnapped child, a multiple murder, or a serial robber whose violence is escalating.

We end the conversation without making a formal alliance, but also without her asking me to stay away from the investigation. I don't need her permission to do what I'm doing, so I'm satisfied I've done my due diligence. As far as I'm concerned, this is my investigation now.

I start the next morning trying to get in touch with Sydney's ex. He doesn't answer when I call, so I call again and leave a voicemail. I decide to go over to the dorm that Jasmine directed me to, but when I get there, I can't get inside. Leaning close to the glass door, I notice a security guard sitting at the desk just inside. It isn't an adult in uniform, just a student wearing a bright red jacket emblazoned with "SECURITY" across the sleeve and the logo of the school on the chest.

He's likely just a student resident who signed up for the work-study program through the financial aid department and ended up with this as his assignment. I knock on the glass and wave when he looks up at me. He looks confused, like he doesn't remember how to answer a door. I gesture to the handle, and he shakes his head. I point to it again and grab on, shaking the door to show him it's locked.

"You have to have an ID card that proves you live here to get in."

I turn around and see a girl with rainbow braids and eyelashes so long they look like they could make her take flight any second. I have a brief moment of envy for her. She flashes her ID at me, reaches around, and swipes it through the card reader, slipping past the door and into the lobby before I can follow her. The envy goes away pretty quickly.

Well, if they need an ID, I'll show ID.

I take out my Bureau badge and hold it against the glass so the security guard can see it. It takes him a second for the shield to register. When it does, he scrambles out of his seat and rushes over. As he opens the door, I grab hold of it so it can close again.

"I'm sorry," he's saying before I can even step inside. "I'm not supposed to let anyone in who doesn't live here. I didn't realize…"

"That's good security protocol," I tell him. "But thank you for opening the door for me. I'm looking for someone who lives in this building. Van Oshanick."

He nods. "I know Van. I live on the same floor."

"Perfect. Do you know if he's in his room right now?" I ask.

"I don't think so," he says. "He's usually in class now."

"Is there a way you can check?" I ask.

"I can call him."

"Would you?"

He looks nervous as he scurries back over to the desk. I should probably tell him that his buddy isn't actually under investigation by the FBI, but I don't. Considering it is my badge and I am here on a case, I'm not impersonating an officer. I'm just encouraging cooperation.

The security guard comes back a second later, and by the look on his face, I can already tell he doesn't have good news for me.

"He didn't answer," he says. "I could text him."

"I have his room number. I'll just go up and see if he'll answer the door. Maybe he has his phone on silent and doesn't know anyone is trying to get a hold of him."

That's a bunch of bull, but the security guard doesn't argue. He nods me across the lobby and into the elevator. I ride it up and head for the number Jasmine gave me, but pounding on the door and calling through it does no good. Eventually, I give up and go back down to the lobby.

"Did you get him?" the kid behind the desk asks.

"No. But let him know to check his messages and give me a call back, alright? It's important I talk with him," I say.

He promises he will, and I leave, dialing Angela Parker as I go.

She looks more tired and sad when I get to the coffee shop where we agreed to meet. She's already sitting at a table near a window, slowly twisting a mug between the tips of her fingers. It looks partially empty, and I wonder if she asked me to meet her here because she was already sitting there.

"Thanks for meeting with me," I say as I sit down across from her. "I'll try not to take up too much of your time."

She shakes her head. "There's nothing else for me to be doing with my time. I'm here until we find Sydney."

"That's why I wanted to speak with you. I wanted to let you know I did talk with the detective who is in charge of her case. Unfortunately, there isn't really any more information for me to share with you, but now that she is aware I'm here, we can streamline the investigation."

"Is there an investigation?" she asks sadly. "Is anyone doing anything to look for her?"

"I am," I say. "And you might be able to help me. I spoke with Sydney's professors and the head of the peer counseling program, and they all said the same things about her. That she's smart and driven. Some talked about how much of an inspiration she is. But one of her professors said there seemed to be something that was bothering her recently. I found out that she and her boyfriend broke up not too long ago, and I've been trying to get in touch with him to talk with him about it, but I haven't been able to."

"Her boyfriend?" Angela frowns.

"Yes. Van. I was hoping you might have his number and be able to call him. I don't know how long the two of them were together and if you were close, but if you could convince him to come talk with me, it would be really helpful," I say.

She shakes her head, looking confused. "Sydney didn't have a boyfriend. At least, not one that I knew of. She never mentioned she was seeing anyone."

My heart drops a little. "Never? She didn't say anything about a guy in her life? Van?"

"No. She didn't," Angela says. Her eyes squeeze shut and she cringes like she's fighting tears and a rush of emotion threatening to overcome her. "I hate feeling like she didn't think she could tell me everything."

"Again, I don't know how long the two of them were together. Maybe it was still new and she hadn't decided she wanted to share it with you yet."

"She did say there was something she wanted to tell me," Angela says.

"When?" I ask.

"I spoke to her Thursday night. I was getting ready to go to a function with an organization I volunteer for, so I didn't have time for a long conversation. She said that was fine, but she just had to tell me."

"What was it?"

"She didn't elaborate. But she sounded so excited. She said she finally figured out what she wanted to do. What she was *supposed* to do, and that spring break had really made all the difference. She said I would find out soon."

"What about spring break?" I ask. "What did she do?"

"She went on a volunteer trip through the school to help rebuild homes affected by a hurricane. She'd been looking forward to it for a really long time. Was planning it for weeks. It was really going to open up the doors to some really big things for her. But afterward, she didn't really talk about it."

"What do you mean?"

Angela shrugs. Before the trip, she'd been telling us all about the details: where they'd be staying, the activities they'd be doing. But afterward… she said it was good, and that was really it. I just figured she was already so focused on the rest of the semester that she wasn't thinking about it, and I would hear all about the trip later. Maybe that's when she met this boy."

"Has she ever been that excited to tell you about a relationship before?" I ask.

"Sydney didn't date a lot in high school. She had a lot of friends, and I guess she went out a couple of times, but there was never one specific guy she had an ongoing relationship with," Angela tells me. "Do you think her ex-boyfriend could have something to do with her going missing? If they broke up, maybe he's angry?"

I don't share with her the information Jasmine gave me. Until I can confirm the details, I don't see a reason to upset her any further.

"I just want to talk to him about Sydney and find out when he last saw and spoke with her so we can keep building a timeline leading up to her disappearance," I say. "I'd also like to speak with the head of the spring break trip. Do you have their contact information?"

Angela nods. "Tracy Gold."

With the name and contact information jotted on a napkin, I leave the coffee shop and start back toward Sydney's apartment to canvass her neighbors. Someone has to have heard or seen something that can tell me when she actually disappeared, and how.

I'm trying to keep myself calm. I'm trying to convince myself that these leads will give me answers. But there's a sinking feeling in my gut that only grows heavier with everyone I speak to.

# CHAPTER TWENTY-ONE

THE LOCATION OF THE COFFEE SHOP HAS ME APPROACHING Sydney's apartment from a different angle from before and adds a little more distance, so I decide to make use of the time by calling the coordinator for the spring break trip. It seems par for the course at this point that I could only leave her a message. It is an in-session college campus, so I get that everyone is busy, but I hate having the dangling threads.

I'm putting my phone back into my bag after talking to Jasmine when I walk into the tiny parking area behind the apartment building. She isn't home, but that doesn't make much of a difference. I'm planning on talking to the neighbors, so I don't need to get into her apartment.

But someone apparently does.

I'm halfway across the dirt and gravel parking area when I notice a young guy slip around the corner of the building. He has his head tucked down and doesn't lift it until he rushes up onto the small porch at the back of Sydney's apartment. He walks right past the door and grabs hold of the bottom of a window I assume goes into her bedroom.

"Hey," I shout, taking off running toward him.

The guy's head snaps to look over his shoulder. When he notices me, he stumbles away from the building and down the steps. They slow him down enough to negate his head start down the narrow alley to the side of the building. I chase him down the alley and catch up to him right before he's able to get out in front of it.

He grunts as I bury my knee in his back and drop him to the ground.

"I wasn't breaking in!" he insists into the ground. "I wasn't breaking in."

"You just make it a habit of visiting people who aren't home and going in through the window?" I snap.

"I wasn't breaking in," he repeats. "Can you let me up? I won't try to run again. I don't really need to have anybody see my ass get tackled to the ground again."

I get off his back and pull him to his feet, letting go of him. "If you aren't breaking in, why are you going to the window?"

"So nobody notices I'm here," he says.

"Wrong answer," I growl, grabbing onto him and yanking him near me again. I have every intention of holding him still until I can get the police there.

"Hey, stop," he whines. "I'm not breaking in. I have a key. It's in my pocket if you let me get it."

"You have a key?" I ask. "If you have a key, whose apartment is this?"

"Sydney Parker," he says. "And her roommate Jasmine. I'm Sydney's boyfriend."

"Van?"

"Yeah."

"I've been looking for you."

"You're Agent Griffin?"

"Yes."

"Shit," he mutters.

"Glad to meet you, too. What do you mean you're her boyfriend? I thought the two of you broke up."

"We did," he admits. "But we're going to get back together. I know we are."

"But you did break up?"

"Yes," he says. "A couple of weeks ago."

"And she didn't want the key to her apartment back?" I ask.

He reaches in his pocket and pulls out a key. "I made a copy."

I grab the key from his hand. "I'll go ahead and keep this. What the hell are you doing sneaking around her apartment building and trying to get into her window? Especially if you're walking around with a key in your pocket?"

"I was going to use the key to go in the front door if I needed to, but I figured it was less likely that anybody would notice me if I was back here. The back door has a deadbolt and the key doesn't work for it, so I checked the window first."

"But that still doesn't tell me why you're here," I press. "You must know by now that Sydney is missing. She has been for a week."

"Of course, I know that," he snaps. "I came here to see if I could figure anything out about it. Maybe I would notice something in the apartment that nobody else had."

It seems like a good answer, but it also sounds like he's coming up with it in real time as it falls out of his mouth.

"I'm not buying it," I say. "Why are you actually here?"

Van lets out a sigh. "Look, I was here with Sydney the night she went missing. I already knew Jasmine was going to be out of town, so I thought it was the perfect opportunity to get us back together. I let myself in with my key and surprised her with dinner from her favorite restaurant. I lit candles and everything."

"And you didn't think it would be important to mention to somebody that you saw her the last night anyone knew where she was?" I ask.

"I didn't want anybody to know. Okay? I was embarrassed and worried that people would think I did something to her because I was here that night. I didn't realize she was here when I let myself in because all the lights were off and she was in her bedroom. She came out and I startled her, and she didn't even give me a chance to really talk to her," he says. "I had to clap my hand over her mouth to stop her from screaming."

"Really not looking good for you here, Van."

"I know. I know. But I didn't do anything. She told me to leave. I wanted to stay. I wanted to tell her everything I'd been feeling and remind her that we were so good together. But I didn't stay. After she told me she wanted me to leave, I left. And that was it. I was just going to pretend it never happened, but then I realized I left something of mine here."

"What did you leave?" I ask.

"My tablet. I had set it up and was playing music we listened to while we were dating. She pushed me out so fast I didn't think to grab it," Van says.

I remember the list of items Sydney's parents and Jasmine said were still in the apartment, and realize one of them was her tablet. Because there was only one there, it means it isn't actually hers, but Van's.

"Give me just a second," I say.

I take out my phone and call Alyssa Bakker.

"What are you doing?" he asks.

"Calling the detective in charge of the case," I say.

His face goes pale. "What? I seriously just explained what I'm doing."

"I'm aware of that," I say. "But that doesn't change that you didn't disclose important information about seeing a girl who is now missing, and who you admit to having a conflict with, and that you were attempting to get into her apartment without being noticed after making a copy of her key. It doesn't look good."

"I would definitely agree that doesn't look good. But I don't think I did any of that." It's Alyssa's voice coming through the phone. I didn't even notice she answered.

"Sorry," I tell her. "This is Emma Griffin. I'm here with Van Oshanick, Sydney's ex-boyfriend." He starts to walk away, and I step toward him. "I don't suggest you go anywhere, Van. I know where you live and it's going to look even worse for you if you try to get away from this. If you haven't done anything wrong, you have no reason not to let the police search your room."

"Search my room? You got to be kidding me. I have rights. This is a violation," he says.

"You live in a dorm on a college campus," I point out. "It's not your personal home and you don't own it. Yes, you have rights, but not nearly as many as you think you do. And, frankly, those rights end where suspicion of involvement in your ex-girlfriend going missing begins."

"Why do we need to search his room?" Detective Bakker asks.

"Because it turns out Van saw Sydney on Friday night. He took it upon himself to use a copy of the key to get into her apartment and was then rejected by her," I say.

"I explained that to you," Van groans. "This is ridiculous."

"I'll meet you there in fifteen minutes," she tells me.

"See you then," I say. I hang up and point at him. "Van, I don't know if you're really grasping how serious this is. This isn't just some college drama. This is a missing persons investigation. I understand you are angry that I won't just take your word that everything's fine, but I don't do that. I've been in the FBI for a very long time, and because of that, I can count the number of people I truly trust without question on two hands. I don't even need to use my toes.

"So, here's what's going to happen. You're going to straighten up and deal with your room being searched. You're going to cooperate, answer every question the police ask you, and give them whatever they need, because right now, the important thing is finding out what happened to Sydney. And if you didn't have anything to do with it, you want to be eliminated as a person of interest and let the investigators use their time and energy on other possibilities."

I can't say Van agrees, but he agrees to meet me at the dorm. He has his car a block away, but I'm not interested in climbing in his passenger seat. I'm just fine walking.

When I get to the dorm, there are two police cars and a black unmarked vehicle sitting out front. I don't see Van's car, but I'm assuming he found street parking wherever he could because he's standing on the patio area out front with a woman in dark gray suit pants and a jewel purple blouse. Much like the rainbow braids I witnessed the first time I came to this dorm, that color is one I wouldn't attempt. But it looks sensational against the detective's rich-toned skin. She reminds me of Bellamy, and I tuck the idea of a sweater in that shade into the back of my mind for her upcoming birthday.

"Detective Bakker?" I ask, walking up to them.

She turns and smiles. "Agent Griffin. It's an honor to meet you."

"Not at all. It's good to meet you, Detective. I appreciate you letting me tag along with this investigation," I say.

"You can call me Alyssa. And, trust me, I'm keeping it together on the outside here, but I'm fangirling on the inside," she says.

I laugh. "Call me Emma."

"This whole bonding thing is really sweet and all, but can we please move this along? I don't really appreciate being put on display out here," Van groans.

I turn a glare in his direction, and he withers back slightly. I look back at Alyssa.

"Let's make sure to make it thorough."

The dorm room Van lives in isn't exactly large, so the search only takes about an hour. By the time the team is done, the desk has a small pile of items they thought might be worth bringing to my and Alyssa's attention. Among them are a t-shirt with blood, several long dark hairs, a bra, and a couple of pieces of what look like a letter that has been ripped up. Not many of the words on the letter are still legible, but I can make out what amounts to a threat against someone who embarrassed Van.

As is standard practice when a location is being processed, Van was kept out of his dorm during the search. Now one of the officers escorts him in. His face registers shock, then anger, when he sees everything upturned and pulled apart.

"What the hell?" he asks. "Was this really necessary?"

"I'm sorry if my team didn't meet your expectations for cleanliness," Alyssa tells him. "Would you like me to ask them to return your partially eaten pizza slices and dirty socks to precisely where they found them?"

"The team found a few things we'd like you to explain," I add, gesturing to the desk.

Van looks over the pile and I can almost see the gears churning in his head. He knows how this looks.

"The blood is mine," he says quickly. "I got a nosebleed the other night. It happens every spring. I didn't have any tissues in the room, and it was the middle of the night, so I didn't feel like going down the hall to the bathroom, so I just grabbed a t-shirt. I haven't done my laundry yet."

"How about the hairs?" I ask. "Looks like there are quite a few of them. And just about the length and color of Sydney's."

"We were dating," he shrugs. "She came over here a few times. Maybe they came out then."

"She just spontaneously lost a chunk of hair while hanging out in your room?" I ask. "And it's just been sitting here for weeks? You did say you broke up a couple of weeks ago."

"Did she lose her bra at the same time?" Alyssa asks. "Seems irresponsible."

"That's..." He stammers, his face going red as he looks at the bra. "Look, I told you I went to her place on Friday. I brought dinner, I lit candles, the whole nine yards. She rejected me. So I left. I wanted to stay, but she made it clear she wasn't ready right then. Yes, I was upset and angry, but I left, and I didn't go back. I can prove I wasn't with her that night after dinner."

"How can you prove that?" I ask.

"Can I use my phone?" he asks.

Alyssa and I nod, and he takes out his phone. Van scrolls through a few screens before turning it to us and starting a video. It appears to be a party. He's the one taking the footage and talking as he moves through a room crowded with people. I notice he'd posted it early Saturday morning.

"This was Friday night?" I ask.

"Yes. If you watch enough of it, you'll see a few seconds of the basketball game that aired earlier. My friend Abbott had recorded it and was playing it back, so I videoed it for a bit."

"Alright. I want you to send me that footage along with a list of the names of everyone you can think of who was there," I tell him.

"Agent Griffin, I didn't have anything to do with Sydney being missing. I loved her. I wouldn't ever hurt her."

"No one knows if she's hurt," I point out.

Bright pink spots appear on his cheeks before I turn and walk away.

# CHAPTER TWENTY-TWO

"That was impressive," Alyssa remarks as we walk out of the dorm. "You had him squirming."

"Yeah, I can terrorize youth with the best of them," I say.

"What do you think about what he said? Do you think he did something to Sydney?" she asks.

I take a breath and look out over the road in front of the dorm. The sun is well on its way down, but students are still shuffling around with backpacks and messenger bags, going to late classes and study groups. A few stare at the phones in their hands as they go, as if they can't exist without a constant stream of input. If I stare long enough, I can see Sydney among them. I imagine her walking down the sidewalk, her head tucked down, sometimes walking alongside others. Sometimes sinking back and walking alone.

I close my eyes and open them again. The image of Sydney is gone. It's not hard to see how easily someone can slip away here.

"Something was suspicious up there," I say. "But I don't know. I want to know more about that party."

"I'll keep you up to date on anything I find out," Alyssa says. "Feel free to call me any time."

"I'll do the same. And you have my contact information."

We part ways and I head for where I parked my car so I can drive back to the hotel. Before I get there, I get a message from Tracy Gold, the sponsor for the spring break volunteer trip. I didn't put my phone in the cradle on the dashboard, so I can't answer the call on speaker, and I let it go to voicemail. I'm listening to the message inviting me to meet with her the next day as I walk through the hotel lobby when a call comes through on the other line.

"Hello?"

"Hey, cuz," Dean starts. "What are you up to?"

"Hey, Dean. I'm just getting back to the hotel."

"Anything interesting happen with the case today?" he asks.

I get to the elevator and hit the up button. "Yeah, actually. But it's too much for me to get into right now. What about you?"

The elevator doors open, and I step in, select my floor, and lean back against the cool brushed metal wall.

"I've just been doing some more digging. I confirmed through a couple more sources that Salvador Marini definitely only has a sister and no nephew," he tells me. "But I was looking through pictures of events and some candid shots from articles about his company, and I did notice a man who seemed to be around him quite a bit for a while. Then he just disappeared. None of the pictures have captions that identify him, which in itself is strange."

"That is strange," I agree. The doors open and I go to my room. I kick off my shoes just like I'm home. "Get in touch with Eric and ask him to get financial records for Marini's company from that period of time. See if there was an assistant or other paid position that isn't being paid anymore. It might help track this guy down."

"I'm not done, yet," Dean says, but his voice is distant like he's pulled his face away from the phone. "I did tell her that, but I wanted to…" He sighs. "Xavier wants to talk to you."

"Bye," I say.

"Emma?" Xavier asks.

"Hey, Xavier. What's up?" I ask.

I loosen the button and zipper on my pants and drop down onto the end of the bed, using my free hand to take my hair down and shake it out. It must have been tied up too tightly because the follicles sting as the strands relax.

"I need you to do something for me," he says.

"What do you need?"

"Can you use your connections to get a guard named Deandre Wright to transfer Benson Mandeville to the hospital for surgery?" he asks.

"Who is Deandre Wright?" I ask.

"A guard at Breyer who drives the transport van."

"And Benson Mandeville?" I ask.

"An inmate at Breyer."

"Okay. And you want me to pull the right strings to make sure that Wright is the one driving the transport van when Mandeville is transferred to the hospital for surgery," I say.

"Yes," Xavier confirms.

"Why would I do that, Xavier?" I ask.

"Because he needs it."

I know that's not the real answer. Not in the broader sense of the word "real." But I don't need to dig. He'll tell me when he tells me. And until then, I probably don't want to be among the ones in the know.

After a shower, I sit down at the desk to watch the video Van sent me. I go through it several times, but there's nothing particularly interesting about it. It looks like Van just started recording because he thought it would be funny, not because there was anything specific happening.

In the email, he'd given me the names and contact information of other people at the party, just like I'd asked. I pull up the list and go through the video, listening for him to call anybody by name so I could start making links. I jot down the timestamps of each of the guys as he mentions them, then start down the line, pulling up the social media for each of them.

It takes a while of tiptoeing through the social media minefield, but I eventually gather several more videos of the same party. It confirms to me that it did definitely happen on Friday night, after when Van said he tried to surprise Sydney with dinner, and he was there. I catch a few instances of clocks, TV shows, and other hints that keep a fairly steady timeline, showing he was at the party well into the night.

On my third run-through of one of the videos, I catch something I hadn't noticed before. Turning the volume up, I listen for the voice I'd heard in the background. It wasn't the person recording that says it, and I wasn't sure I heard it correctly the first time, but when I play it through again, the voice definitely says Van's name.

The camera swings over the people at the party and locks for a second on a figure across the room. It looks exactly like Van. And in his hand, making his own video evidence of the party, is his tablet.

This happened long after he left Sydney's apartment. But if he had the tablet at the party, how did it get back into Sydney's apartment?

I am definitely going to need to speak with him again.

There might not be enough coffee on this campus to help me deal with this level of bullshit so early in the morning.

Tracy Gold insisted on us meeting early so that she wouldn't interrupt her faculty schedule. That means it's barely eight-thirty in the morning and I am already fuming as I take long, aggressive strides across campus toward Van's dorm. I know for a fact he doesn't have a class this early, which means I have a good chance of catching him as he leaves.

I decide not to force my way inside this time. Being out in the fresh air is probably good for me right now.

It takes nearly ten minutes of waiting before Van comes out. He falters slightly when he notices me there, then sets his eyes in front of him and continues on. I jog to catch up beside him.

"I need to get to class," he says.

"You don't have a class until ten-thirty," I reply. "What you probably mean is you need to get to breakfast, which means you have plenty of time to tell me about your tablet."

Van rolls his eyes and doesn't stop walking.

"I already told you. When I went over to Sydney's apartment to try to surprise her, I put our favorite music on the tablet and had it near the table. I thought it would be nice, and it would give us something to reminisce about. But she didn't care. She told me to leave, and I forgot to get my tablet."

"Right," I say. "But I mean after that."

"After that? It's been sitting in Sydney's apartment."

"Then how did you use it to record that video of the party?" I ask.

He blinks in surprise and opens his mouth to answer, but before he can I stop him with a serious look. "You better be very careful about what you are about to say to me. I don't have the patience to deal with more of your lying and forgetting to mention things right now. So, why don't we just go ahead and agree you're going to tell me the truth and we'll go from there?"

Van tightens, looking like he's debating with himself, then his shoulders drop.

"We broke up because I cheated on her," he admits. "It was with a girl named Lila who I met in a study group. Sydney found out and I broke things off with Lila because I wanted to be with Sydney. But then I ended up falling back into things with Lila. When Sydney found that out, she broke up with me. She was really angry and upset, and I was worried about her. She's been through a lot, and I'd started noticing some strange things. I didn't want to think I'd made things worse."

"What do you mean strange things?" I ask.

"Before everything happened with Lila, I was at Sydney's apartment, and her computer was open. There were searches on it for places like the desert, a really remote mountain resort, some white water rapids," he says.

"Why is that strange? From what I understand, she did some traveling," I say. "Maybe she was planning a trip with some friends."

"That's the thing. She wasn't. The searches were for remote locations in those areas, specifically for trips as a single traveler," he says. "There were some searches for just words, too. I don't know what exactly she was looking for, but I didn't like them."

"What kind of words?" I ask.

"Water needs. Fall injuries. Reception in national forests. Just strange things. Like she wasn't just planning a trip. She was preparing for something to go wrong," he says.

"Alright. So, you thought she was planning on going on a trip by herself," I say. "And that worried you."

"It probably doesn't make sense to you, but that's because you don't know her. You don't understand," he says.

"If this worried you so much, why didn't you say something to someone about it?" I ask.

"Because she asked me to stay out of it," he replies. "She'd gone through down periods before and I asked about what her parents and her doctor thought, and she told me to stay out of it. She always said it was her business and her decision, and since I'd never been through any of the mental health issues she has, I didn't have a place to say anything."

This immediately strikes me as strange.

"But she was a peer counselor, an advocate for mental health awareness and removing the stigma," I say.

"And I think that's what she thought she was trying to do," he nods. "She'd been treated like she was helpless before. Like just because she dealt with depression and anxiety it meant she couldn't make her own decisions or live her own life, and that wasn't the case at all. But I thought I was doing the right thing by respecting what she asked of me."

"All of that aside, I'm not sure I understand what the searches you found on her computer have to do with your tablet being in her apartment after you had it at the party," I say.

"I went back to the apartment on Monday because I'd been trying to get in touch with her and hadn't been able to all weekend. Lila was pressuring me to tell Sydney about us, and I just wanted to make sure she was alright and try again to let her know I wanted to get back together. She hadn't been answering my calls or texts, and she didn't answer the door when I knocked. I let myself in and when I saw she wasn't there, I just assumed she was in class.

But as soon as I saw that computer, the searches I'd found came back to me. I thought if I deleted her search history, maybe she wouldn't think about them anymore. If it wasn't right there, maybe she'd snap out of those thoughts."

It's all I can do to stop myself from rolling my eyes right here and now. None of this is adding up.

"What I really want to know is why you cheated on her. You're trying to convince me you love her and that you really want to be with her. So, why hook up with Lila?" I ask.

"The first time, it was just a mistake. I can't explain it any other way than that. It was something stupid I did because the opportunity presented itself. And, yes, I realize just how utterly horrible that makes me sound. But it's true. I felt invincible and like there was no way I'd ever have to face consequences for it. But then she found out and I realized I wanted to be with her. I knew I'd hurt her, and I tried hard to make her trust me again. The second time was because I found out about the guy from spring break," he says.

I give him a quizzical look. "What guy from spring break?"

His eyes narrow slightly.

"Jasmine didn't tell you?" he asks.

# CHAPTER TWENTY-THREE

I WAS SPITTING ANGRY WHEN I CONFRONTED VAN THIS MORNING, but by the time I used his spare key to go into Sydney's apartment and sat down in one of the oversized chairs in the living room, I start feeling calm. It may look like I've come to a place of peace and control, but I know what's actually happened is I've gotten so blindingly angry I've just whipped right back around to fine again.

The inside of the apartment is quiet and still as I wait. I take my focus out of the apartment itself and instead listen for anything happening beyond it. There are only four floors in the building, each with four apartments taking up the corners of the larger square.

Like Sydney's apartment, the ones on the back of the building have porches. I assume the layouts of the units vary slightly so that the same rooms of each don't stack on top of each other, which means some of them have the porches coming from their kitchens like this one in apartment 9, and the others are likely twisted so the porch is from the side of the living room.

The upper apartments have narrow balconies on the upper floors and patios to the front. I would guess those come off of the living rooms of some of the units and the bedrooms of others. Closing my eyes, I visualize the building cut in half so I can see all the rooms and what it would look like for people to be milling around inside. They would be able to hear each other at least to a degree, and after a few seconds, my ears start to tune into the sounds of the people around me.

Somewhere, a TV is playing. I can't discern what it is, but it sounds like it's coming from the apartment to my right. Water starts running above me. Footsteps sound from the apartment in the front and a door slams.

With sixteen apartments in the building, it's unlikely there's ever a time when only one of the apartments has someone in it. Which means there's a good chance someone could have heard Sydney Friday night. Even if they can't specify what they heard, or didn't hear anything significant, they might be able to help narrow down the timeline.

I've been sitting in the apartment for probably half an hour before the door opens and Jasmine comes in. She doesn't realize I'm there until she's come all the way inside, and she jumps when she sees me.

"Agent Griffin," she says breathlessly. "I didn't see you. What are you doing here?"

"What did you do for spring break?" I ask.

She looks at me quizzically. "Spring break?"

"Yes. What did you do for spring break? It wasn't that long ago, so you should be able to remember."

She shakes her head slightly as she puts her bags down and goes to put her keys in a basket hanging on the wall.

"You want to know what I did for spring break, so you broke into my apartment?" she asks incredulously.

"I have a key," I say, holding up Van's copy and giving a shrug. "Apparently that means something around here. But that's not really the issue at hand right now, because I'd venture to say a little bit of mild breaking and entering doesn't really compare with potential conspiracy in relation to a disappearance."

"Wait, what? You don't think …"

"I think you should tell me what you did on spring break," I insist.

"I didn't really do anything. Just stayed around on campus."

"So, you didn't go anywhere? Do anything special?" She shakes her head again. "Volunteer, perhaps?" Her face goes red and I stand up to walk toward her. "Because I hear you had signed up for a trip to travel to a village destroyed by the hurricane and help with the rebuilding efforts. You and Sydney signed up together. A little roommate, best friend bonding trip. Saving the world together."

"We..."

"I talked to Tracy Gold. She told me the two of you signed up for the trip, did the orientation and meetings, and then pulled out at the last second. Neither one of you gave an explanation. She was really disappointed, and it put her in kind of a lurch. I don't understand, Jasmine. You just keep lying to me and leaving things out that you really should be telling me," I say. "And it's making me start to wonder why it is that you're not being straightforward when one of your closest friends is missing and no one knows what happened to her. Only, I think you might know."

Her eyes widen and she shakes her head adamantly. "No. I don't. I really don't know where she is or why she left."

"Then why the secrets and lies, Jasmine?"

She groans, wincing as she realizes she's snowballed her way to the bottom of the hill and is now going to have to come clean.

"I've been seeing someone I shouldn't be seeing. Okay? I didn't plan on it happening, it just happened, and I can't make myself stop," she admits as she drops down to sit on the couch.

"Can I take a wild guess that it's one of your professors?" I ask.

She nods, looking defeated. "Yeah." Her eyes move over to me. "Do I have to tell you who it is?"

I shake my head. "No. At least not right now. Depending on how this investigation progresses, I might have to know at some point just to corroborate what you're saying. But for now, you don't have to say anything."

"Thank you." She runs her fingers back through her hair. "I feel like the worst person in the world."

"Why?"

"Because I left her here. Maybe I could have done something if I'd been here," she mutters.

"Was she upset when you told her you weren't going on the trip with her?" I ask.

"No. I was talking about when she disappeared. It was Sydney's idea not to go on the spring break trip. I was still thinking about going, but then my boyfriend's plans fell through, and I decided to stay here to spend time with him."

It makes my stomach turn a little to hear her refer to the professor she's having an affair with as her "boyfriend," but I have to move past it.

"Why did she decide not to go?" I ask. She looks resistant, staring down at her hands and rocking slightly back and forth. "Jasmine, now is not the time for you to cherry-pick what you tell me. I need to know everything."

"She asked me not to say anything about it because she was really embarrassed."

"You can't worry about that right now," I tell her. "Her being embarrassed and possibly being upset with you because you told me something is way less important than her being missing and very likely in danger."

She nods. "Sydney was starting to do some odd things. I don't really know how to describe it other than that. It was like she'd go through these periods where she disconnected and was totally different for a while, then she'd be back. I thought maybe she'd gotten into drugs, but she said she'd never do that. About a week before spring break, we were supposed to meet up here to go get some dinner with a couple of friends, but she didn't show up.

"I called her a couple of times, and she didn't answer, but I just figured she'd gotten wrapped up in a paper or a project and had lost track of time, so I decided to go by the library to find her. She has a couple of favorite places in there, so I usually just do the rounds to find her when I need to. But because we were already late, I called her when I was going up the steps to the upper floors of the library. I heard buzzing, realized it was her phone, and followed it.

"She was at the bottom of the stairs, curled up in a ball against the wall, crying. I thought someone had attacked her or she fell, but she told me she had forgotten how to get to the research section. She couldn't figure out how to open the door and go through it."

Her voice catches and she looks down again like she's trying to get ahold of herself. "I got her up and calmed her down. I reminded her about dinner, and we went. By the time we got home, she was tired and went to bed, and the next morning she seemed fine. She was embarrassed and asked me not to tell anyone. I figured she was just exhausted and had a moment. I didn't…"

She shakes her head, hanging it down and wiping tears from her eyes.

"I talked to Van," I tell her. "He mentioned something about a guy over spring break. That was part of why he ended up cheating on Sydney again. When I said I didn't know what he meant, he seemed surprised that you didn't tell me about it. What's he talking about?"

"After the staircase incident, she spent a couple of days just staying in the apartment. I assumed she was getting some rest. That's when she told me she decided she wasn't going to go on the spring break trip. She said she didn't think it was a good idea for her, and that she would rather stay here and focus on some other things. I wasn't sure what she was talking about, but I went along with it.

"During spring break, everything seemed pretty much back to normal, but then there were a couple of days when she seemed jumpy. I don't really know how to describe it other than that. She wasn't upset about anything, I didn't think. She just seemed like she was always on edge, like she couldn't relax, and any little thing would send her off skittering around. But she wasn't sad or angry.

"Then one night she told me she wanted to go out. I wasn't feeling great, so I decided to stay home. She said that was fine because there were some people she knew who would be there. I should have gone with her. But I wasn't worried about her. She stayed out so late I thought she might have gone to someone else's place to spend the night. Then she showed up stumbling around, laughing and whispering really loudly.

"I came out of my room, and she had some guy with her. I had never seen him and had no idea who he was. She was hanging on him and he was trying to get her into the bedroom. I managed to stop them by introducing myself and convincing her to watch a movie with me. They both fell asleep by the end of it, and I stayed there in the living room with them for the rest of the night. I didn't want him to wake up and something bad to happen."

"Did he stay all night?" I ask.

Jasmine nods. "Sydney woke up the next morning and didn't even remember how she got home, much less that she brought the guy with her. She didn't know his name or anything about him. It was really awkward. She couldn't even tell me where she was the night before or anything that happened. I'd never known her to drink or anything, so this was really out of character.

"We managed to get the guy to leave by telling him we had plans, but he didn't get the hint. He started showing up at the apartment, running into her on campus, even showing up outside the counseling building. He was obviously really interested in her and thought there was something between them, but she didn't even know him and wanted nothing to do with him."

I close my eyes and rub them with my fingers for a second.

"Jasmine, do you not understand how that information is important for this investigation?" I ask.

I'm trying to stay calm and patient, but it's getting more difficult.

"She didn't want people to know," she insists. "She was embarrassed and didn't even want to talk about it with me. She didn't even want to acknowledge it was happening. I talked to the guy, and he said he didn't even see her on Friday."

"You aren't an investigator," I snap, my anger slipping through more. "You don't get to make that choice. This is something you should have told the police or at least Sydney's parents right from the beginning. Is there anything else you haven't told me? That you're holding back because you think you shouldn't say it?"

She shakes her head. "No."

"Are you absolutely positive?"

"Yes."

"Consider this a warning. If you know anything else about what was going on in Sydney's life, or what happened to her, you need to come forward. Continuing to conceal things could be seen as obstruction at best and could put Sydney at dire risk at worst. Do you understand?"

"Yes," she says meekly.

"I need to know how to find that guy."

# CHAPTER TWENTY-FOUR

Jasmine is able to give me Steven Bender's phone number and social media since he pressed it on her during his pursuit of Sydney. I fold the paper with the details written on them and put it in my bag, then ask her to call him.

"He's less likely to answer if he doesn't recognize the number or if I message him. If it's you, he'll answer. Just get him on the phone, introduce me, and I'll take care of the rest."

Just like I suspected, Steven answers instantly when Jasmine calls him. The expression on her face tells me just how much she doesn't like this plan, but she's not about to argue with it considering just how much she's kept from the investigation. She can't really make up for not being honest from the beginning, but cooperating now is at least a start.

I keep the details of what I want to talk to him about brief and vague, not wanting to get into it too much over the phone. People tend to be jumpy, even if they haven't actually done something wrong. If they think they might be under suspicion, a lot of people will just completely avoid any type of interaction. They feel like not participating will make things better, like the whole situation will just go away if they don't talk or get involved.

That's not how it works. At least, not with me. The ones who don't talk are the ones who stay the most on my radar, and I do whatever it takes to get under their skin and find out what I need to know. Fortunately, this kid doesn't seem to want to hide anything. As soon as he finds out I'm trying to find Sydney, he's all in.

He has a class, so he can't meet with me for another couple of hours, but that gives me enough time to canvass the neighbors the way I'd planned. Jasmine comes along to tell me their names and to offer a friendly face that can put the other student residents at ease. By the time I'm heading up toward the building where I am supposed to meet with Stephen, I have a better idea of the timeline leading up to Sydney's disappearance.

Some of her neighbors told me they heard something that sounded like arguing coming from her apartment Friday evening, then the sound of the TV later in the evening. One neighbor told me they could smell something like bacon burning early Saturday morning. If all of these are accurate, it tells me we've been thinking a few hours too short. Sydney was still at home through Friday night and into Saturday morning, which meant she didn't go missing until the day after we thought.

I finish talking to all the neighbors and head off to meet with Steven. I'm walking across the grass in the middle of campus when I hear somebody calling my name behind me. Pausing, I turn around and see an unfamiliar girl walking up.

"Are you Agent Griffin?" she asks when she's a few steps away.

"Yes," I say.

"You've been talking to my boyfriend," she says.

"Your boyfriend?" I raise an eyebrow, wondering if she might be talking about Steven.

"Yes. I know you're trying to find out what happened to that girl, but you need to know he didn't have anything to do with it."

"I'm sorry," I say, shaking my head slightly, "what's your name?"

"I'm Lila Kellerman."

The name registers and I nod.

"Van," I say.

"Yes. You really upset him with that stunt you pulled, you know."

"Excuse me?" I'm stunned by the way this girl is talking to me.

"Harassing him and having the police dig around in his dorm room just because you didn't like what he had to say to you. He didn't do anything wrong, and you are being completely unethical about the way you're treating him," she presses.

"I have somewhere I need to be right now because a girl is missing and I am trying to find her, but we're going to clear something up real fast. I am not harassing anyone. Van was known to have a personal relationship with Sydney. He may have been the last person to have seen her. No matter how pissy you are going to be about it, that makes him someone we want to look at," I tell her. "He went to her apartment in an effort to rekindle their relationship and was rejected. The fact that he didn't come forward to tell investigators that, or at least talk to her parents, only makes him look more suspicious."

"No," Lila says, shaking her head. "No, that's not what happened. He went to talk to her that day, but he wasn't trying to get back with her. He was going to tell her that he wanted to be with me and that Sydney needed to leave him alone. She'd been clinging to him and trying to get him to choose her. She was totally obsessed with him and was getting really out of control with it. I told him he should just call her and tell her and get it over with, but he said he should do it face to face."

What a tangled web we weave. I raise an eyebrow.

"Is that what you think happened?" I ask.

"That *is* what happened. Van wanted to be with me. He only got back with her for that short time because she was being weird, and he didn't want her to feel like he abandoned her. But he wanted me. Now we're together and that's not going to change just because she's missing. If you ask me, I think Sydney is just doing this to get attention. She's going to pop back up in a couple days waiting for everyone to fawn all over her and tell her how worried they all were and how much they missed her."

"I don't think I asked you," I tell her.

I walk away, thinking of the long dark strands of hair in Van's dorm room, and the thick ponytail hanging down past Lila's shoulders.

Steven is waiting for me on a bench in the courtyard just like he told me he would be. As I approach, he jumps to his feet and takes a couple of steps toward me.

"Agent Griffin?" he asks.

There's something in his voice that tells me I'm not the first unfamiliar adult woman he has launched himself at that way this afternoon. I nod and extend my hand.

"Steven?" I ask.

"Yes."

I gesture at the bench. "Want to sit down?"

We sit and I dispense with the small talk, jumping right in so he can relax a little. I tell him what Jasmine said and watch as his face contorts and his head shakes with increasing speed and intensity.

"No," he finally says when I'm done. "No. That's not it at all."

"You didn't come home with Sydney Parker during spring break?" I ask.

"I did," he nods. "That part is right. She did bring me back to her apartment with her and I spent the night. We weren't even alone together. We fell asleep in the living room with her roommate right there. Then in the morning, they had plans, so I left."

"And you expected Sydney to call you, but she didn't. So you started stalking her," I say.

"No," he replies insistently. "I didn't stalk her. I was just showing her I was interested. I didn't want her to think it was some sort of one-night stand thing for me. That's not what it was. We had something really amazing."

"But you followed her and showed up at her apartment and her work," I say.

"She's busy. It's not a surprise. Someone that amazing is bound to be busy. But I wanted her to know I wasn't discouraged or deterred by that. She deserved to feel special and pursued."

"Even if she didn't want to be?" I ask. "Jasmine says Sydney didn't have any idea who you were and didn't even remember seeing you that night."

"That's not how it was. Sydney was interested in me. It wasn't like we met that night," Steven says.

"You'd met before she brought you to her apartment?" I ask. "When?"

"A few weeks before spring break, I was at a party at my cousin's place. I don't usually go to parties, but that night I ended up going. I'm glad I did because it was the first time I saw her. I remember being really shocked because there was this gorgeous girl, and she was there alone. No guy, not even any friends with her. She just walked in and started talking to people and dancing like she owned the place. I was immediately drawn to her.

"The whole night she was basically the life of the party. She was constantly on the move, going from room to room, laughing, dancing. It looked like she knew everybody there, she was so comfortable just joining in conversations or hopping in to dance with people. I couldn't take my eyes off her. I'd never seen anyone like that before.

"I lost track of her at some point and didn't see her again that night. Then when I asked my cousin about her, and I found out no one there actually knew who she was."

"No one knew her?" I ask.

"No. The party wasn't on campus and a lot of the people who were there were from other schools, or friends of my cousin's from back in high school. All of them were trying to figure out which of them had brought her. That actually made it even funnier when I saw her again."

"What do you mean? Why was it funny?" I ask.

"I didn't think I was ever going to see her again. And I knew I had to. I asked around about her. I even searched the school website for any mention of her, but I couldn't find anything. Then that night at the bonfire she was just there. She appeared, just like she did at the party. It was fate."

"The bonfire?" I ask. "That's where you met up that night?"

"Yeah," he nods. "A couple of on-campus groups were doing different activities and events for people who decided not to go out of town or home for spring break. I heard about the bonfire and thought it sounded like fun. It wasn't, by the way. Not until Sydney showed up."

"Why do you say that?"

"It was just a bunch of loud music and people acting like idiots. Essentially the whole reason I avoided going on a regular spring break trip in the first place. I was actually about to leave when she showed up. I saw her through the light of the fire, and it was like a vision. Like I had conjured her up out of my imagination." Steven stops and lets out a puff of half-laughter. "I guess that sounds pretty ridiculous, doesn't it?"

"You said something was funny when you saw her again," I say, prompting him.

"Right. Well, it turned out the reason I couldn't find her when I was searching all over for her, is because I didn't actually know her name," he says.

"What do you mean you didn't know her name?" I ask.

"When she was at the party at my cousin's place, she told everybody her name was Rio. I even made a joke about her dancing in the sand. She laughed. No one else seemed to get it, though."

I don't tell him that song reference is so outdated I'm amazed he even knows it, and I highly doubt Sydney actually did.

"Did anyone at the party know that wasn't her name?" I ask.

"No. Everybody she introduced herself to there thought her name was Rio. So, when I was searching for her, I was searching for a girl named Rio, and there isn't one. When I asked her about it at the bonfire, she said she was playing a game with some of her friends. A scavenger hunt thing. She was embarrassed, but I told her I thought it was adorable. I just wished I'd known that before I went searching all over the place for her."

He starts laughing, but I don't find that anywhere near as amusing as he seems to. Why would she lie about her name? The scavenger hunt reasoning doesn't make sense, even if smitten Steven wants to pretend it does.

"So, that's when you found out her name is Sydney," I say.

"Yes. Then we hung out at the fire for a little while before she invited me to her place," Steven replies.

"Did you know she'd been drinking?"

"I didn't see her drink. But it was difficult to ignore the signs," he says.

"And yet, you decided to go with her anyway?"

He can hear the accusation in my voice and it's clear he's torn about his own actions.

"I didn't want her to be alone," he insists. "By the way she was acting, I didn't think she would be safe if I just let her go home by herself. Other guys were noticing how she was, and I thought it would be better if I was there with her so she wasn't completely vulnerable."

"And since you were there already, you didn't see a problem with trying to get her into the bedroom with you," I say.

Steven cringes slightly. "We didn't end up there. I told you. We stayed in the living room with her roommate."

I nod, deciding not to press the issue. "Alright. I need you to get in touch with your cousin."

"Why?"

"I want to find out more about this party."

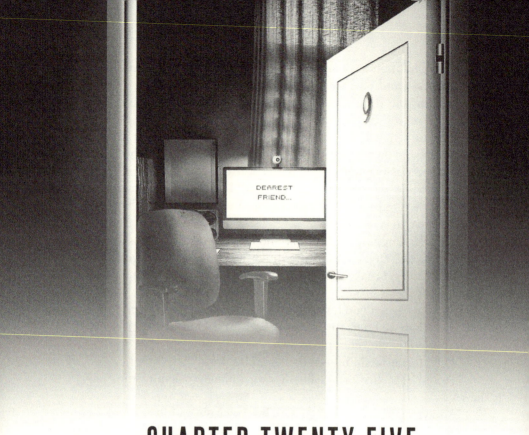

# CHAPTER TWENTY-FIVE

Steven's cousin Brent was at work when Steven called, but he said things were slow, so I could come by and talk with him. I sit at the last table at the restaurant's bar and watch him move around behind it preparing for tonight's dinner service.

"Honestly, at first I didn't really think much of it. At house parties like that, usually you're going to end up with at least a couple of random people. Even if you invite just specific people, inevitably a dozen people you've never met show up. It isn't that big of a deal. When I saw her and didn't recognize her, that's just what I figured it was. I asked around some, but it turned out nobody knew who she was, and everybody was trying to find who brought her."

"Why was it such a big deal to find out who brought her?" I ask.

He hesitates slightly like he doesn't really want to answer that question. "The way she was acting was kind of over-the-top. I know my cousin got all moony-eyed over her and thought she was charming, but everybody else noticed that she was kind of out of control. She was going around people who had no idea who she was and just putting herself in their conversations, taking food out of people's hands, jumping up on furniture, and dancing. I'm all for having fun, that's the point of having parties, but it was all just a bit much."

"So you wanted to know who brought the troublemaker, essentially," I say.

"Yeah. It wasn't that I wanted to take her out or embarrass her or anything. But if I was able to figure out who got her there, maybe they'd be able to rein her in a bit. But I noticed that Steven was watching her all night, I got more uneasy about it."

"Why is that?"

"Steven is smart. Really smart. When it comes to books. He gets good grades and got scholarships, the whole nine yards. But when it comes to people, he sometimes isn't the most aware. He just doesn't have a ton of social experience. Especially when it comes to girls or dating. I think he went on like one date in high school, and there was some girl a couple of years ago who he said he was dating, but I never actually saw them spending time together. Other than that, he hasn't had a real girlfriend."

"So, you feel like he might not have really been aware of the way she was acting," I note. "He was attracted to her, so he was able to ignore what she was doing."

"Essentially. It was a relief when he came up and asked where she was, and I realized she'd left the party. Steven ended up going home and it wasn't until a couple of hours later that I found her," he says.

That perks up my attention and makes my stomach lurch a little.

"Found her?" I ask.

"Yeah," he nods. "The party was slowing down, and I was doing the rounds making sure people who shouldn't be driving weren't and that everything was good, and I found her out by the pool, totally passed out. She was right on the edge, with one arm down in the water. She was just about to slide the rest of the way in. I got her up and brought her inside."

"You didn't call the police?" I ask.

"This girl was clearly underage and drunk out of her mind. It wasn't something I intended to have happen at my party, but there we were. I really didn't feel like getting myself into that kind of trouble. I mean, she was really hot, but not worth that kind of headache over. I don't live on campus and everybody I invited was twenty-one or older, but police don't really care about intentions. You should know. They'd find out I had some undergrad at my house drunk until she passed out, and they'd have my ass.

"If something was wrong with her or I thought she was actually in danger, I would have brought her to the hospital or something, but she was just passed out. It's not like there aren't girls who get black-out drunk at parties every week, right? She was breathing fine and I had a couple of girls I know bring her into one of the bedrooms and watch out for her until she woke up. They got her back to her dorm."

That makes me pause. I get out a picture of Sydney and show it to him.

"Is that her?" I ask.

"Yeah," he nods. "That's Rio."

I nod. "Did Steven tell you why I needed to talk to you about her?"

"No." Brent finishes putting away clean wine glasses, grabs a tray with salt and pepper shakers and large containers of the seasonings, and walks out from behind the bar to sit at one of the tables and fill them. "He just said a cop needed to ask some questions about the party and the girl Rio. What happened? Is she in some kind of trouble?"

I take out my phone and pull up one of the few articles that had been written about the disappearance. The picture on it is a bit grainy and the angle doesn't clearly show Sydney. It's clear the writer took a screengrab in order to add a picture to the article but wasn't able to use any good images because they all belong to the college and he wasn't authorized to use them.

"Have you seen this?" I ask.

Brent shakes his head, then leans closer to look at her. "Oh, shit. Is that her? That doesn't even look like her."

I understand the motivation and sentiment behind her parents wanting to keep Sydney's disappearance out of the mainstream media as much as possible, but this is the flipside of that. Keeping her image away from the public in an effort not to embarrass her, the family, or the school, means people who were aware of her and might have important insight into her state of mind leading up to her disappearance haven't been able to come forward and share that information.

"It's her. And I'm not a cop. I'm an FBI agent. This girl's name is not Rio, it's Sydney Parker, and she's been missing for more than a week."

Brent holds up his hands, his eyes wide as he shakes his head like he's pushing away all possible blame.

"Whoa—I didn't have anything to do with that. Like I said, she came to that party, acted up, I found her outside, and I let the girls take care of her and bring her home so she'd be safe," he says.

"You let the girls bring her back to the dorm," I say.

"Yes," he nods. "That way she wasn't alone and couldn't get up to anything else."

"I have a problem with that," I say.

"Why?" he asks.

"Sydney doesn't live in a dorm. She lives in an apartment off-campus," I explain. His face drops. "I need contact information for everybody you can think of who was at that party, especially those girls who supposedly brought her home."

Brent does me one better and calls up several of the people who were at the party, telling them to meet up at the bar after he got off work so I could talk to all of them at one time. I thank him and leave, his words resonating in my head. He's the second person to describe Sydney as losing control or being out of control and it's starting to get under my skin.

The longer I look beyond the glossy, inspirational exterior of her life, the more I'm seeing a different picture of Sydney than the one she wanted the world to see. Her mental health, or at least how she handled it, was slipping, and no one around her seemed to notice.

# CHAPTER TWENTY-SIX

"**N**ONE OF YOU REALIZED THE GIRL MISSING FROM CAMPUS WAS the one you saw at the party?" I ask the group gathered at the bar later that night.

They all shake their heads without hesitation. None look uncomfortable or like they're trying to hide something. I've more than learned throughout my career that a convincing facial expression and calm demeanor don't always mean anything. People can hide a lot, especially when they are around a group of people unknowingly giving them an alibi. But I'm not seeing anything in any of these people that makes me think they actually know more than they are saying.

Their voices overlap in a chorus of denials, and they look at each other as if hoping to see one of them nodding so they can find out more.

"Are you sure it's her?" a girl asks from across the table. "If she was using a different name and none of us recognize her, could it actually be someone else?"

"No," I say, cutting off some mumbles agreeing with her. "It's her. I have witness statements confirming the girl at the party calling herself Rio was actually Sydney Parker. I need to know everything that you saw that night. Even if you don't think it matters or that it's too small to mean anything. If you saw her that night, interacted with her, watched her interact with anyone, I need to know about it."

For the next hour, I listen as they unspool events in the manner of the old movie *Rashomon*—every one of them telling the exact same story with a slight difference in perspective. Some say they actually witnessed Sydney drinking that night. They say she was taking shots and had pulled drinks out of people's hands. Others said they didn't see her drinking at all, she was just acting up from the second she got to the party. When one implied he'd seen her possibly doing drugs, another nodded and got the look in his eye that said he wanted to think he'd seen the same thing, that maybe if he had, he could be helpful.

To further sort out the responses and streamline my understanding of how the party unfolded, I ask some basic questions. What she wore. How her hair was styled. What color lipstick she was wearing. Who she danced with. What she ate.

The questions might seem like they don't mean anything, like useless details that won't actually make a difference. But gathering the answers from the group and evaluating the variations in what they say gives me a better grasp of who might be telling something closest to reality.

"Brent told me that after he found Sydney passed out by the pool, he brought her inside and had two girls take care of her. They brought her back to what they thought was her dorm. Who was that?" I ask.

"I helped her," a girl who had introduced herself as Topaz pipes up. "He brought her in, and she looked really rough. Something was definitely going on with her. I didn't actually see her drink anything, but I don't know what else could have been affecting her that way. Brent didn't want her to try to get back home by herself, but he also didn't want to just trust anybody with her, so he had us watch over her for a while and then walk her back to the dorm."

"Okay, the issue with that is that Sydney doesn't live in a dorm," I reply. "She has an apartment. So, who told you that she lived in the dorm?"

"She did. We told her we were going to bring her home and asked where, and she said Murray Hall."

The name jumps out at me. That's the dorm where Van lives. I remember that at this point they hadn't broken up. I wonder if he had already started cheating on her, and if that was something she knew about yet.

"What happened when you got to the dorm?" I ask. "You can go inside without being a resident and swiping your ID card."

"We were going to bring her up to her room, but she said she didn't have her ID card on her, so she couldn't get through the door. At this point she was starting to sober up a little bit. Still not really functional, but she was calming down. I was going to bring her back to my place, but then a friend of hers came out of the door and offered to bring her in," Topaz says.

"A friend? Did you get their name?"

"No. It was a girl. Short blonde hair. We didn't stand around and talk," she tells me.

I nod. "Alright. Thank you." I take cards out of my pocket and hand them out to each of them. "Call me if you think of anything else."

It's getting late when I leave the bar, but I call Jasmine anyway. She answers on the second ring without a trace of sleep in her voice.

"Is there something else you're keeping from me?" I ask. "Something else Sydney didn't want you to tell anyone about so you haven't said anything?"

"No," she says, sounding confused. "Why? What's going on?"

"Are you sure?" I press. "Because I'm really getting tired of chasing people around trying to get everything out."

"I'm sure. I'm not keeping anything from you. What did you find out?" she asks.

"I'm coming over tomorrow morning to talk to you," I tell her.

"Sydney's parents are going to be here, too," she says.

"What time? I want to be there to talk to you about this before they get there. I'm going to need to talk to them as well."

I go to bed thinking about my shifting view of Sydney and what brought her to the moment when she decided to completely break with herself and be someone else for the night.

The next morning, I arrive at the apartment early enough for the smell of shampoo and heat to still be coming from the bathroom. Jasmine's wearing thin sweats and a t-shirt, no makeup, and the air of someone who has no intention of leaving their home that day.

She offers me coffee and we sit down in the living room while I tell her what I learned about the party. For a second, Jasmine looks confused, like she can't place the night I'm talking about, then realization settles over her.

"Oh, god," she whispers. "I remember that night."

"So, you were there," I say.

She shakes her head. "No. I wasn't there. What I remember is that we were kind of settled in for the evening when Sydney suddenly decided she wanted to go out and do something. We didn't have a plan, so we just headed out and were going to look around to see if anything was going on that sounded like fun. I found out about an open mic night at an eighteen-and-up club not too far from campus. I thought that would be a good time, but she wanted to do something more wild, as she put it.

I tried to convince her to just go with me, but she wasn't having any of it. She said she didn't care if I went with her, she was going to go find something fun. I shouldn't have let her go. I find myself saying that a lot recently. I shouldn't have let her do this or that. I shouldn't have just trusted that everything was going to be okay because Sydney was always okay. I shouldn't have left her alone.

"But, like I've heard so many times over the last week, she is an adult. She can make her own decisions. And this campus is safe. That's what we've been told countless times. A couple of bad things have happened, of course, but they happen everywhere, all the time. Especially on bigger campuses. And Sydney didn't come to school to be babysat, just like I didn't come to be a babysitter."

"Where did you leave her?" I ask.

"It's not like I just abandoned her. We went our separate ways in the quad. She said she saw some people she knew and was going to go and join up with them and see what they were doing that night. I saw her going toward some people, so I figured that's where she was going. I went to the club and hung out with some people, but my boyfriend ended up calling me and I went to his place. Usually, I don't spend the night over there, but that night I did. So I didn't see her again until the next night.

"But we had texted a few times and she seemed perfectly okay. Then, when I got home and she was here, I didn't notice anything about her that was strange. She seemed kind of tired and said she had a headache, but that's not really that weird. We had dinner and watched TV for a while. I asked her what she ended up doing that night she said she just hung out with the people she met up with on campus. She never mentioned going to a party."

"And you never heard anything about an off-campus party with a girl nobody knew who was acting out a lot?" I ask.

"I hear things about stuff like that all the time," Jasmine shrugs. "I'm in college. There's always some sort of off-campus nonsense going on. And there's always some girl who's acting up. Or some guy who's being an idiot. It's kind of the soundtrack of every Monday. What kind of craziness did people get up to over the weekend? But, like you just told me, nobody knew it was Sydney at that party, so I would have no reason to hear about it specifically. I don't know if I even heard about that party or anything that went on with it."

This is only getting more confusing. I need to talk to her parents.

# CHAPTER TWENTY-SEVEN

I T'S OBVIOUS THAT SYDNEY'S FATHER ISN'T HAPPY TO SEE ME WHEN he comes into the apartment. Angela is surprised I'm there, but seems willing to accept it if it means we can get closer to finding her daughter. It seems the longer this stretches out, the sadder Angela gets, and the angrier and more defensive Wesley gets. The schism between the two of them is more evident. I wish I knew what their relationship was like before Sydney disappeared, and at what moment everything changed.

Did this friction start because of her disappearance? Or did she disappear because of it?

"This is one of those moments when I need both of you to be really honest with me," I say a little while later when we are all sitting in the living room. I've asked Jasmine to give us some privacy so they might feel more comfortable opening up to talk to me about Sydney.

"Have either of you been aware of your daughter drinking heavily or doing any kind of recreational drugs?"

Angela's eyes widen and she lets out a small gasp.

"No," she says. "No, of course not."

"Why would you ask us a question like that?" Wesley asks.

"I'm not going to get into details about it, but I am following through with some information I learned about her in the weeks leading up to her disappearance," I tell them. "I can't get her side of the story, so I need to get as much as I can from other people in her life to try to piece it together."

"You're saying someone told you that our Sydney is an addict?" Wesley presses. "Or some kind of drunk?"

"That's not what I said," I reply. "I'm just asking if she has ever experimented with alcohol or drugs, or if you know of her having a problem with them. Even a minor one."

"Never," Angela answers quickly.

"I really want you to think and answer me honestly," I say.

"Why do you keep saying that?" Wesley asks. "We are being honest with you. Sydney has always been a responsible girl. She is too driven with too many dreams to get wrapped up in stupid behavior like that."

"He's right," Angela concurs. "Her goals are so important to her. She wouldn't throw it away like that. And she was a good girl. *Is* a good girl."

"I'm sorry if you feel like I keep asking the same questions, or like I'm not listening to you. That's not the case. I just need to be the sometimes-uncomfortable voice of reality in situations like this. I have encountered many parents whose teenage or young adult children have gone missing, or who have gotten involved in serious crimes or other trouble. Parents have an extremely difficult time accepting that and admitting that their child could be doing anything wrong."

"We raised her well—" Wesley starts, but I hold up a hand to silence him.

"I'm sure you did. And I promise, I'm not trying to imply anything about your parenting ability. The unfortunate truth is, even the best parenting in the world can't prevent a child from making bad decisions, especially when off on their own for the first time. That's part of life. And all too often, when I deal with parents in situations like these, it's almost as if they refuse to see that. They become so stuck in what they believe their children to be that they don't realize that those children have changed. Especially in times of their lives like college, where so much change is happening all around them.

"I know it can be hard to come to terms with, but the image you are holding onto of who Sydney is may simply not be accurate anymore. That doesn't mean she's any better or worse a person for it, nor does it mean anything about your parenting. I'm just trying to figure out the truth of who Sydney is *now*, not as she was when she was younger. That will be the only way we can find her."

My words leave both of them in silence for a minute. It's Wesley who finally breaks it.

"Do you have children, Agent Griffin?"

"No, I don't," I admit. "But—"

"So you feel completely entitled to talk about what we feel even though you have no firsthand experience with it?" he doubles down.

I glare at him for a long moment, trying to plan my next words carefully. I don't know why he's being so defensive, but I can't afford to let this spiral out of control.

"There's a recent case you might have heard about, out of Richmond involving a freshman in college. She left her dorm one night under the guise of going out skateboarding and didn't return home.

"Her mother was completely frantic and broadcast out to the entire world, anyone who would listen, that her daughter had never been in any trouble, never drank or did drugs, and didn't associate with anyone who did. She insisted that there was no way her daughter would ever get into a bad situation like that. Her insistence on her daughter's innocence led to a panic throughout campus because everyone believed there had to be some sort of random attacker free in the city.

"In the end, it didn't turn out well for her, and it was quickly revealed she wasn't nearly the angel her mother made her out to be. She'd been sleeping with a man twice her age, doing drugs, and making all kinds of reckless decisions."

"So, now you're saying someone attacked Sydney, and if she has made some bad choices, it makes her less worthy of being found?" Wesley asks.

"That's not what I was saying," I reply. "It doesn't matter what she chose to do. She deserves to be found, and if someone else is responsible for her going missing, they will be held accountable. But we're not going to get anywhere by holding onto beliefs about her behavior that may simply not be true."

"Oh, sure. So you want to make sure that you take every opportunity to judge us and our daughter, and to scare the hell out of us," Wesley snaps. "And to make sure that nobody just thinks about Sydney as a girl who is missing, but as someone they can also judge. That's just perfect."

He gets up from the couch and storms out of the apartment, slamming the door behind him. I look at Angela, whose face holds the sustained wince of someone who has seen more than one of those temper tantrums in her marriage.

"I'm sorry," I tell her. "I know the two of you are under a tremendous amount of strain. I didn't mean to upset him."

Angela shakes her head. "Don't worry about it. You're doing everything you can to find our girl. Wesley is just sensitive about what happened when Sydney was younger."

"What do you mean?" I ask. "What happened?"

She draws in a breath, her shoulders rising up tight close to her ears, as if to pull in all the air she will need to carry her through if the words she's about to say take her breath.

"Her depression and anxiety started when she was in middle school. It was always manageable, and we did what we could to make sure she could handle it. And she always seemed to without much difficulty. They were bad days, of course, but that's to be expected when you're dealing with something so serious with someone so young. She was going to weekly therapy and it really did a lot of good for her. But in high school, it got worse.

"She didn't want to talk to us or tell us what was going on. We thought everything was fine. But we noticed her grades were starting to slip, and found out she was lying about her extracurricular activities. Eventually, we learned she had fallen in with the type of friends we definitely didn't want her to have. They were drinking and committing petty crimes together.

"I was completely shocked. This just wasn't my daughter. And then on top of everything else, we found out she had stopped going to her therapy appointments. We would schedule them, and she would either contact the office and cancel them, or just not show up."

"The therapist didn't tell you this?" I ask.

"That particular doctor had a policy of interacting only with a patient after the age of 16, so we were never notified of her missing the appointments."

"That seems like the kind of policy that could end up causing trouble," I say.

Angela nods. "Exactly. I can understand the sentiment behind it. I know teenagers need their independence. But at sixteen and seventeen, they are still children. I honestly hate to even think of an eighteen-year-old as an adult. They need our guidance, and she wasn't getting it.

"We ended up getting her to a new doctor who recognized that her conditions had worsened. He explained to us that the feelings of depression and anxiety can become overwhelming, and be frightening for anyone, but especially a teenager who is also going through so many changes, surging hormones, new levels of stress. It's a lot to deal with, and they have to develop coping mechanisms to manage them.

"Unfortunately, the coping mechanisms Sydney had developed weren't really coping mechanisms at all. She thought they were making things better because the drinking would temporarily dull the feelings, and all the drag races or shoplifting gave her a rush of adrenaline. What she didn't understand was that those things then exacerbated the feelings of depression and anxiety. Which meant she just kept looking for more.

"It was a really difficult time for our family, but we worked hard together to get her life back under control. We brought her to her therapy appointments every week. The doctor prescribed her medication for the first time. She was really resistant at first, but after a little while of taking it, she realized how much it was helping her, and how much more clearly she was able to think about things. I think that was the biggest life-changing factor for her. She realized that the depth to which she had sunk was stopping her from being able to honestly evaluate what was going on in her life. She realized that she was feeling hopeless. But the medication helped reclaim her life.

"Wes and I were so proud of how hard she worked to fix the mistakes she had made and move forward. Everything was different after that. She became the Sydney people here know. Ambitious, confident, open, and honest about her struggles. She became an advocate for mental health awareness for young people, trying hard to reduce the stigma surrounding talking about things like depression. She wants so much to normalize going to therapy and taking medication if people need it."

"So, that's why you are so sure she hasn't been drinking or doing drugs," I say. "Because she got through that difficult phase and changed her life."

"Yes," Angela nods. "She swore she would never do any of that again. She knew how much it hurt her, and she never wanted to relinquish that kind of control again."

I can tell by the look on her face she isn't fully believing the words even as they come out of her mouth. She knows that just making that kind of promise, or even being openly against those behaviors, doesn't necessarily stop a person. Angela is leaning into hope and wishful thinking to get her through this. But it's not enough.

"Have you spoken with the doctor she sees here?" I ask.

She shakes her head. "No. She's nineteen years old. I don't think they would speak to me."

"We have to try," I reply.

Dr. Villarreal is understandably reluctant to open up to us when we go to her office. Her receptionist has the two of us wait in the waiting room for nearly an hour before we are ushered back into an office. Stepping in there brings back a rush of memories. There was a time, a few years ago now, when the Bureau required me to participate in mental health counseling. A couple of extremely difficult cases on top of the extreme emotional pressure of digging deeper into my mother's death, my father's disappearance, and Greg's disappearance and eventual murder had me spiraling.

I hated it. I resisted it. I resented the woman who sat in the room with me, watching my reactions, listening to the words I said when I was willing to speak, and evaluating me. I didn't want to hand over any pieces of myself. I felt like that was my pain. I was entitled to it, and I clung to it as hard as I could. Now I wonder about the real effect of those months of sitting, often silent, in Katherine's office.

Because I feel better now. I found ways to process and manage my pain, to come to terms with the way my own mental health would spiral out of my own control. It's taken me a lot of work both inside and outside therapists' offices to come to this point. And it's still a struggle I deal with every day.

But after all, it may have been worth it.

# CHAPTER TWENTY-EIGHT

"I DO HAVE TO TELL YOU RIGHT FROM THE BEGINNING THAT I won't be able to share much information with you about my time with Sydney," the doctor tells us as we sit down. "Regardless of the fact that she is a student and is missing, she is owed privacy."

"We understand," Angela nods.

"We are just looking for you to give us any of your thoughts about her that you can," I say. "Right now, we're having a difficult time even knowing where to start when it comes to looking for her or figuring out what happened. I'm asking for as many people as possible who have been around her to give me their insights on her life, her state of mind, anything that could point the investigation in the right direction."

"Absolutely. Have there been any developments at all? I know the last article I read said there weren't any leads, but there wasn't any indication of any violence. I'm hoping that's still the case," she says, sitting down in front of us and crossing her long legs.

I notice she's not wearing pantyhose under her knee-length skirt and her fingernails are painted a deep ruby shade. She looks around the same age as the therapist I went to, maybe even slightly older, but the bare legs and nail polish make her come across as younger. There's a different energy to her, and my immediate thought is that maybe I would have felt more comfortable talking to her when the Bureau sent me for therapy.

"Some new information has come up," I tell her. "But I'm sure you'll understand I have to keep some things to myself as well."

She nods. "Of course. I didn't mean to pry. I was just…" She looks like she's thinking for a second. "I'm not as familiar with the building Sydney lives in as I am with the dorms, but I would think there are security cameras there like there are at the dorms. They're not very visible, but you could check."

"Not very visible?" I ask.

I'd assumed the police would have asked for camera footage if there was any, but now I'm kicking myself for not thinking of getting it myself.

Angela nods beside me. "They do have them. When Sydney moved in, the housing department head let us know they were there, but said the apartment buildings were designed with hidden cameras so the students wouldn't feel like they were under surveillance all the time. It's supposed to create a more welcoming and independent environment."

"That's a philosophy, I guess," I say. "But I'm independent and the cameras we just installed at my house are right out there for the world to see and I feel very welcomed."

Dr. Villareal laughs. "I like that approach. Let people know you're watching them."

"Exactly," I say.

She checks the time. "I have an appointment in just a few minutes, but I'm glad you came to talk to me. Sydney has really been on my mind since the last time she came to see me. Then when I heard she was missing, it got me worried."

Angela and I notice the choice of words at the same time.

"How long has it been since you saw her?" Angela asks. "Didn't she have an appointment with you just a couple of days before she went missing?"

The therapist looks like she's regretting her words a little. "I thought she would have told you. Sydney decided to stop regular meetings with me. I've seen her twice in the last two months. She's been attending her small group therapy more frequently, but I am not the facilitator of that group, so I can't speak to what's been said there. I only know she's been attending because I oversee the department."

I remember what Angela told me about Sydney not going to her therapist in high school when her mental health was starting to deteriorate. It's sounding like she hit the same pattern.

"Did she give you a reason why she wasn't going to come regularly?" I ask.

The doctor shakes her head. "I have a feeling she didn't like the direction our sessions were going. Again, I can't get into specifics with you, but I can tell you I had some real concerns. Her behavior, some of the things she was saying… there was a distinct change."

"What was she saying?" Angela asks. "What were you worried about?"

"I'm sorry. I can't tell you that," she says.

"You are a mandated reporter," Angela insists. "You can't just hold information like that back."

"Unfortunately, mandated reporters only apply to children, and Sydney is nineteen. That legal obligation doesn't apply here," Dr. Villareal replies. "Legally and ethically, I am under no requirement to bring any of Sydney's sessions to the attention of law enforcement."

She's careful with her words, making sure she sets firm guidelines in place. But it goes a step further than that for me. By her making that statement as clearly as she did, she's giving me a lot of the information I asked for. She might not be able to tell me what Sydney said to her, but she can tell me what she didn't say.

"She was still taking her medication, right?" Angela asks. "Surely you can tell me if the prescriptions have been refilled."

The doctor hesitates again. "I can tell you that I have submitted refill authorizations for medications for your daughter."

That's enough for Angela. She nods, looking somewhat relieved.

"You said Sydney was on your mind after your last appointment," I say, making a leading statement rather than asking a question so she can decide for herself how she's comfortable answering.

"Yes. Sydney has been… showing signs of greatly altered thinking. That's really all I can say about it, but it has made me worried about her."

"There have been some reports of uncharacteristic behaviors," I say. "Wanting to do things she generally doesn't do. Saying things that people close to her find odd. Does that sound like it aligns with what you noticed?"

"Yes," she nods. "That would make sense." Her eyes flicker over to the desk on the far side of the room, then back to us. "I'm walking a very fine line here ethically, but I feel it's important for you to have some idea of what's been going on, and since it is addressed to you, I think it is appropriate to give it to you."

"What is addressed to me?" Angela asks.

Dr. Villareal goes over to the desk and opens one of the drawers. She takes out a manila envelope and withdraws a mailing envelope she brings over to Angela.

"One of the exercises I do with my patients is to have them write letters to people in their lives who they want to say something to, but haven't been able to bring themselves to say. Most of the time these letters are designed to never be sent. They are just an opportunity for the patient to express themselves openly and work through emotions. Sometimes, however, I encourage my patients to consider allowing the recipients to read the letters.

"Sydney wrote a series of letters over the course of several weeks a while ago. Some of them she said she absolutely did not want to send, and actually burned a few of them. But a couple of them she allowed me to keep and said she did want to give them at some point. One of them, in particular, she intended to give during a planned family session she and I were talking about having next month.

"It's addressed to you. She isn't here to give her express permission, but I'm going to use my professional discretion and say that because we'd already discussed her plans to give you this letter in a future session, it's yours to read if you want to."

Angela takes the envelope out of the doctor's hand and looks at it. From where I'm sitting, I can see "Mom" written across it in tight, jagged handwriting.

"This is what her handwriting looked like in high school," she whispers, more to herself than to us. Her eyes lift to the doctor again. "Do you know what it says?"

"No. I didn't read it."

Angela nods, letting out a breath as she looks down at the envelope again. She's holding it carefully, like she's almost afraid to open it. Like if she does, she's going to know something she doesn't want to. Or that she'll finish the letter and still not know something she does.

Finally, she peels open the adhesive and takes out a folded piece of printer paper. The handwriting on the paper is at an angle, filling the white space until there's only a corner left at the bottom. Her eyes look teary as she reads through the harshly slanted words, but the further she gets, the more confused her expression becomes. She shakes her head and looks up at the doctor.

"I don't understand," she says. "So much of it doesn't make sense. What is she talking about?"

"You'll have to tell me what it says," Dr. Villareal tells her. "I didn't read the letter and I can't conjecture on what she might have put in there based on anything she said in the sessions to protect her privacy."

"She's talking about her past chasing her no matter how hard she tries to hide from it. That she turned into a different person so that *they* couldn't find her again, but they did, and no one knows. She says she's been searching and she knows Ab… someone is there, but she can't find her, and she keeps looking. Then she says the most important thing she has to say is that she wants me to know that she knows that blue is her color." Angela looks up, the tears sliding down her cheeks seemingly forgotten in her bewilderment. "I don't understand."

"I can't tell you what she's talking about. Not because of her privacy, but simply because I don't know. I was hoping you might be able to shed some light on it," Dr. Villareal says.

"These are things she said in her sessions?" I ask.

"Similar," the therapist admits. "She didn't elaborate, but it always seemed like these things were extremely meaningful to her. They definitely weren't just random statements. I take it they don't mean anything to you, either?"

"Here, where she says that blue is her color, I… that's something I used to tell her when she was younger and feeling self-conscious. I'd tell her how beautiful she was and that she looked great in blue because it contrasted with her hair and brought out her eyes," she says. "But I don't understand why she would say it in a letter like this. I don't know what she's trying to tell me."

The doctor nods. She looks like she's debating with herself, but then her shoulders drop slightly. "I'm concerned we might be dealing with something more than we thought."

"What do you mean?" Angela asks.

"Your daughter's mental health struggles don't come as a surprise to you. You've been aware of her depression and anxiety for some time and have been a part of her management approach," Dr. Villareal says.

I notice her wording and my mind goes to Xavier. I can't help but wonder what he would think of the letter.

"Of course," Angela nods.

"Well, considering what I've observed, and what Agent Griffin has suggested, I believe what Sydney is facing goes beyond that. She's clearly exhibiting signs of greatly altered thinking and compromised processing. I don't want to put specific words to it because I haven't formally diagnosed her, but I believe she could be moving toward a psychotic break."

# CHAPTER TWENTY-NINE

ANGELA STILL LOOKS PALE AND TREMBLING WHEN I GET HER ONTO the couch at Sydney's apartment and go into the kitchen to search for something warm to give her to drink. When I was in college, I always had tea bags somewhere. Many of them ended up chilled and set over Bellamy's eyes when she was feeling stressed, but I got to drink a lot of them, too. Angela could use some of that soothing right now.

I'm happy to find a box of raspberry tea in one of the cabinets and go to work boiling water. My mind is still churning, trying to process everything we learned from the doctor. I understand her professional constraints in not being able to italicize everything, but I can't help but be a little frustrated by them.

Sydney is nineteen, so she is an adult in the eyes of the law, which means she has the right to privacy and discretion when it comes to her medical treatment. But it's hard not to look at the picture of Sydney and still think of her - as a child. The pain on her mother's face is so clear.

She wants nothing more than to protect and take care of her daughter, and she can't.

She thanks me when she takes the cup of tea from my hands and holds it in hers, not drinking it, but holding it close enough to breathe in the fragrant steam.

"She needs to tell me what's going on," she says. It's obvious she's thinking about the same thing I am. "She knows something about where Sydney is, and she isn't saying anything."

"She can't," I tell her. "Mandated reporting laws are mainly for child abuse or elder abuse. If I force her to tell us what's going on, that would get her—and me—into huge trouble. Dr. Villareal can't give us any information without a court order, and there's no way we can get a court order with what we have now."

Angela lets out a pained breath. "She thinks Sydney is really sick."

I wish I had a better idea of what I could say to her. I can't even begin to imagine what she's feeling right now. Not just the fear, but also the helplessness. And maybe even the guilt. Wesley made it a point to mention she's the one who encouraged Sydney to have more independence. It's a completely normal thing for parents to want for their college-age children, but it has to feel different when that child goes missing.

"I know. And I'm not going to pretend to understand how that might feel for you. All I can say to you right now is this makes the situation much more serious than we thought. Understanding all the steps that led to her going missing is critical. Before we were just dealing with the possibility she wanted to get away from everything, but now I think we need to accept the reality that it could be something else. I need to tell you what I know about the timeline of her disappearance. It's not going to be easy for you to hear, but we need to all be working together. Is it possible to get your husband here?"

She bristles and shakes her head. "No. He went home."

"He went home?" I ask.

I'm stunned. His daughter is missing. I can't understand what would compel him to leave.

"We've been arguing a lot. He said it wasn't doing any good for him to be here and he should be back home working and talking to as many people as he can who know her. Maybe she would try to get back home or go to stay with friends or something from back there. I just think he doesn't want to be near me," Angela says glumly.

"This is going to be an extremely personal question, and I apologize in advance, but can you tell me if the problems with your husband have been going on since before Sydney's disappearance? Things like this cause a tremendous amount of tension, and it's very common for couples to experience a lot of difficulty after a child goes missing. So it would make sense…"

"It's not new. I mean, it's gotten worse since all this has been happening, but things haven't been good between the two of us for a while," she admits.

My phone alerts on the coffee table where I put it. I pick it up and see I have a new text from a number I don't recognize. I handed my cards out to several people, so it could be any of them. I'm expecting the message to start with a name or at least some sort of clue about who it might be, but there's nothing to indicate who sent it. It's only one sentence.

"Look for *ReuniteInOrion*."

"Reunite in Orion," I mutter, seeing if it will trigger anything.

"What's that?" Angela asks.

I shake my head. "I don't know. But I think we need to find out."

I don't have my computer with me, so I have to settle for searching on my phone. The way the words are written make it look like a screen name or a handle, but without knowing what it's attached to, the easier first step is just to type it into the search engine. The search results bring me to an alternative living forum. A place where people can share their darkest secrets, their whispering thoughts they dare not share under their real names. It's like the photo negative of social media, where the dark underbelly is right at the surface.

I can't search for anything or read any of the posts without creating an account, so I throw one together, using one of the disposable email addresses I use when I don't want something going to my personal address. Once my account is verified, I'm able to scroll through posts and look at the various forums and video categories available.

They're all dark, some of them dipping into the disturbing. People talking about their forbidden, taboo desires. Their darkest pasts. The thoughts they could never tell anyone—barely even themselves. This is where the search results brought me, though, so I know it has something here. I type the name into the search and a profile appears. The avatar is appropriately an image of the night sky with the Orion constellation visible against the inky blackness.

There aren't any written posts, but I see a collection of thumbnails associated with videos. The most recent one is from the night before Sydney disappeared. The image of the thumbnail is small, but it looks like the back of a girl's head, her dark hair streaming down her back and only the tips of her shoulders visible.

"Have you ever seen this?" I ask.

"No," Angela says. "I have no idea what this is. Is that Sydney?"

"It looks like it could be."

"Play it," she says.

I hesitate. "I don't know what could be on these videos. You should let me watch them first."

"Play it," she insists. "I want to know."

I look at her, searching her eyes. Now I see it. She's melting, too. I turn back to the screen and start the video.

# CHAPTER THIRTY

S YDNEY DOESN'T TURN AROUND DURING THE ENTIRE VIDEO. As much as I want her to, so I can confirm it is actually her, I'm glad to only be looking at her back. Angela looks like she's starting to crumble just hearing her voice. I don't know how she would react if she had to look into her daughter's face as Sydney emptied her pain out to anyone listening.

At the end of the video, I move out of that screen to get to the keypad.

"What are you doing? I want to watch the others," Angela says.

"I need to call Jasmine," I tell her. "We need to find out if she knew about this."

It turns out Jasmine is only a few minutes away, so I call Van and ask him to meet us at the apartment. He's hesitant, but finally agrees. Angela is pacing through the living room, on edge. She wants to watch more of the videos, but it would be better to be able to see them on a larger screen rather than the phone.

When Jasmine comes into the apartment, she looks anxious and is already pulling her computer out of her bag to hand to me. I asked her to use it while we were on the phone, hoping she would say it was in her bedroom.

"What's going on?" she asks.

I put the computer on the table and open it. Jasmine tells me her passcode and sits beside me while I bring up the website.

"I got a message from someone who didn't identify themselves directing me here," I tell her. "Do you know anything about it?"

Jasmine leans slightly closer to look at the screen. She shakes her head.

"No. I've never heard of this site."

"How about this?" I ask, pulling up Sydney's profile. "Did Sydney tell you anything about making these videos?"

"I have no idea what this is. She never said anything about making videos. And I never saw her do any of them." She looks closer. "ReuniteInOrion. What does that mean?"

"I don't know. But I have a feeling it carries a lot of meaning for Sydney. Enough that she referenced it even when she didn't want to openly talk about it," I say.

"What do you mean?" Jasmine asks.

I point to the words. "Reunited. In. Orion. R-I-O."

"Rio," she murmurs.

I nod.

"Rio?" Angela asks. "Who is that?"

I explain the party and Sydney's strange behavior.

"Part of the reason I want to talk to Van is to ask him about that night. I spoke to one of the girls who thought they were bringing Sydney home that night and she said Sydney told them to bring her to Murray Hall."

"The dorm?" Angela frowns.

"It's the one Van, her ex-boyfriend, lives in. They apparently got her to the door and couldn't get in, but another girl came out and said they were friends and brought her inside. I haven't been able to find who that girl is, but I'd like to know if Van has something to say about it," I say. "Jasmine, watch this. I have to make a call."

I leave them sitting with the computer while I call Detective Bakker.

"Hey, it's Emma," I say when she answers. "I have a quick question about the investigation. Have you contacted the school's housing department to ask about security cameras at the apartment building?"

"I did, but they're giving me the runaround. Apparently, they think it's an invasion of the privacy of the other residents of the building to simply release the footage because we asked them to. They need proof something occurred that justifies it," she gripes. "A girl being missing from the building is apparently not urgent enough to compel them to share the footage without a court order from a judge who also believes there is enough evidence to justify it."

"What the fuck is wrong with people?" I ask. "Somehow the people who are not missing and who are by all accounts perfectly fine and safe in their homes going about their lives have more value than a girl who could be in significant danger? We're going to worry more about them not wanting people finding out they order pizza every night or who is coming in through their back doors and doing the walk of shame at three A.M. than we are finding out if Sydney left alone, if she looked distressed, and if anyone came into her apartment?"

"That's the basic gist of it," Alyssa says.

"Fantastic. Alright, get that order. And throw in the security footage for Murray Hall and any businesses that might have views of the building in their footage. I'd like to get as much of the front patio space and the streets around it as possible," I tell her.

"Sounds like you might be on to something," she says.

"I am, and I might be calling in your services again soon."

"Anything you need, just let me know."

"Great. Thanks. I will. Give me a call when you have that footage," I say.

I get off the phone right as there's a knock on the front door. It's as I'm walking to it to open it that I remember Angela has never met Van. She didn't even know her daughter was dating anyone, and now she's going to be facing down the ex who is still in so many ways tied up in Sydney's disappearance. I don't know how she's going to react. I don't know how I would react if I were her. But right now, playing referee between the two has to be the least of my concerns. I need the information both of them can give me, and they can deal with any conflict on their own time.

Opening the door, I step back to let Van inside. He looks at me suspiciously as he steps past, only coming in far enough for me to close the door.

"Why am I here?" he asks.

"A few things have come up in our search for Sydney, and I need to talk to you about them," I tell him.

"Why do I need to be here?"

"Why do you sound so uncomfortable?" I ask. "It isn't like you haven't been here before."

I meet his eyes and he knows I'm threatening him. His thwarted attempted break-in and copying the key aren't much to hang over his head, but it's enough to keep him from arguing. Perhaps it isn't the most ethical approach, but I'll take some gray area in this situation if it gets me the answers I need.

We go into the living room and I carefully introduce him to Angela. She looks at him with the kind of mixed set of emotions I expected, and I brace myself for something to bubble up to the surface and make her lash out. But she doesn't. She stays calm and steady. I admire her a bit more in that instant.

"Go ahead and ask me what you need to know," Van says. "Though I really don't know what could be left for you to do. You already had my room trashed and my privacy violated."

"Trust me," I say, "there's plenty left for me to do, and I wouldn't have so much attitude if I was in your position. This isn't about you. You strike me as the kind of guy who might not have heard that very much in his life but get used to it. This is about Sydney and what happened to her, starting with the night she was brought to your dorm after the party."

"What are you talking about?" Van frowns. "What party?"

"The party at Brent Bender's house," I tell him.

I say the name casually and without any emphasis so I can gauge his reaction to it.

"I don't know Brent Bender," he says.

"Sydney went to a party at his house a few weeks ago and ended up at your dorm," I say. "From there, we lose track of her until the next night."

"She wasn't with me," he insists. "I don't know what you're talking about." He looks around. "Is that why I'm here? You want to grill me about Sydney going to some party and ending up at my dorm?"

"You're here because every time I turn around it seems like something else is coming up to point at you having something to do with her disappearance, or at least to you knowing more about what happened to her than you want to say. You told me the first time I talked to you that you were deleting search history from her computer."

"I was. I told you, she was looking up strange things and I wanted to get them off her mind, so I deleted the history. I hoped it would help her to push those thoughts away."

"And what about the videos?" I ask.

He looks genuinely confused. "What videos? I didn't delete any videos, just search history."

"You didn't delete any of the videos of her talking? The ones that she posts on the forum?" I ask.

Van shakes his head. "I didn't see any videos. What forum? What is she talking about?"

I bring him into the apartment, and we all sit down to watch the videos. I'm uncomfortable doing it. It feels voyeuristic. Sydney posted these videos on purpose. She created them and put them up on a forum where she knew other people would watch them. But it still brings me painfully close to the feeling I got when I was stretched on that sofa in the therapist's office, answering her questions. It feels like we're cracking Sydney open and digging around inside her and prying out the quivering, vulnerable pieces she keeps hidden.

The more she talks, the more I want to stop. I don't want to split her open further. I don't want to watch as her words reveal her veins and ask us to slowly slit them with every intimate bit of knowledge of her so she doesn't have to.

And yet, I can't stop. As long as there are more videos to play, I feel the compulsion to watch them. They exist, so I need to experience them. Like I owe it to Sydney for me to listen to what she has to say.

*There used to be light ahead of me.*

*When I thought about the future… there was one.*

*I wanted to do things. I wanted to be things.*

*And I believed I could.*

*That's not there anymore.*

*The light is gone.*

*Sometimes I wonder if it was really ever there to begin with. Maybe it was nothing but an illusion.*

*M says I'm right.*

*The light, the aspirations, the beliefs. They were there only because I was told they were.*

*I believed what I was told to believe.*

We're all breathless and silent listening to her. The tears falling down Jasmine and Angela's faces make no sound. Van looks like stone.

Suddenly, I notice something in the background of the video we're watching. I track it backward by a few seconds and pause it, pointing at the now-still image.

"What's that?" I ask. There's something metallic on the table off to the side of the image. "Does that look like a computer to you?"

Angela leans forward to look more closely at the object. She nods. "That's her computer."

"But then what is she recording this video on?" Jasmine asks.

I look at Van. "When you were deleting the search history, are you sure you were on her regular computer? The one she uses all the time?"

"Yes," he nods. "I mean, that's what it looked like. It was just her computer. The one that was in her room. It was open and the search was there."

"Is there anything about her computer that's distinctive?" I ask.

"She has a sticker on it from the peer counseling program," Jasmine says. "Right on top."

We examine the still image more closely, and I notice what looks like something round and colorful on the top of the computer at the side of the screen. I point to it.

"Is that it?" I ask.

She nods. "That looks like it."

"So, Sydney recorded these videos on a different device," Angela notes. "Why would she do that?"

"So no one would find them," I say. "And possibly so it would be less noticeable when she took it with her."

When we've watched all the videos, we take a few moments to process it all, then I turn to Angela. She jumps in and speaks before I have a chance to.

"Who is 'M'?"

"I was going to ask if any of you had any idea about that," I say.

Jasmine and Van look at each other like both are expecting the other to know who she's talking about.

"I've never heard her talk about anybody she called 'M,'" Jasmine says.

"Neither have I," Van concurs.

"How about any friends she has with names that start with 'M?'" I press. "Can you think of anybody?"

"There was a girl in one of her classes who she studied with a lot last semester whose name was Maggie," Jasmine offers, "but they weren't close. And after the class ended, I didn't hear Sydney mention her again. I can't imagine she'd have suddenly gotten that close to her."

"I need both of you to talk to anyone you can think of who might know about these videos," I tell them. "Think about the people you know who have the kind of taste who would like these things. Find out if anybody watched them and what they know. By the sound of some of these comments, what she's saying really resonates with some of the viewers. Someone sent me that message directing me here. If we know who did, we might be able to focus in on M, and maybe have the chance to find Sydney before this gets worse."

# CHAPTER THIRTY-ONE

Angela swallows hard beside me. Jasmine and Van leave and I go back to watching the videos again. I don't want to see them again, but I know I have to. I take notes about the comments, writing down names that appear on multiple videos and any messages that stand out to me in particular. It's going to be difficult to trace these to the users and find out their actual identity if they don't expressly state it, but I'm going to try.

As I listen to Sydney's confessions, a recurring theme becomes obvious. I pause the current video I'm watching to look at Angela.

"In several of these videos, Sydney talks about her past and the guilt she feels about specific people, but she doesn't name them. In the letter she wrote you, she mentioned people as well, saying they were with her or something like that," I say. "I noticed that you stumbled a little when you were talking to the doctor about it."

"What do you mean?" she asks, though I can tell she knows exactly what I mean.

"When you were telling us about the contents of the letter, you were starting to say something else, but changed it to 'somebody,'" I tell her. "It sounded like you were going to say a name."

There's a brief second where it seems she might try to cover it all up again, but then her shoulders fall, and she relents.

"Abigail. Sydney's cousin," she says.

"Are they close?" I ask. "Could that be someone she's staying with?"

Angela shakes her head. "No. Abigail is dead. But they were very close once."

"What happened to her?"

"She and her boyfriend were murdered," she tells me.

I'm shocked by the revelation, but it brings up even more questions.

"Why would Sydney feel guilty about that?" I ask.

"It's a long story. When Abigail was younger, her mother gave birth to a baby boy. He was perfectly healthy when he went home from the hospital, but he died in his crib three weeks later. The doctors said it was SIDS. There was nothing they could have done. Her parents were devastated, but especially her father, who had always wanted a son. A year later, it happened again."

"That's awful," I whisper, still not understanding how any of this went together, but letting her talk.

"It was. Abigail's mother, Beth, knew how desperately her husband wanted a son, so she went against her doctor's recommendations and got pregnant again. It was another boy, and they were thrilled. Everyone was nervous, but when they brought him home, he was fine. He was healthy and it seemed like the tragedies were behind them.

"When he was three years old, Sydney was babysitting him. She put him down for his nap and sat in another room doing homework. When she went to check on him, he wasn't in his bed. She found him at the bottom of the pool in the backyard. He'd gone through the door in his parents' bedroom. They'd left it unlocked and they had disconnected the alarm because it bothered them that it went off every time they wanted to go out and swim. She was overcome with guilt."

"That isn't her fault. The parents should have taken more precautions," I say. "It was a horrible accident, but if there was anyone at all to blame, it wouldn't be Sydney."

"I tried to tell her that, but she was inconsolable for a long time. Beth was beside herself and her husband, Barrett, Wesley's brother, fell apart. They changed as people. It's hard to describe, but it was frightening watching it."

"And Abigail stayed with them?" I ask.

"There didn't seem to be a reason for her not to. They were hurt and angry, but they were good to her. We were hoping they would get through it together, heal, and be able to move forward. But soon Beth started talking about having another baby. She wanted to give Barrett back his son. We all tried to convince her that wasn't a good idea, but she got pregnant a few months later.

"We tried to be happy for her and got her gifts when she announced her baby boy's name. But then when it came time for her to have the baby, there was no announcement. We waited and didn't hear anything, then we got a call from Barrett. He said Beth had stopped talking about the baby and didn't look pregnant anymore. He asked if I could make plans with her and see what was going on.

"She had me over to her house for lunch and as soon as I saw her, I could tell something was wrong. Her belly was gone, but it wasn't like she'd been wearing a fake one and was back to having a flat stomach. There was still a pouch there like a woman who has given birth. She looked pale and wild-eyed. That's the only way I can describe her.

"It was like she was too energetic. She was talking nonstop and doting on Abigail. I tried to figure out a gentle way to ask her about the baby and when I did, she made it seem like I was crazy. She said she wasn't pregnant and hadn't been. When I pressed her on it, reminding her of the name she announced and the gifts we'd given her, she burst into tears and told me I was being cruel and tormenting her after losing her children. I didn't know what to think, but later when I went to the restroom and went to get a hand towel from the closet, I noticed there were a lot of towels missing."

"Is that significant?"

"Beth was meticulous when it came to designing her home," Angela explains. "Everything matched, everything was always just so. And she was fanatical about towels and sheets. They had to be white, she bleached them every wash, and replaced them every couple of years so they were never worn out. She always had so many the closet was full even when there were several in the dirty laundry. But that day, the shelf in the closet was nearly empty."

The end of the story is starting to form in my mind before Angela even says it, and it makes my stomach turn. I brace myself to hear it.

"She gave birth to a girl, didn't she?" I ask.

Angela nods. "In her bathtub at home without telling anyone. She was completely convinced she was going to give Barrett the son he wanted so much and told everyone she was pregnant with a boy. But then when she had an ultrasound, she found out she was actually carrying another girl. Barrett wasn't there for the ultrasound, so she lied. And the lie turned into a deep belief that she could somehow will the baby to change. That maybe they were wrong reading the image and it really was a boy.

"But she had another ultrasound, and it confirmed the baby was a girl. She couldn't bring herself to tell Barrett and something inside her snapped. When she went into labor, she gave birth by herself at home, then disposed of her. After cleaning up, she went about convincing the world around her that she hadn't been pregnant to begin with.

"When the police got involved, they found the baby girl's body and Beth was charged with murder. She ended up in a mental hospital rather than prison, but it still left Barrett alone with Abigail. Everyone was devastated for him and couldn't imagine how he was going to get through. He'd now lost four babies, something so overwhelmingly tragic it was difficult to even fathom it could happen. And he was left with a young girl to raise on his own. She was thirteen and the loss of her mother was extremely difficult for her. But her father was right there with her and seemed to swoop in even more adoring than before.

"What we didn't realize at the time was that Barrett had become obsessed with her. Even before the last pregnancy, his focus on his daughter took a very dark turn. No one knew what he was doing to her until she was fifteen and told Sydney. Sydney didn't tell us, but later I found out she'd tried to convince Abigail to tell her teachers or the police, someone, but Abigail refused. She was too embarrassed, and she swore Sydney to secrecy.

"Everything came to a head when Abigail was sixteen. Things had gotten worse with her father, and she decided to run away with her boyfriend. Sydney didn't want her to, she was afraid for her, and Abigail convinced her that she should go with them. They could all go together. Wesley caught her as she was leaving. He forced her to tell him what was going on, and he called Barrett.

"Abigail and her boyfriend left, but Barrett chased them. He ended up running them off the road and shooting both of them. Sydney felt like she should have been there with them. If she hadn't gotten caught and had been with them, they wouldn't have been killed. That was when her spiral started. She couldn't handle what happened and felt like all of it was her fault, starting with the drowning."

"Angela, forgive me for asking you this, but did Wesley ever hurt Sydney? Have you ever had any suspicions that he might have treated her the way that Barrett treated Abigail?" I ask.

Angela shifts uncomfortably. "I didn't want to think so. There were a couple of times when I noticed strange things, but I told myself they weren't anything. Just things like him adjusting her bathing suit or commenting on the clothes she was wearing. She never said anything, and I never saw anything, but after she went missing… I'm scared I missed something the same way we did with Abigail. That that's why she wanted to leave with her."

Angela lets out a sob, then looks at the screen again, the look in her eyes painful as she struggles to keep herself together.

"What is it?" I ask.

"This," she says, reaching out and briefly running her fingertips over Sydney's screen name. "After Abigail died, we were cleaning out her room and found journals full of poems she'd written. In one of them, she says 'when I leave, look for me in starlight, I'll find my way to the hunter.'"

"Orion," I whisper, and she nods.

My lungs fill with air that stays there until they ache. Somewhere along the line, Sydney went from living to suffering, and no one noticed. She was right there, and no one saw her.

It's on me now.

I have to see her.

# CHAPTER THIRTY-TWO

F EELING LIKE I NEED SOME TIME TO MYSELF, I GO BACK TO THE hotel and order dinner from a little local restaurant that had a flyer tucked into the welcome book sitting on the dresser when I checked in. While I'm waiting for the delivery, I call Sam. It feels like it's been so long since I heard his voice and I need it now.

I sit curled in a chair next to the window, looking out over the dusky evening falling across the campus in the distance, while I catch him up on what's been going on here.

"I don't understand. If she's so open about her mental health and acted as an advocate for other people going through similar things, why did she hide the videos?" he asks. "I'd think that would be something she would talk about."

"When she first started making the videos, I think she thought of them more like an online journal. They were her way to talk through the things she was feeling and what was happening around her so she could process them. Just because someone is open about the fact that they are experiencing issues like depression or anxiety doesn't mean they don't have negative feelings about them. I think the videos were part of her coping strategy. And maybe she did tell people that she made them.

"But then they started getting darker and more intense. They take on a different feeling and it's almost like she was living a double life. There's the Sydney who confidently faces life dealing with her mental illness as just another part of her. As something she can not only manage but use to reach out to others. And then there's the Sydney who is battling constantly and feels like she's losing. The Sydney in those videos definitely didn't want the people who she helps, or even those close to her, to know what she's going through. The only exception to that is this person she calls M."

"And you haven't figured out who that is?" he asks.

"No. Her mother, roommate, and ex-boyfriend all said they didn't know of anyone in her life with that initial, or with a nickname that would use that, and the comments on the videos didn't point me toward any specific person who seems like the right fit, either," I tell him.

"There are comments?" Sam asks.

"So many," I tell him. "More than I even want to think about, honestly. It's almost like she built up a fan base. It kind of makes me sick to even think of it that way. That there would be people who would be attached to her and get entertainment from listening to her talk about being in so much pain. Some of the comments are encouraging, like they want her to get through everything and to know she's not alone. There are the classic helpful, not helpful things that people say when they know that someone's going through a hard time. You know: *You're going to be alright. Everything's going to work out. You'll figure things out. At least you're healthy. You're too young and have too much to live for to feel like this. I'm sending you hugs!*"

"All the greatest hits," Sam notes.

"Yup. Then there are other ones that are commiserating with her, saying they know just how she feels. She's in their heads. She's their voice. On and on. Like they were looking up to her in some way.

"And of course, it wouldn't be the internet without the really vicious ones. People telling her that she's too broken and damaged for this world. She should just give up. That she's just looking for clout and she isn't actually feeling any of those things. She just wants to be dramatic and have people fawn on her. A couple of people tell her she should just go ahead and kill herself."

"Damn. That's harsh," Sam mutters.

"It is. But it's not unusual, unfortunately. As great as the internet can be to get information and stay in touch with people, share ideas, all of that, it's definitely got a horrific underbelly. When they don't have to be face-to-face with other people and can just hide behind the keyboard, people get puffed up and say horrible things. It's like they forget that there's actually a person on the other end and they aren't just playing some sort of elaborate video game.

"There was one person who commented on a lot of the videos who stood out to me. The name they use is Shepherd. All the comments are this strange blend of encouraging and morbid. The person will say Sydney is beautiful and loved and wonderful, and then say that she shouldn't have to keep struggling if she doesn't want to. That she makes so much of a difference in the world and has touched so many people, and it's alright if her work is done and she's ready to rest."

"They're telling her to commit suicide," he says.

"Or at least that it's a fine option if she decides to," I say.

There's a knock on the door and I get up from the chair, grabbing my bag so I can get out some cash to tip the delivery driver. But when I look through the peephole, I put it back down.

"Babe?" Sam says. "Everything okay?"

"Yeah. I'm going to need to call you back. I love you."

"I love you. You're sure you're alright?"

"I'm fine. I'll talk to you in a bit."

I hang up and open the door. Detective Bakker turns back from where she was looking down the hallway and meets my eyes.

"Hey, Emma. I'm sorry to just show up like this, but I couldn't get through on your phone," she says. "Are you going somewhere?"

I look down and realize I'm still holding my bag. "Oh, no. I thought you were the delivery person bringing me my dinner. And I'm sorry about not answering my phone. I was on a call with my husband and didn't notice another call was coming in. Come inside."

I step out of the way to let her into the room, but she hesitates.

"I can't stay. I came by hoping to pick you up," she says.

My head tilts to the side and I give her a questioning look. I might have only known her briefly, but I wouldn't put it past Alyssa to decide she was having a slow evening and show up wanting to go out and find some fun, but I'm not getting that vibe from her right now.

"What's going on?" I ask.

The elevator opens and the delivery driver comes out. He pauses when he sees us standing at the door as if he doesn't know how to process not having to come knock. I accept the bag and tip him as fast as I can to get him back in the elevator.

"A call came into emergency dispatch about twenty minutes ago. Some students going to a study group found a body. It looks like a girl jumped off one of the buildings."

My stomach sinks and I nod.

"Give me a second to put this inside and get dressed. I'll be right there."

## CHAPTER THIRTY-THREE

ALYSSA AND I ARE SILENT AS WE DRIVE FROM MY HOTEL TO CAMpus. We don't have to talk. Both of us have the same thing on our minds. The details she got about the discovery are vague. The student who made the emergency call only said they found a body behind one of the academic buildings and that there was a lot of blood. It looked like the female victim jumped.

The responding officers called Alyssa before the crime scene investigation unit even arrived. They obviously know of the investigation into Sydney's disappearance and thought it would be a good idea to have her available just in case. I hate the concept of 'just in case,' but I'm glad they called her. It meant she came to me and as much as I don't want this to be how the search for Sydney ends, I want to be there.

We park along one of the streets surrounding the buildings and hurry toward the bright yellow tape visible even from the distance. There's a crowd already gathering to watch the proceedings. I'm disappointed that it seems to not just be students but staff and faculty among the onlookers. Most of them are hanging back several yards away, just curious about what's going on and wanting to watch it unfold in hopes of getting the details. Others are more brazen. They creep up as close to the tape as they can get and crane their necks, trying to get a look at the body.

I notice one holding his phone as I approach. He lifts it up and a light pops on, indicating he's recording.

"Put that away," I demand.

He whips around, starting to protest, but when he sees the badges Alyssa and I have visible on our hips, he backs down.

"I just ..."

"If you took any pictures or video of anything, you better delete them. Right now," I say.

We duck under the tape and two of the responding officers come toward us.

"What do you have?" Alyssa asks.

I can hear in her voice she really wanted to ask if it's Sydney, but she knows the young officer can't make that determination. In all reality, neither of us can, either. Until the medical examiner takes the body and does the postmortem, there can't be an official identification. And it might not be easy to make a presumptive identification, either.

Unfortunately, I know firsthand the damage a fall from a building can cause to a body. I've seen the aftermath and am familiar with just how devastating those kinds of injuries can be. It can leave the person wholly unrecognizable, even to someone who has seen their face daily.

"Female. Late teens, possibly very early twenties. We're assuming she was a student here. Injuries are consistent with a jump. Looks recent. Likely within the last couple of hours."

One of the CSU investigators covered the body with a tarp and the bright blue stands out against the darkened sidewalk as we approach. A voice goes through the back of my mind, hoping it's not Sydney under there. It's a strange feeling, but one I've had many times before. Any time I'm searching for someone, and a body is found, there's that thought hoping it's not the end.

It always takes a few seconds for the alternative to settle in. There's someone under that tarp. A human form is creating the mound that's been concealed from the prying eyes around it. That was a life not too long ago. Just a few hours ago, that was a walking, breathing, speaking person. Thoughts were churning through her brain. Blood was pumping through her veins—the same blood that is now seeping into the concrete beneath her head.

I'm hoping it's not Sydney, but there's still someone dead. There's still a victim representing friends and family who are going to be destroyed by the news. But that doesn't change that when the officer leans down to pull back the tarp, I'm bracing myself and hoping not to see her.

The tarp comes back and the first thing I see is blood-stained blonde hair. The pixie cut frames a face battered by the impact with the sidewalk. Her eyes are closed. I'm glad for that. I've become accustomed to seeing corpses and can disconnect from them when I need to, but there's something raw and intimate about seeing the open eyes of a person who has recently died. You become very aware of occupying the space that was the last thing they saw.

"It's not Sydney," Alyssa says.

I shake my head. "It doesn't look like it."

"Shit," she mutters. "Have her pockets been checked? Any identification on her?"

"No identification," the responding officer says.

"Alright. Get her to the medical examiner's office. We need to get an ID on her."

"Did you look at her fingertips?" I ask as the officer pulls the tarp over her again.

"Her fingertips?" he frowns.

I nod. "Did you look at her hands?"

"No," he says.

The medical examiner comes up and I repeat the question.

"Not specifically," she says. "Is there something specific you want to know?"

"Can I check?" I ask.

She nods and I crouch down beside the tarp to lift the edge. One hand is lying on the ground, resting palm-down. I lift it and carefully turn it over. Except for a couple of small abrasions and some bits of cement embedded in the skin from the force of the impact, her skin is smooth and unbroken.

"What were you looking for?" Alyssa asks when I stand up again.

"Cuts or scrapes on her hands," I explain. "Something that might indicate she was holding onto the edge of the building or fighting against going over the edge."

"You think she might not have killed herself?" the detective asks.

"I don't think there's anything to indicate that," I say. "I just wanted to make sure the bases are covered."

We linger at the scene for a little while longer gathering all the details we can, then Alyssa and I walk back to her car, and she drives me back to the hotel. I tell her everything about the videos and my concerns.

"I'm working on getting access to her phone records and to the security footage as fast as I can," she says. "I'll keep you updated."

"Thank you."

The next day I'm back at the apartment watching the videos again. Angela bursts into the apartment and comes toward me in a rush.

"They found a body?" she demands. "Is it Sydney?"

I stand and shake my head. "No. It's not her. I was there at the scene last night. We don't have an identification of the body yet, but she was too small, and her hair was very short and blonde. It wasn't Sydney."

Angela lets out a breath like all the air inside her has been sucked out and she drops down onto the couch. Her hand shakes as it comes up to cup her forehead and her eyes close.

"Thank God," she says. "I heard it on the news, and I thought…"

"I would have called you," I say. "You wouldn't find out that way." I sit back down in front of the computer. "But that doesn't mean there's any less urgency. I'm going through the videos again, trying to find any clue she might have dropped about what she planned to do."

"She only has a few days left of her medication," Angela says.

"Her medication?" I ask.

She nods. "She has them with her. That means she's taking them, right?"

I remember the prescription she'd talked about when I first met her.

"We can only hope she is," I mutter.

If Sydney is taking her medications, it means she's still alive and is taking steps to take care of herself. That gives at least some indication she isn't hopeless. But I'm very aware of the amount of medication she has left dwindling. It etches a line in the sand, giving what could be a bright, firm ending to the time I have left to find her.

I've just started another video when the computer chimes and a bubble appears at the corner of the screen. I call out to Jasmine in her room to let her know about the notification before I notice it's from the forum. I click on it hoping it will be a message. Instead, a new video pops up.

A girl with short blonde hair stands at the edge of a building's roof, staring forward and not saying anything. Her hands curl and clench by her sides before releasing and then clenching again. She suddenly looks back over her shoulder like someone said something to her, but there was no voice. I see her face and the image of it superimposes on the memory of the bloody sidewalk.

She approaches the camera and adjusts it. It looks like she set it up before going to the edge of the building. When the angle is what she wants, she returns to the edge of the building. She turns around so she's looking into the camera and for a long second, I wonder if she'll walk away, even though I know what's actually about to happen.

"Oh, god," Angela whispers beside me.

"Agent Griffin," Jasmine says, coming into the room with her phone in her hand.

"Angela, don't—"

I don't get the full warning out before the girl on the screen tips backward and falls out of view.

Angela's hands fly up to cover her mouth. What we just watched was horrifying and I'm trying to process how it appeared on the forum. Jasmine comes over to me with her phone and holds it out to show me a thumbnail image of the video on one of her social media channels.

"Where else is it?" I ask.

She pulls the phone back and scans through a few screens. Her breath catches in her throat.

"It's everywhere."

I grab my phone and call Detective Bakker.

"I've seen it," she says when she answers. "What the hell is going on?"

"I don't know, but we need to shut it down. Now."

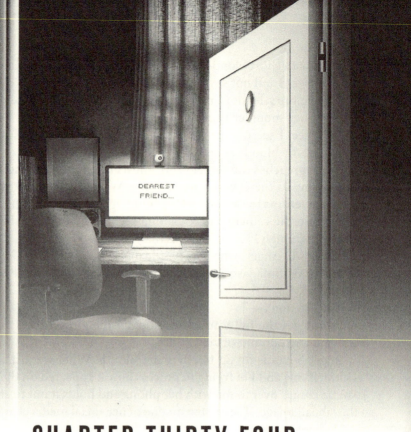

# CHAPTER THIRTY-FOUR

After the release of the video, it doesn't take long for the identity of the victim to seep through.

Cora Gough, a sophomore at Baxter and a resident of Murray Hall.

The patio that has been nearly empty the last couple of times I came to the dorm is crammed full when I arrive later that evening to attend a candlelight vigil arranged to honor Cora. Around me, people are clutching tapers poked through paper cupcake liners. Some are alone, staring at the cut stones at their feet, others in small clusters. Every person there is alone, but together.

Van comes through some of the people in front of me and his face drops when he sees I'm standing there.

"Don't worry," I say. "I'm not here for you. I'm here for Cora."

He nods. "All of us are. This is terrible."

"Did you know her?" I ask.

"No," he says. "Not personally. I probably saw her at some point, but I can't remember ever talking to her. But she was still a person."

"Of course," I nod.

I feel a touch on the back of my shoulder and turn around to see who it is. Topaz is holding a taper and looks shaken.

"Agent Griffin," she says. "I thought that was you."

"Hi, Topaz," I say. "How are you tonight? Except for all this?"

"I'm alright," she says. "But I wanted to tell you—this is the girl who I left Sydney with the night of the party."

"Cora?" I ask.

She nods. "She said she knew Sydney and would take care of her. I didn't know her name. That's the only time I met her. I didn't put it together until I got here tonight. I just wanted to pay my respects."

I nod. "Thank you."

A red-faced girl wearing a thick sweater against the breeze of the evening steps up onto a chair close to the building. The candle she's holding is lit and I notice two others starting through the crowd lighting candles and encouraging people to light the candles of the people around them. I can't help but think of the last vigil like this I attended, only weeks ago, in the parking lot of an abandoned store where another young woman had been found lifeless.

The circumstances are completely different, but the feeling is the same. Even if they go all but unnoticed in life, death puts a spotlight on a person. It brings people together out of the innate, indescribable compulsion to gather and commemorate the loss of a fellow human being.

"Thank you, everybody, for being here tonight for Cora," the girl starts. "For those of you who don't know me, I'm Bailey Collins. Cora was my best friend. Tonight we're here to remember her and celebrate every second we had with her. If you knew her, you understand when I say she left us far, far too soon, and I can only wish I knew why. But I don't. I knew she was going to group therapy. I knew she'd gone through some difficult things in the last year. But I didn't know how hard it had gotten for her. I wish I'd listened harder. I wish I'd stayed longer. I wish I'd done anything differently. And the only thing I can say is we all need to do better."

"Agent Griffin," Dr. Villareal frowns the next morning as she walks through the doors to the counseling center to find me already waiting there. "I'm sorry, did we have an appointment?"

"No," I say. "I just hoped you might have a quick second for me this morning."

She looks at the time and nods. "If it's brief. I have quite a few appointments today and I've opened up sessions for grief and trauma counseling."

"Because of Cora Gough's death," I say.

She nods. "Yes. As you can imagine, many students are going to have a hard time processing this."

"I understand. Cora is actually why I came to speak with you. Last night at her vigil, her best friend mentioned that Cora was doing group therapy. You mentioned you don't facilitate the groups, but I was hoping you'd be able to point me in the right direction of who I can speak with about it," I say.

"Absolutely. James Underwood facilitates the group therapy program. I don't know how much he'll be willing to share, but you can find him in his office. I'll show you."

"Thank you," I say and follow her down the hall to an office across from a glassed-in conference room.

Dr. Villareal knocks on the door to the office and opens it when a voice calls out, leaning inside without stepping past the threshold.

"Good morning, James. This is Agent Emma Griffin. She's on campus investigating Sydney Parker's disappearance. She wanted to speak with you about Cora," she says.

Emotion flickers across his eyes before he stands up and comes from around his desk toward me, his hand extended.

"Of course. Agent Griffin, I know all of us appreciate you being here."

"Thank you," I say. "I don't mean to intrude. I'm sure you're very busy today."

"Yes," he says, his voice sounding strained and tired. "Please, sit. Can I get you a coffee?"

"Oh, no. Thanks. I don't want to take up too much of your time. I just wanted to find out what I can about Cora. Her best friend mentioned at her vigil last night that she did group therapy."

"Yes," he nods, letting out a breath.

"I'm so sorry this happened," I say. "It can't be easy for you."

"It's not. It isn't the first time I've lost someone this way, but it never gets easier. Unfortunately, some don't understand that suicide is not a viable option. Despite what a few want to say."

"I know you can't get into any specifics with me, but what can you tell me about Cora?"

"When she first got here, she had a harder time than others getting acclimated to the different environment. She came from a very close family and was the first to leave home to go to school, so I don't know if she was really prepared for how big of a change it was going to be to live in a dorm, be responsible for herself, and not see her parents and siblings all the time. But over time, she found new friends and was really starting to thrive in her community.

"She went through a hard breakup before this semester started and she was having difficulty in a few of her classes. As you said, I can't get into details about anything we discussed in the group or in her sessions with me, but I can tell you she was going through a lot of the same challenges as other students who come to college thinking they are prepared and realize they've gotten in over their heads. We'd been working on finding ways to cope with and manage her stress, and the demands she put on herself."

"Can you tell me if she ever had peer counseling with Sydney Parker?" I ask.

He shakes his head. "No. Cora didn't participate in the peer counseling program. And they weren't in the same small group."

"Okay. I don't want to keep you any longer. Thank you so much for your help." I give him one of my cards. "Feel free to get in touch with me if you think of anything I might need to know."

I leave the office unsure of what to think about Cora's death. It sounds like the pressure around her just got to be too much and she couldn't take it anymore. Though they didn't share a therapist, the counseling center seems to be the link between Cora and Sydney, and I wonder if that's why she took Sydney in the night of the party. Even if she didn't know her well, she would likely be concerned enough about her to not want her with strangers.

I just need to know what happened once they got inside that night.

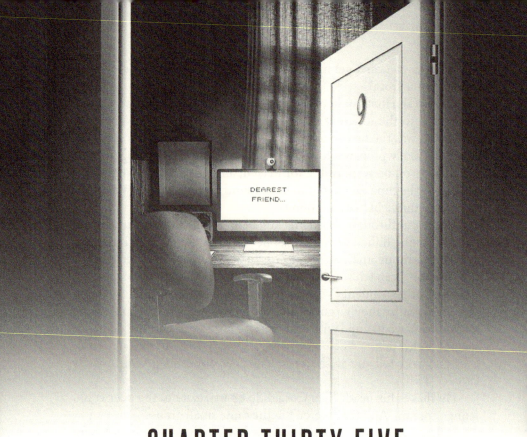

# CHAPTER THIRTY-FIVE

THE SAME SECURITY GUARD WHO WAS BEHIND THE DESK THE DAY I came to see Van is walking across the patio toward the doors when I get to the dorm after leaving the counseling center. He looks at me and visibly lets out a sigh.

"I'll call him," he says.

"No, I'm actually not here to see Van," I tell him. "I'm here to see Bailey Collins. Do you have a way to get her for me?"

He shakes his head. "I don't know her. But you can wait if you want."

"I will," I say and sit down on one of the metal chairs arranged around round tables on one side of the patio.

I don't know how long it's going to take for me to catch Bailey, so I take my computer out of my bag and open it, ready to pull up all the information I have and go through it again. Before I can do that, I notice a couple of new emails in my inbox.

One from Alyssa briefly tells me they got access to the security footage, and she attached the relevant clips. She's still working on the phone records but is hoping for them within the next day or two. The email has three video clips attached to it. The first two are of Sydney's apartment building, one from a camera focused on the back parking lot, and another from a building across the street showing the sidewalk in front of the building.

Both show Sydney walking alone, but at different times. The first appears to show her getting back home on that Friday after class. She doesn't look upset or hurried. She even waves at someone offscreen and pauses to check the mailbox attached to the front of the building. Then she steps inside and the clip ends. The second one shows her early Saturday morning in the very first light of the sun coming out of her back door carrying a bag of trash.

She goes to the dumpster, tosses the bag, then stops in the middle of the parking lot and looks up at the sky, appearing to close her eyes briefly before going inside. The clip shows a time-lapse of a couple of hours before she comes out again with a bag over her shoulder. She walks across the lot and disappears out of frame.

That tells me wherever she was going in that image, it was the last time she left her apartment.

The third clip shows the patio where I'm currently sitting. A few people are milling around and the street lamps around the edges create pools of illumination on the concrete that break up the darkness of the late-night hour. It takes a few seconds before Topaz and another girl appear from the corner of the screen. Both have their arms around Sydney's waist and seem to be helping her walk across the patio.

At one point, the girls look at each other behind Sydney's back and laugh. It seems cold and callous watching it now, but I have to remind myself these girls have no idea what's coming. They don't know the kind of danger Sydney is actually in. They've probably seen plenty of girls end up in sloppy condition after parties, and it never occurred to them that it could have much more serious consequences than embarrassing memories and a hangover the next day.

They wait there for a few minutes in the darkness as Sydney seems to awkwardly rifle through her pockets, but they're interrupted when Cora comes out. She places her arm around Sydney's shoulder, thanks Topaz and the other girl, and ushers her inside. The two of them walk back inside and that's the last I see of them.

I close out of the videos and return to my email. The next message makes me pause. It's from Nathan Klein. The name comes at me like through a fog. I know it's only been a few days, yet it feels like so much longer since I last sent an email to him. I wanted to create distance, to make my questioning seem less threatening to Marini himself so the lawyer wouldn't be as defensive.

I stopped thinking about him as I got more tangled in Sydney's disappearance, and the forward part of my brain had all but forgotten about him. Now it rushes back, and I open the message quickly, wanting to see what he might have to tell me. It doesn't offer me much, but it's enough for the questions to rise right back to the surface.

*"Mr. Marini had no nephew, therefore could have no connection to a missing person. Thank you."*

I'm so invested in the email I nearly miss Bailey Collins walking past. I catch her only because someone calls out to her, asking if she's doing alright. She's only a couple of feet away from me and I say her name to get her attention. She turns and her face falls slightly, an expression of anticipation like she's been hearing the same things all day disappearing and giving way to confusion.

"Yes?" she frowns.

I close my computer and put it away, swinging my bag over my shoulder as I stand.

"Hi. I'm Agent Emma Griffin. Can I talk to you for a couple of minutes?" I ask.

"Agent?" she asks, then something like recognition flickers across her eyes. "Oh. You're that FBI agent who's been asking around about the missing girl."

"Sydney Parker," I say.

She nods. "I'm sorry, but I don't know her. I know her ex supposedly lives in this dorm, but that's all I can tell you about her."

"I actually wanted to ask you about Cora."

The red appears across her cheeks again and tears spring to her eyes. They're already baggy and rimmed, but it's obvious she is far from running out of them.

"I don't..." she whispers. "I can't..."

"Please," I say softly. "I'm sorry. I know this is extremely difficult for you and I'm not meaning to make it any more difficult. But it's very important that I get some things straightened out."

"Why?" she asks. "I just told you I don't know Sydney, and I don't think Cora did, either."

"But she did," I say. "Can we just go somewhere to talk for a few minutes?"

Bailey straightens her spine with a deep breath and glances around, then nods.

"We can go to my room."

"Thank you."

I follow her inside and she brings me up the elevator to the third floor. There are fewer doors on this hall than on Van's floor, and when she opens the door to her room I immediately notice this room is bigger than the typical dorm room.

Rather than the somewhat utilitarian look of the other rooms, this one looks more like a hotel suite. The door opens into a dining area with a living space beyond it. Doors on either side lead into bedrooms. I remember rooms like this from when I was in college. Each of the bedrooms accommodates one or two people and has a private bathroom. It was the bathrooms that made these rooms the envy of everyone living in one of the tile-floored basic rooms.

Bailey drops her bag and sits down in the living room. She doesn't invite me to sit with her, but I take a seat anyway.

"This is a really nice room," I observe, trying to break through her cold exterior.

She looks around, then back at me. "Thanks."

I bob my head toward the two bedroom doors. "You have a roommate?"

She draws in a sharp breath and I know instantly what she's going to say.

"I did." She points at one of the doors. "That's Cora's room."

"I'm so sorry for your loss," I say. "At the vigil, I heard you say the two of you were best friends. How long did you know her?"

"Since middle school," she says. "We didn't like each other at first. Then we got used to each other. Then we became friends. Then we fell in love. I guess you can say we've been through all the different relationships together."

"Cora was your girlfriend?" I ask.

Bailey shakes her head. "We broke up in between semesters. But we'd been together for a few years. Things were so great between us at first, but when she started getting more stressed and depressed, I shifted to being her friend and taking care of her more than anything. Eventually, we broke up and just decided to remain best friends."

"How were you dealing with that?" I ask.

"About as well as I could. I love her and I would have rather us be friends than nothing, but it was really hard seeing her with…"

Her voice breaks and she seems to be fighting tears.

"She was with someone else?" I ask.

Bailey wipes her eyes and takes a deep breath. "She wasn't in a new relationship, but she'd started dating a little. I didn't want to see it.

When she brought a date home, I would just go in my bedroom and stay locked in there until I knew they were gone." More tears puddle on her cheeks. "What does any of this have to do with Sydney Parker?"

"A couple of months ago, Sydney went to a party and left in a compromised condition," I explain. "She was pretty out of it, so a couple girls from the party were bringing her home. They said she told them to bring her to Murray Hall. I'm assuming she wanted to speak with Van Oshanick, but he says he didn't see her that night. But then she couldn't get inside. In reality, of course, it was because she never had access to this building. But Sydney told them that she did live here and she'd just forgotten her ID card. After a while, a blonde girl came out, recognized Sydney, and brought her inside."

"Cora did that?" she asks.

I nod. "One of the girls who brought Sydney home that night identified her as Cora yesterday. And today I got a clip of surveillance video of that night—it definitely was Cora who brought her inside. Sydney wasn't heard from by anyone until the next night when she got back to her own apartment. We don't know what happened between those two events, and I'm trying to piece it together. I'm wondering if Cora brought her up here and you didn't see her because you were in your room."

Bailey's eyes narrow. "She would never hurt anyone. She wouldn't take advantage of someone drunk."

"I'm not saying she would. I'm just trying to figure out what could have happened and if there's any chance Sydney could still be alive. I'm going to be very blunt and honest with you, and I'm sorry, this isn't going to be easy to hear. Sydney is missing and considered in very serious danger. She's been posting videos that seem to express suicidal thoughts. Someone she clearly had contact with killed herself less than two weeks after the last time Sydney was seen. If they could have anything to do with each other, I need to know."

Bailey's eyes water. She looks down at the ground and back up at me, seemingly lost for words.

"I don't know," she whispers. "I wish I could help."

I open my mouth to try to comfort her, but my phone rings.

# CHAPTER THIRTY-SIX

"Have you had any contact with Cora Gough's parents?"

"They are making arrangements to fly into town tomorrow," Alyssa tells me. "They should be here sometime in the afternoon to collect her belongings."

"By any chance did you..."

"I told them that her death was not considered suspicious, but it was tangentially linked to a missing persons case and we would deeply appreciate permission to search her room and access her phone and computer," she says.

"Oh, my lord, you're amazing," I say.

She laughs. "I'm going to make that my ringtone."

"I will happily repeat it for you," I say.

"I'm sending officers to the dorm to get those things. You should be able to come get them in a bit."

"No need," I tell her. "I'm actually here talking to her roommate right now. If I have your permission, I'll go ahead and take them now."

"Absolutely. Did she have anything? Did she see Sydney the night of the party?" she asks.

"No. But she didn't deny it was possible. She just said she always went into her bedroom when Cora brought somebody up into the room."

"Okay," Alyssa notes. "At least that's something. Not another person trying to cover themselves by saying they have no idea what happened. She at least admits Sydney could have been there that night, she just didn't interact with her."

"It's a step in the right direction," I say. "I'm going to get her phone and computer. I'll let you know if there's anything on it that could be useful, and I'll get it back in time to turn over to her parents tomorrow."

"Thanks. Talk to you soon."

As I get off the phone, Bailey steps out of her bedroom again. She'd gone in to splash water on her face, but I can tell by her expression she heard the conversation.

"Why are you interested in Cora's phone and computer?" she asks. "Isn't her death tragic enough for those of us who knew her? Why do you have to drag her into some other girl's disappearance?"

"I'm not trying to make anything harder for anyone," I say. "I understand how painful and shocking this is."

"No, you don't," she snaps. "Don't do that. Don't be that person who tries to pretend they know what someone is feeling. You don't know what this feels like."

I take a deep breath and look at her seriously.

"It might not have been the exact circumstances, but I have lost people extremely close to me in violent, horrible ways. And I have stood in front of people as they made the decision to end their lives and tried to pull them back. It's not exactly the same, but I know better than most people you'd encounter," I tell her. "And I also know how hard it is to have to share that person and your grief with someone else. Especially a stranger. But I promise you, I'm not here to cause any extra pain. And I'm not here to bring any negative attention to Cora. This is only about finding Sydney and trying to prevent another tragedy."

Bailey is trembling, but the anger is gone from her eyes. She nods.

"I didn't know," she manages to whisper. "I didn't know this was going to happen. I should have known."

"You can't put that on yourself," I tell her.

She nods again and brushes tears from under her eyes as she gestures at Cora's bedroom door in an invitation for me to go inside. I know there's no one inside, but I open the door cautiously. It smells like perfume and fabric softener, with a faint hint of cold, stale coffee.

Everything in the room looks like any second Cora will just walk back through the door and grab her books for class or tug on the sweatshirt draped over the end of the bed.

My eyes scan over the surfaces, checking for a note. There wasn't one visible with her body, and the medical examiner didn't find anything in her pockets. The truth is, most people don't leave notes when they decide to take their own lives. It's a deeply personal moment they don't choose to share with anyone else, forgetting in that moment how many people they are going to affect with this one choice.

I don't see anything that looks like a note, but her computer and phone are sitting in the middle of the bed like she just used them. Her death isn't considered suspicious and there won't be an investigation, but I still take pictures with my phone before I touch anything. I've learned to take extra measures when I'm handling a situation like this. It's better to go a few steps farther at the beginning and never have to use the pictures than to get to a point where I could use those details and not have them.

When I've documented the room, I pick up Cora's phone. I swipe the screen to turn it on and it presents me with a grid of dots.

"I can do it."

Bailey had been hesitating at the door, but comes in and reaches for the phone. I watch her use her fingertip to draw the shape of a heart through the dots like the games in the old coloring books from when I was a little girl. She hands it back to me with a faint smile on her lips.

"I set that as her passcode when she first got the phone. She didn't change it when we broke up," she says.

"Thank you," I say. "Do you know the passcode for her computer?"

"I think so." She goes over to the computer and opens it. After a few seconds of trying numbers, she turns it toward me. "It's 1106. Her birthday. She wasn't great at cybersecurity."

Bailey laughs softly, sadly, giving herself a moment just to remember Cora for the girl she was rather than the painful memory she's become.

"I appreciate it," I tell her. "I know you said you kept yourself out of her relationships with other people since your breakup, but can you remember her ever talking about someone she called 'M' or 'Shepherd?'"

She thinks for a second, then shakes her head. "No. Neither of those sound familiar."

"Alright." I rest my hand over the computer and hold up the phone. "Thank you, again, for these. And when her parents come, thank them for me. Give them my card and let them know they are more than welcome to call me and talk to me about anything they need to."

I bring the computer and phone back to my hotel and settle in to search through the computer first. Almost immediately, familiar names and phrases start to rise up out of the rest of the messages, notes, searches, and other miscellaneous content. I immediately zero in on all mentions of Shepherd.

Most of Cora's email conversations with the person called Shepherd are fragmented, leading me to believe some of the messages have been deleted. But I can still piece together enough to make a cold chill roll down my spine.

*You don't owe anything to anyone, Cora. You belong to yourself and no one else. Don't let them guilt you into being tortured for years just because it's easier for them.*

*You're the only one who has to live in your body and your mind. Only you know what it can take.*

*My sister was the strongest person I have ever known. She always will be. She chose every second of her life. And she chose when it was time for it to be over.*

*I'm here. You're not alone. You never have to keep anything from me.*

*You promised to love her for the rest of your life. Even if you close your eyes tonight, you will have kept your promise.*

I move on to her phone and discover texts from Shepherd. The conversations are similarly segmented and incomplete, but they have the same chilling effect.

**Shepherd:** *Did reading M's story give you any comfort?*
**Cora:** *He seemed so sure.*
**Shepherd:** *He was. He was so at peace and happy when it was all over. I wish those moments could last forever, but they can't.*
**Cora:** *What if they could come again? Later?*
**Shepherd:** *They might. But they might not. That's something you have to think about.*

The conversation breaks. The next messages are from weeks later.
**Cora:** *What should I do?*
**Shepherd:** *I can't tell you that. You have to make the decision. I'm only here to help you with whatever you choose. I can guide you, but only in the direction you want to go.*

The last interaction is dated the day Cora died.
**Shepherd:** *I'm happy for you.*
**Cora:** *I am, too. I'm glad to know how M felt.*

**Shepherd:** *Is it everything you wanted?*
**Cora:** *It really is. It's finally right. Thank you for everything.*
**Shepherd:** *Don't thank me. You didn't need me. I feel lucky to know you. Tell me if there's anything I can do.*
**Cora:** *Just make sure to pick up the camera.*

What the hell is this?

# CHAPTER THIRTY-SEVEN

THE NOTIFICATION THAT POPS UP IN THE CORNER OF MY COMputer screen later that afternoon makes my heart clench. I stare at the bubble, my hand reaching for my phone before I even open it. I anticipate the ring. I know someone else has seen whatever is waiting behind that notification.

The photo that comes up when I click the bubble isn't what I'm expecting. It's not an image of Cora's body or even of the aftermath of her death. A few of those have circulated around from people who were there that night and managed to snap pictures before we stopped them. Most didn't bother to zoom in, and they were taken from such a distance there wasn't much to see in them, but a few were graphic and didn't last long before being removed.

But this isn't one of those, or even another person testing the waters and trying to see if they were able to get in under the radar. Instead, the image is of a small clearing in what looks like a fairly dense area of woods. At first, it seems like there isn't much more in the picture than the trees and the sunlight peeking through the thick leaf cover at the edges, creating a dappled pattern like the doilies I remember on my grandmother's side table when I was young.

Then I see it. My phone rings at the same moment the image registers. I answer it without looking.

"Who is hanging from the tree?"

"It's fucking everywhere," I growl into the speakerphone as I drive toward the police station. "It's all over the forum Sydney uses, all over every social media platform. It's showing up on searches for the college."

"And nobody knows who posted it?" Dean asks.

"No one even knows who the victim is. Or where, by the way. The body hasn't even been found and there are pictures of it swirling around all over the internet. Shit!"

I slam my hands on the steering wheel.

"Where are you?"

"I'm in the car trying to get to the police station, but these damn cars are going about a mile an hour," I say.

"Emma, are you doing okay?" he asks.

"Right at this particular moment, no, I am not doing okay. I'm pissed off and I don't know about you, but it really gets under my skin to think there's a boy hanging from a tree somewhere without anyone to find him," I say.

"I understand that," my cousin says. "But I mean everything else. Are you doing okay dealing with all of this?"

I know why he's asking me. He's witnessed some of my slide into the depths of my own mental health. People describe it as a slippery slope, but it's not. At least it wasn't for me. The hill was gritty and rough, puncturing the thickest protections I put up and leaving me with bits of stone in my blood.

There's silence on the line as the cars in front of me start to move faster.

"I'm fine."

"We're going to be nearby there in a couple of days. If you want us to come by..."

"Dean, I'm fine. I can handle this," I insist.

"I know you can. You can handle anything."

I wish I could have said the same about Davi Barbosa. There was something he felt he couldn't handle. Something that caused him to kick away a paint bucket with a noose around his neck. It took Detective Bakker and me, along with a task force she built up, hours to pick apart the images of the body and identify where the twenty-two-year-old had hanged himself. By the time we got there, it was obvious he'd been dead for more than a day.

Within an hour of the body being cut down and brought out of the woods on a gurney, video of his suicide started making the rounds. Just like with Cora's death, the camera captured the moments leading up to the actual act, showing him making his preparations and seeming to take a final second to absorb the world around him before passing into whatever was next.

The video is even more disturbing and gut-wrenching than the one of Cora's death because of the gruesome nature of it. In Cora's video, the tension is horrifying when watching her stand at the edge of the building, and seeing her disappear makes my stomach drop to my feet, but there's a distance about it. I feel guilty to think of it that way, but not being able to see the moment of her death, only to hear the impact of her body hitting the sidewalk, creates a buffer that makes it easier to process.

There is no buffer between us and Davi's death. Watching all the way through the video means seeing him twist the rope and choose the right tree, toss the noose over the branch and position the bucket. His face is visible at every step. He occasionally looks over at the camera, like he's wondering if anyone is watching.

Or he knows for certain someone is.

His eyes meet the camera in the seconds he's standing up on the bucket, the rope around his neck, his fingers coiled around just in front of his throat like for a few heartbeats he's considering pulling it away. But he doesn't. His hands drop down to his sides and he says nothing before lifting one foot and kicking the bucket away.

The violence of his death is raw and startling. It's easy to pretend the depiction in TV and movies is accurate, that it's just a matter of gravity taking over and a second later, it's done. That's not how it happens for most who die this way. For a very fortunate few, the length of the rope and the distance of the drop along with the positioning of the knot is just perfect to ensure the neck snaps as the body falls. For those, it's quick.

For most, it's not that easy. Rather than the neck breaking, the victim asphyxiates to death, caused by the rope slowly crushing down on the neck and restricting breathing as the person dangles helplessly. It can be a long, painful, and terrifying death, and those witnessing it watch as the person struggles and thrashes, their instinct compelling them to try to find something to stand on, to lift their weight to ease the pressure, to find breath.

In this video, Davi's body going still and the realization settling in that he is dead come as a relief. And that relief allows the video to take hold of the viewer and drag them into the brutality. It turns the viewer into a monster.

"What the hell is going on here?" Alyssa asks later when we meet up at a coffee shop near campus. "I thought there was a pattern. Sydney and Cora are both students at Baxter. They knew each other. But I just notified Davi's mother and she says he never went to college and isn't somebody who would have gone to parties and things with students from there. He has no reason to have known either of the girls. But I can't stand here and say a second suicide in just a couple of days at the same time as a high-risk disappearance is a coincidence."

"I always say there's no such thing as coincidences," I say, watching a group of young people walk past and wondering what was going through their minds.

"I'm beginning to agree."

"These deaths are clearly suicides," I say. "We can watch them go through with each step. But it's obvious someone else is involved with each one. Cora and Davi didn't record themselves dying just because they wanted to. They were directly appealing to someone. I know from going through her computer and phone that Cora was communicating with the person called Shepherd. And if I had to take a wild guess, I'd say a search through Davi's phone and computer would turn up conversations with him, too. This is the same person that's been having direct, frequent contact with Sydney for months. If we don't find her, she's going to end up a victim, too."

"Then we don't let that happen," Alyssa says. "I'll get orders for his phone and computer. We'll find out who this is, and we'll nail the son of a bitch."

# CHAPTER THIRTY-EIGHT

Later that afternoon, I finally get what I've been waiting for since the beginning of the investigation. Alyssa calls to let me know the phone company sent over Sydney's records and she would send copies of them to me. It's a bit of hope. Adding the information from her phone to what we have from Cora's could start clarifying what's happening. It could finally give us a chance to narrow down the possibilities of who is luring these people to their deaths. When we have Davi's information, it will be even better.

The files that appear in my cloud drop file are much the same as I'd expect from any college-age girl. Page after page of text messages and phone calls, almost like she was attached to it every second of her day. But that's exactly what I want.

The information we have from Cora's phone is abbreviated. We can only see what she didn't delete until we get some of her records from her phone company. As of now, we still haven't been able to find Davi's phone, but even when we do, I'm expecting the same results.

Conversations with most of the messages deleted, texts that seem to dangle without any context anchoring them on either side. All I can hope for is crumbs, but with the right ones, they'll lead us where we need to go.

But Sydney's interactions with Shepherd are laid out in their entirety. I remember what Angela said when she was explaining Wesley's frustration about having to request the phone records rather than the company just sending them when he asked. Sydney probably didn't even know the records exist.

The sentiment is likely not too far off. Many people these days, not just children and teenagers, but adults as well, don't realize just how much of their lives is documented. They believe if they delete something, it's gone forever. That nothing they can't see is permanent. But it's all there if you know where to look.

Sydney must have been using her computer and an email address not synched to the phone when she first came into contact with Shepherd, because there's no initial interaction. The conversation starts on what seems like tenuously familiar grounds. It's the kind of exchange that happens between people who have a basic knowledge of each other and are gradually building a closer bond. But it has the feeling of something arranged rather than organic. These two were put together and are slowly stitching themselves together with the common thread promised to them when they were first linked.

The first few messages feel exploratory, like they are finding their footing, and trying to settle on the language they're going to use. It's careful at first with a lot of euphemisms and allusions, then gradually becomes more comfortable and open as the two settle into something like a friendship.

Three days after their first recorded interaction, Shepherd offered Sydney a glimpse into their life. I'm reading the long message when a video call from Xavier comes in. I answer and minimize the screen so it's just his face taking up the top right-hand corner of the window.

"Hi, Xavier," I say. "What are you doing?"

"Calling you," he says.

I walked myself right into that one.

I nod. "Yes, you are."

"Did you get a chance to call the prison?" he asks.

"I haven't," I say. "I'm sorry. I'll call today, I promise."

"You look distracted. Are you multitasking? Did you minimize me?"

"I did beca—"

"Dean, she minimized me," he says, disappearing out of the frame. "How is she supposed to witness all the facial expressions I've been practicing?"

Dean's face appears on my screen.

"He's been practicing facial expressions?" I ask incredulously.

"A few. He says he wants to be able to communicate and connect better, so we're working on looking like he's not only actually listening to another person, but sharing some sort of engagement with them and reacting appropriately," he explains.

"Well, it's good to hear you have a project," I say absently, still reading over the page in front of me.

"I can see why Xavier is miffed. What are you paying such close attention to?" he asks.

I fill him in on having access to the phone records and going through, reading along the conversation thread between Sydney and Shepherd.

"I was just reading this message that this Shepherd person sent to Sydney. It's really long and intense, so I'll just summarize it for you. They talk about their older sister Lisa. They were extremely close while they were younger, and she and her husband had been working hard to make a better life for all of them. Their parents had died when they were very young, so Lisa had been like a mother figure as well.

"She worked hard and finally got the family to a point where they were financially stable and life was looking really good. Then Lisa's husband was killed in a drunk driving accident. It was so sudden and tragic it came as a complete shock and really threw them both into a tailspin. Not long after that, Lisa was diagnosed with a terminal illness. Shepherd doesn't specifically label it, but says it was a very painful disease and the doctors told them she would gradually lose her physical and mental functioning until she was just lying in a bed wasting away.

"Shepherd didn't want to accept that. They thought they could get another opinion and maybe a doctor somewhere else would be able to help Lisa. But they went through all the options and realized there wasn't anything that anybody could do. A few months after her diagnosis, when the effects of the disease were really starting to show, Lisa sat Shepherd down and said she wanted to die on her own terms.

"This disease was going to take everything from her. Her body, her mind, her dignity. She couldn't stand that thought, so she had come to the conclusion that she wanted to take her own life. Shepherd said the thought was devastating and they couldn't bear to look forward to a life that Lisa wasn't in. At the same time, seeing their sister suffering so much and slipping into being a different person was also horrific.

Shepherd decided it was their responsibility to the sister who had always loved and taken care of them to now be the one to support and take care of Lisa. Together they researched and found a person willing to help with the details.

"Of course, the doctors couldn't know what was happening. At the time, assisted suicide was still illegal across the entire country. They requested Lisa be released from the hospital into at-home hospice care, and from there they made the arrangements for her to die. She could choose the date and the time, even the method. Once everything was in place, Lisa wasn't upset anymore. She was peaceful and happy, and even felt better for the first time since her diagnosis. She knew everything was going to be alright.

"Lisa chose to die on the first day of spring. It was symbolic, representing her going on into her new life. She died serenely, surrounded by her favorite flowers and music, and holding Shepherd's hand. It was sad as any death is going to be, but Shepherd said they felt better knowing it was the way Lisa wanted it, and her tremendous pain and suffering were over. It happened the way Lisa felt it should. From then on, Shepherd was committed to the belief that life belongs to the person living it, and every person should have the choice over how long it lasts and how it ends.

"They dedicated themselves to helping those who were struggling through life and trying to decide if it was time for them to bring it to an end. Now they guide people to the decision that is right for them, whether that is that it's time to die or not, and then if it is their time, they help them choose the method and are there for them during the process. Sometimes in person, and sometimes over a video call. It's their way of honoring Lisa."

"Holy shit," Dean whispers.

"I know. It's quite the introduction," I say.

"Emma, that wasn't an introduction. That was an origin story. You've been saying Shepherd like it's this person's name. I don't think it is. I think it's *the* Shepherd. A title."

"Like some supervillain?" I ask.

"Or superhero. Who's to say who is a villain and who is a hero? It depends on how you're looking at the story."

# CHAPTER THIRTY-NINE

THIS TIME, THE VIDEO FEED IS LIVE.
I'm walking across campus so I don't get a notification. Instead, I hear Van screaming my name from behind me. I stop to let him catch up and see the look of horror stretching and exaggerating his features.

"What is it?" I ask. "What's going on? Is it Sydney?"

He shakes his head, catching his breath and pushing a lock of sweaty hair away from his forehead as he holds his phone out to me.

"I heard somebody in the dining hall talking about this. They were watching it," he tells me.

The thumbnail of a video has a small lock icon over it and a title warning viewers that they could bear live witness to "sensitive, mature content."

"Live?" I ask. "This is happening right now?"

Van nods. I read the description, but there's no indication of where it's happening. When I click on the video, it won't open. He points out the lock.

"It's a paid stream," he says.

"Are you fucking kidding me? People are paying to watch this?" I ask.

"Yes. A lot of people sell live streams and pictures…"

"I'm familiar, but they're usually selling their bodies, not their deaths." I think only for a second. "Shit."

I can't believe I'm actually doing this, but I click on the payment link and purchase the stream. I need to be able to see it. It's a relief when I see a girl sitting on a rock next to what looks like either a large stream or a small section of a river. She's staring down into the water and it sounds like she's humming quietly to herself.

"She's still alive," Van says.

There's a lilt in his voice that says those words are carrying more responsibility than just the girl we can see. He's hoping for Sydney.

"Look at the jacket beside her," I say, pointing at a hooded sweatshirt jacket folded in half and draped across the rock at her side. "That's from Baxter. Maybe she's another student here. Do you recognize her?"

He shakes his head. "No. I can't really see her, but I don't think I know her."

The girl leans back a little away from the water and tilts her head up toward the sun like she's enjoying the feeling of it on her face for a few seconds. Even though I've only been on campus for a short time and haven't interacted with many students, I still search her face, hoping I've seen it somewhere and will be able to recognize it. But I don't.

"Hi, everyone," the girl suddenly says, twisting her head just enough to look into the camera. "It's Rachel Fleming. Thank you for being here today. Even though you're only joining me virtually, I can feel every one of you with me. It means so much to know I'm surrounded by friends as I take this journey. I've been looking forward to and preparing for this day for a long time."

My heart sinks. I already know what she's planning.

"There have been moments when I wasn't sure if it was what I really wanted, or if there was something else out there. But now that it's here, it truly feels like a celebration. This isn't something to be mourned or feared. It's my going away party, and I can't think of anywhere more beautiful than this to have it."

She glances at the fitness tracker watch on her wrist. "I'm going to wait just a little longer. It's not quite time yet. I chose the exact time I want to enter the water because I want to leave this life as close to twenty years to the minute from when I entered it as I can."

"Oh, god, it's her birthday," I whisper.

"I want to thank the people who helped me get to this place, to where I knew what's right for me. I've never felt so comfortable and at peace. It's like now that I don't have to worry about anything that's to come, I can just let myself be happy. Like I'm finally enjoying life. That's why I came here. It's one place I remember feeling good. Let me show you more of it."

Rachel picks up the camera and turns it slowly to give a panoramic view of the area surrounding the creek. I was expecting her to be in the woods, but instead, there are only a few trees around and beyond them, I can see a field. Van gasps beside me.

"I know where that is," he says. "I know where she is."

"Where?" I ask, already moving toward where my car is parked.

"It's an old farm not too far from here. A friend of mine showed it to me when I first came to Baxter. It's a good spot to hike and bring girls. I've seen that part of the creek. People go skinnydipping there in the summer because that's where the water is the deepest and goes the fastest," he says.

"Charming. You need to get me there."

"I can bring you right to it," Van tells me.

Rachel's voice continues on the screen as we run to the parking lot. "I already said I want to thank the people who helped me to get here, but I don't feel like I can say it enough. I went back and forth so many times, wondering if I even could make the right decision. After all, I've made so many bad choices getting to this point. Why would I be able to make the right one now? But then I met the Shepherd, who introduced me to my angel. They talked me through everything and really helped me to understand what I was feeling and what I wanted."

"Angel?" Van asks.

I shake my head, my feet going faster across the open section of campus. "I don't know. I haven't heard that."

"But the most important person in this is M. I don't know if I'd ever have had the courage to do this if it wasn't for hearing his story. And soon I'll be able to thank him face to face."

We get to my car and I'm hitting the pedal before the doors are even shut. Van directs me off campus into the small town bordering it. It only takes a few minutes to get past the town and into a stretch of neighborhoods and farmland, but I feel like it's too long. Van is still gripping the phone, watching the video.

Rachel lets out an audible breath. "It's time."

I glance over to see what's happening and watch her step down into the water. For a second she's just standing, then the force of the current pushes her and she falls.

"Shit! How far are we?"

"We're almost there. It's just up the road."

Still gripping the wheel with one hand, I use the other to dig through my bag and take out my phone. I call Alyssa and tell her what's going on.

"We're almost there. Send everybody."

A few seconds later, Van points me to an old broken wood gate across a dirt road dotted with plants and grass. There are tire tracks in the dirt and a few yards away, I see a car parked just out of view of the road. I stop and we jump out. Van takes off and I run after him. He's still holding his phone and I can hear splashing and gurgling from the video playing on it. That's what I want to hear. As long as I'm hearing that, Rachel is alive.

We're still running across an abandoned field toward the trees in the distance when the sounds stop. All I can hear through the video is the mirroring of the birds singing around me.

"Right there," Van points. "It's just through those trees."

He runs toward them, but I notice his steps falter as he gets closer. I run past him. There's no time to pause. Breaking through the line of trees, I find myself at the edge of the stream. I scan the water for Rachel and the bank for the boulder where she'd been sitting. It takes several seconds of running along the muddy edge, grasping onto trees and hanging vines to keep my feet under me, screaming her name as I go, until the rock comes into view. A phone is set up on a stand with a ring light surrounding it. I briefly see myself on the screen as I run by.

The water is moving swiftly, fed by the spring rains and snowmelt. I have no idea how deep it is. I stare down into it, searching for any indication of her. I shout her name again and I hear a soft, strangled cry in return.

Fighting the sliding earth beneath my feet, I run around a bend toward the sound and finally see Rachel clutching a smaller rock in the center of the widest part of the stream. The water is rushing around her, tugging on her as she tries to hold on.

"Rachel! Pull yourself up! Pull yourself all the way up onto the rock."

She groans and tries to hoist herself higher, but she's lost strength. "My foot is stuck."

She sounds weak and I know the last several minutes of the fast, hard water beating on her and tumbling her down the stream have worn her body out. Her hands slip and she's pulled backward away from the rock.

"Van!" I shout as loud as I can, hoping he can hear me. "Watch out for the police and ambulance! Get them down here!"

I let go of the tree I've been holding and jump down into the water. It immediately catches me and starts dragging me, but I fight against it. Using all my strength, I defy the force of the water to move toward her. Rachel's head breaks the surface for a second and she gasps for breath, but is taken down again. Each time she surfaces, it's for a shorter time, and less of her face is visible out of the water. I press forward against the current, willing my arms to move faster, but the current is intense. The last time I see her, I'm only a couple of feet away, but her eyes are rolling in her head and her hands float beside her rather than grasping for the rock.

Finally close enough to her, I dive down under the water. It's murky, filled with mud and debris, and the visibility is next to nothing. I use my hands to search and look for any change in color or movement that might show me where she is. My hands hit her legs and I grab onto them, using them to lead me down to the rock where her foot is stuck.

The water is trying to rip me away and force me downstream, and fighting it is quickly depleting my energy. But I won't give up. I find her foot and pull it out from where it's wedged in rocks jutting up from the bottom. The rest of her body moves up and I grab onto her, forcing both of us up to break through the surface.

As soon as we are in the air again, I flip her over in my arms and push her chin down to let out the water. She chokes, but draws in a gurgling breath. I get us to the edge of the stream and drag her up onto the grass. Rachel turns to her side and coughs out more of the murky water. I rub her back hard to push more of it out. Her head tilts and her eyes meet mine. I give her a trembling smile.

"Hey, Rachel. Happy birthday."

# CHAPTER FORTY

"I NEED TO SPEAK WITH MALLORY KELLEN, PLEASE."

The woman behind the desk in the counseling center nods and picks up a phone beside her. As she's calling into the back, I hear footsteps coming up behind me and I turn just as Dr. Villareal is starting to speak.

"Agent Griffin. I was hoping I would see you here today. I heard what happened yesterday. That's incredible you were able to save that girl like that."

"Rachel Fleming," I say. "She's going to be okay. The doctors are keeping her in the hospital for a couple of days just to make sure there aren't any lasting effects from being underwater, and then her parents are bringing her to an inpatient mental health treatment program."

She lets out a relieved breath. "That's good. She clearly needs intervention. The fact that she grabbed onto that rock shows she wasn't really completely sure of her decision to end her life."

"Hopefully now she's going to get the support she really needs. And maybe she'll be able to help us find Sydney."

"Do you believe she's still alive?"

"Agent Griffin?" the woman behind the desk says and I turn to her. "Mallory will be out in just a few moments."

"Thank you." I turn back to the therapist. "Yes. Until I have absolute proof otherwise, I will continue to believe she's alive. We have strong evidence to indicate she is connected to these three victims and is in extreme danger, but the fact that we haven't heard from her and no one knows where she is actually gives me hope. So until I have a reason to, I won't stop looking for her, not her body."

"I'm glad to hear that. No one should ever just give up on another person. My schedule is very full today, as you can imagine, but if you need anything from me, please don't hesitate to call. I'll help in any way I can."

"Thank you. I'll let you know if I can think of anything," I say.

She nods and turns to walk back to her office. She passes by another woman who glances at her by way of greeting before walking up to me.

"You must be Agent Griffin. I'm Mallory. Please, come to my office."

"I appreciate you talking to me this morning. I know I don't have an appointment and I'm sure you're busy," I say.

"No worries at all. Situations like these take absolute precedence over everything. Besides, I don't have a schedule like Dr. Villarreal. I'm only a counselor, not a psychologist. I don't do individual therapy here. Just small group."

"James Underwood directed me to you. He said that you are the facilitator for the small group Sydney participates in," I tell her.

Mallory nods and sits down on a pink velvet couch in the corner of the room. It's not so much an office as it is a meeting room, with several clusters of furniture arranged throughout it, white dry erase boards attached to the walls, and bookshelves overflowing with books, art supplies, and other materials. I'm assuming since she isn't an individual therapist, she doesn't have a private office and instead just meets with people in the same space where she does her small group sessions.

"She's a really active part of the group, really inspirational to the other participants. At least she was before…"

Her voice trails off and I pick it up.

"Sydney has been missing for two weeks now. I have to ask you this: do you have any idea where she is? Did she mention to you she was planning on going somewhere? That she wanted to get away?" I ask.

"No. In fact, the last time I saw her, we were talking about an upcoming event for the counseling center. We are planning a mental health fair to try to encourage more students to take advantage of the peer counseling program, small group, or individual therapy," Mallory tells me. "She seemed really excited about it."

"Did she ever express any suicidal thoughts to you?" I ask.

She isn't surprised by the question.

"She never said those words or opened up to me about any plans or anything. But she did participate in an intense retreat at the end of spring break," she tells me.

That catches my attention. "Spring break?"

"Yes. It was for a select group of students who have been active participants in therapy. We held a two-night retreat designed to be an intensive healing opportunity, time for them to really dig deep into their past trauma, their emotional scars, and their current mental health challenges so they could address them honestly and constructively," she explains. "Sometimes getting people out of the traditional therapy environment is an extremely effective way to help them further examine themselves and get in touch with elements of their journeys that are more difficult to reach."

"What happens at a retreat like that?" I ask.

"The goal is to help them express themselves in a way that might be more accessible than just words. So there are small groups, and communal activities, such as art, writing, dance. Hiking out and communing with nature. There was also a confessional box that gave them a chance to be alone and speak about what was on their mind without the other participants hearing."

"A confessional box?" I ask. "Like a church confessional?"

"Essentially. A small room where they could speak and get advice and guidance from an unseen advisor."

"Unseen?" I ask.

"Yes. For some, even dealing with a therapist they know and trust can still feel intimidating when dealing with some of their deepest inner thoughts. This is an opportunity to unburden themselves completely anonymously. It's a time for them to open up about anything without the potential discomfort of talking to someone face to face, especially someone they haven't met with individually before, and receive support and guidance. It's surprisingly a pretty positive experience."

"Do you know if Sydney participated in that?"

She shakes her head. "Even if I could divulge that information, I don't know. It's kept entirely anonymous."

"Alright," I nod. "I appreciate your time. I'll let you know if I have any other questions."

"Please do," Mallory says. "I really hope you find Sydney."

"I do, too." I'm starting out of the room when something comes to my mind. "Just one more thing. Did Sydney ever talk about someone she called the Shepherd?"

Mallory makes a slight face in reaction to the title, but shakes her head. "That doesn't sound familiar."

"How about a friend of hers she called M?"

Her face lights up a bit. "Yes. She actually did talk about him in our group sessions occasionally. She didn't mention him until recently, but she said they'd been friends for a little while. They met online and had been talking just about every day. She called him her dearest friend and said he was a really valuable support system for her because he understood what she was feeling and never tried to judge her. He gave her an opportunity to feel like she was helping someone and making a difference in their experience."

I think about this for a second, then offer a brief smile and nod. "Alright. Thank you."

Dean is calling me as I leave the counseling office.

"Hey," I answer.

"You sound tired," he observes.

"I didn't get a lot of sleep last night." I start to tell him about Rachel, but pause when I see her face on the shirt a guy is wearing as he walks past. "I'm going to have to call you back."

I don't wait for a response before shoving the phone in my pocket and chasing the guy. Grabbing him by his shoulder, I turn him around to face me.

"Hey, what are you doing?" he asks angrily.

"What the hell is that?" I demand, pointing at his shirt.

The image of Rachel is surrounded by text that reads *'we deserve a refund.'*

I'm so infuriated that dots dance in front of my eyes. How could somebody do something like this? And why would anyone want to wear it?

"It's a shirt," he answers snidely.

"Cut the attitude. This is absolutely disgusting," I say.

"Calm down. It's just a joke," he replies. "It's funny."

"A girl nearly killing herself on video and people using it as entertainment isn't fucking funny. That girl on your shirt is a human being, and she almost died yesterday."

His face drops slightly. "It was just supposed to be a joke."

"You have a seriously sick sense of humor," I say.

"It's not like I made it," he says. "I just bought it off the girl selling them in the green."

"There are more?" I ask. I notice the sleeves of another shirt sticking out. I let out a growl. "Take it off."

"Excuse me?" he asks.

"Take off the damn shirt. Right now."

He looks for a second like he's going to protest, but sees the intensity in my glare and falls back. He takes off the shirt and I snatch it out of his hand before taking long strides toward the green in the center of campus.

There's a small crowd gathered around and I notice people walking away from it carrying what look like folded t-shirts. Pushing through the people, I find a table with stacks of shirts of several different designs, all featuring Cora, Davi, Rachel, Sydney, or a combination of them. And each has an offensive phrase written across it that just spirals me further into my rage.

"Get out of my way," I demand, stepping in front of the girl standing at the edge of the table.

The person behind it is crouched down on the other side of the table, the tablecloth draped over her head. When I slam my hands down on the table and tell her to stand up, she pushes the cloth away. My mouth falls open when I see Lila Kellerman.

"Agent Griffin," she says.

I turn around to the students still standing nearby.

"Clear out. All of you. Get out of my sight."

They dissipate and Lila rolls her eyes.

"Did you seriously have to do that? I was really starting to make some money."

"What in the living hell is wrong with you?" I demand. "You are exploiting victims of suicide and attempted suicide, as well as a girl who is still missing."

Lila smirks. "Don't judge me. Call it capitalism."

"I call it sickening. You clearly still harbor ill will against Sydney. You need to let it go and stop hurting other people for your own amusement just to feel like you're getting something over on her," I say.

"I don't care one way or another about Sydney. This isn't about her. This is about getting my own little slice of that pie," she replies.

"What pie?" I ask.

"You know those videos Sydney posted? They're all monetized. Every time she goes on there and rambles on about her life and gives her little shout out to M—who doesn't know where she is or what happened to her despite them being just so very close, which I find interesting—people come to watch and she gets paid for it. And there are paid streams of murders, accidental deaths, and other suicides, and people selling books full of crime scene images and autopsy reports. It's what the people want. And, excuse my quote here, sometimes you just have to give the people what they want."

"You are going to stop this right now," I tell her. "And I'm going to make sure that the families of the victims you are exploiting for your own gain are fully aware of what you're doing. And if they decide to sue you, I will very happily help them in whatever way I can."

# CHAPTER FORTY-ONE

A NGELA TEXTED ME THE NIGHT BEFORE ASKING IF WE CAN MEET, and I'm running late after my showdown with Lila. She's already sitting at the table at the coffee shop, a partial croissant in front of her, staring into her mug when I get there.

"I'm sorry I'm late," I say as I sit down in front of her. "There was an issue I needed to take care of."

"She only has three days left," she says without preamble.

"Three days?" I ask.

"That's all the medication Sydney has left. She's going to run out in three days," she clarifies.

"I'm doing everything I can to find her," I say. "These deaths…"

"These deaths are why I'm as worried as I am. She didn't order a refill for her prescriptions. She is never without her medication. If she's willing to let it run out, maybe that means she's not intending on needing it."

It's hard for her to say the words, but she forces them out, keeping her voice as steady as she can.

"I need to ask you again if you ever heard her mention somebody named M or who she calls the Shepherd," I say.

"The only time I ever heard her say anything about somebody called M is in those videos. And she never talked to me about a Shepherd. But I know both of them have something to do with her going missing. This Shepherd person had something to do with the others, too. People are talking about it," she says. "I want to know what they said to my daughter."

I stiffen. The messages I read between Sydney and the Shepherd are something I'll never be able to get out of my mind. They will haunt me for the rest of my life, and I've never even met the girl. I don't want to think of how deeply they would cut into her mother.

"I don't think that's something you need to know," I say.

"I do," Angela says firmly. "She is my baby. My only baby. I have the right to know what's going on. If someone hurt her, I need to know."

There's desperation in her eyes and pain in her voice. I'm not going to be able to convince her that she shouldn't know about the conversations, even if I think it would be better for her to keep that aspect of Sydney's disappearance at a distance. I'm not a mother. I've never experienced that bond and can't understand what it would feel like. But I have been on the other side. I've been the child with a missing parent, and I know how desperately I clawed for even the smallest detail about what happened to my father and where he could be. If someone knew something, I wouldn't have cared how painful or difficult to hear it would be, I would have wanted to know.

"If you really want to know, I will tell you. But I'm going to warn you that none of it is easy to hear. If it gets to be too much, I'll stop."

"Go ahead," she says. Her spine straightens and her hands tighten around her cup as she braces herself for what I'm going to say.

"She came into contact with the Shepherd a few months ago. I haven't been able to pinpoint exactly when or how they first encountered each other, but the first conversations I've found put it in the fall. From that first interaction, it's obvious the Shepherd knew about Sydney's mental health issues. It's a topic of conversation right from the beginning. They are pretty cautious about it at first, but then the conversations get more blatant."

"Blatant how?"

The Shepherd tells Sydney about their sister, who was suffering from a terminal illness and made the decision to kill herself. It's clear this person is very much in support of assisted suicide. They talk about it openly and without any negativity. Most of the messages are initiated by the Shepherd and sound like they are in response to Sydney, but there aren't always messages that correspond. I have a feeling there are videos Sydney created that were taken down from the forum, or there are more conversations on her tablet or other computer that we can't see. But there are some messages from Sydney that express suicidal thoughts."

"Oh, god," Angela whispers, covering her mouth with her hands and shaking her head. "She never said anything to me."

"Do you want me to stop?" I ask.

"No." Her hands fall back to the table and she assumes a stoic expression. "Go on."

"She asks about different methods and which one would be the best. The Shepherd tells her that the entire process is a very personal choice, but offers suggestions. Overdosing or carbon monoxide poisoning are usually gentler, good for those who don't really want to experience their death. But some people want to experience it. They want the feeling or to make their death a form of expression. That's when the other methods become options.

"There are several conversations of them discussing the different methods and how much they appeal or don't appeal to Sydney. Throughout it, this person tells Sydney it's up to her to make the decision and that she should be happy no matter what she chooses. Either she chooses to continue with life and see what it has to offer her, or she chooses to take control, claim her life as truly her own, and end what she sees as something not viable. They promise either way that they are there for her. I believe that's why they refer to themselves as the Shepherd. They see themselves as watching over the people who come to them, and guiding them to where they need to be."

"You're telling me my daughter is out there preparing for some kind of ritual suicide because a faceless person online told them to?" she asks.

"There's no way for me to know if she ever encountered this person in person or if their entire relationship was through these messages. From what I've been able to find from her interactions with M, I don't think they encountered each other in real life. It seems he lives somewhere else and they only communicated through emails and messages," I tell her. "He's very supportive and caring, but also talks about his own struggles. A couple of times, they discussed the possibility of going through with their suicides together."

"Are they connected? Shepherd and M? Do they do this together?"

"They are connected," I nod. "Cora's phone had messages from the Shepherd that mentioned M, asking if his story was comforting to her."

"So, they're accomplices," Angela says. "They murder people together."

It's a blunt, viciously angry statement and I don't know how to respond.

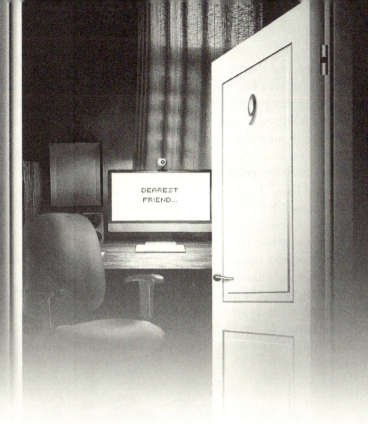

# CHAPTER FORTY-TWO

"That's seriously messed up," Dean says when I call him back after my meeting with Angela. "She was just standing out there selling those shirts?"

"Yep," I confirm. "Like it was absolutely nothing. One of them actually had a picture of the tree where Davi had been hanging, there's still a piece of frayed rope on it, and she had 'want to hang out?' written on it. I can't even begin to wrap my mind around what a person has to be thinking to come up with something like that and think it's a good idea."

"She has no empathy," Dean says. "She's not thinking about how anyone else would react to that. From what you've told me about this girl, it seems like she doesn't really care about what anyone thinks or feels but herself."

"I'm not so sure," I say.

"What do you mean?" he asks.

"She said something when I was talking to her about the shirts that really got me. I pointed out it seemed she's still wrapped up in her issues with Sydney, and that she can't just let go of it. She's clearly still angry at her, or just has a lot of bad feelings toward her, and she argued with me. She said that wasn't why she was doing it, she just wanted to make money off it like other people do. Apparently, death is big business. She was talking about Sydney's videos and she mentioned M."

"You said you asked Van about M," Dean points out. "Maybe he said something to her about him."

"That's true," I acknowledge. "He could have. But Lila said M doesn't know where Sydney is or what happened to her, and made a snide remark about them being so close."

"But how would she know that?" Dean asks.

"Exactly. And the way she said it was almost like she was jealous. Like the way she talked about Sydney and Van," I say.

"Do you think she could have something to do with this?"

"I think she's closer to it than any of us thought. I want to know how she knows M, and why she hasn't mentioned it to anyone," I say. "I don't think she even realized what she said. I need to figure out the connection."

A quick call to Eric gets the ball rolling for accessing the records of the forum. By now, they are very aware of what's unfolding around Baxter's campus and don't want to be highlighted as a cause of the tragedies. I expected a bit of resistance from them the same way the phone company didn't want to give up Sydney's records, but there's none. They don't want anyone placing blame on them or thinking they are causing any of this to happen, so they are more than willing to offer up any information they have. Which includes access to messages and user data.

By that evening, I have printouts of the profile and messages of a user calling themselves MirrorMirror. It didn't take long to figure out it's Lila.

There are no videos, no pictures, and only one written post. The post is nothing but a single statement.

*Is anyone out there?*

Within days of that post, messages started coming in from an anonymous user. I found out from the moderators of the forum that there is no requirement for messages to be sent with a user's name, much less their real identity or information. The comment box is completely blank and could be from anyone. The idea is to allow for total anonymity and safety from it leaking into real life.

I understand the sentiment. I appreciate the intention. I also see the danger.

The messages are friendly and supportive, and though there are no introductions in them, I recognize some of the language patterns as sounding like the snippets of Sydney's conversations with M. After a few messages, the anonymous user suggests they bring their communication off the forum, and the interactions end. Without being able to sift through Lila's emails and phone, I'm not going to get any more insight into what they talked about.

But all that matters to me is they talked. There is a connection there that links her to Sydney's disappearance in a very tangible way, and I want to know more about it.

Lila lets out a heavy sigh and adjusts her backpack over her shoulder when she sees me coming. She tries to walk around me, but I stand in her path to force her to look at me.

"I got rid of the shirts, okay?" she says. "You can get off my ass about it. You cost me a month of grocery money, so that's fantastic."

"Seriously the least of your worries right now. I want to know about M," I tell her.

A startled expression flickers across her face for a brief second before she pulls on a mask of confusion.

"What are you talking about?" she asks.

"You are familiar with Sydney's videos and I have no doubt you've talked about the investigation with Van," I say. If you're going to try to lie about something, at least try to be more convincing about it."

"Fine. M is that guy that Sydney talks about in her videos, right? She calls him her dearest friend," she says.

"Now we're getting somewhere. Let's go a little further. How do you know him?" I ask.

She shakes her head and adjusts her backpack again. "I don't know him. I've just heard her talk about him because I've seen those videos. Like everybody else on campus, by the way."

"I'm sure they have," I nod. "But none of them have made a comment about him not knowing where Sydney is. You did."

Lila's eyes dart to the other students walking around us. A few of them glance over at us and some slow down like they want to overhear what we're talking about, but are trying to be casual about it.

"Can we talk about this somewhere else?" she asks.

I sweep my hand through the air in an inviting gesture. "Lead the way."

She brings me back to her dorm room and tosses her bag onto her bed.

"I've never met him in person. He lives in Oregon, so it's not like it's easy for us to just get together for a quick dinner," she says. "And before you ask, no, I don't know his full name. He only ever calls himself M. He says that's what his family always called him, so that's what he goes by."

"Alright. How did you meet him?" I ask.

She shrugs, her arms crossed over her chest and her hip cocked defiantly. She hasn't asked me to sit and hasn't moved from the spot she took in the center of the room.

"I don't know," she says.

"Come on, Lila. You've already cost this investigation two weeks by not telling us about this. Don't make it worse."

She scoffs. "I'm the one costing the investigation time? Why is it me? Cora knew him, too. I don't know the guy who hanged himself, but I bet if you did your little scavenging thing through his life, you'd see he does, too."

"Why would you say that?" I ask.

"He mentioned helping a guy and that he was looking forward to seeing the video," she says.

I do my best to withhold the shudder that ripples through me.

"The difference is that none of them have the link to Sydney that you do. Cora may have known her in passing, but *you* are the girl her boyfriend cheated on her with. Can you see why it would be of interest that you also know the person she considers her closest friend?" I ask.

She sighs. "Look, I don't know how he got in touch with me. That's the truth. I joined that forum a while back, which I'm sure you already know about."

"Yes, I do. And I've read the messages," I say.

"I figured. I don't even remember where I first heard about it, but I was going through a rough time and I joined it. I posted once. Then I just read things and watched videos. I don't like to talk about my childhood or the things I went through. But it was reassuring to see other people who maybe felt something like I did.

"Then I got a message. It said a friend of mine had given him my contact information and thought we would hit it off. I actually deleted that message and the next couple of them because I thought it was just spam. No one knew I was on the forum or about anything that happened to me, so I didn't know how he could have found out about me. But eventually, he started giving little details about me and I realized he did actually know things. I asked him who our supposed mutual friend was, but he wouldn't say. At first I thought it might be Sydney, not that either of us would ever describe each other as friends, and not that I think she would give half a damn even if she knew what I was dealing with. But she didn't. That's the thing. She didn't know any of it," she says. "But I started talking to him. He was a good listener and helped me work through when I was having a bad day or dealing with bad thoughts. I decided not to hold it against him that he was friends with Sydney."

She smirks, but I don't crack a smile.

"Bad thoughts?" I ask.

Her face falls and her eyes darken. "I don't want any of this to go outside of this room. I'm only telling you because you obviously think I have something to do with Sydney's disappearance or those people killing themselves and I didn't."

"Well, it's not looking good for you. I suggest you start telling the truth. Now," I reply.

Lila lets out a heavy breath. "I didn't have a happy time growing up. I have nothing to do with my family now and it's completely because of what they let happen to me. There were a few years there when I was really depressed and I did try to kill myself once. But obviously, it didn't work. That's something I never told any of my friends, not even Van. M went through a lot of the same things and understood what I was feeling."

"I don't understand. If you went through all of that, how could you mock people who went through the same thing? Especially ones who didn't make it?" I ask.

"I wasn't mocking them. I was making the most of the situation. They had a choice and they made it. That's all any of us really have in this life, isn't it? A bunch of choices. I just decided to capitalize on that choice," she says.

It doesn't make sense to me, but it's all she's giving me.

"Thank you," I say.

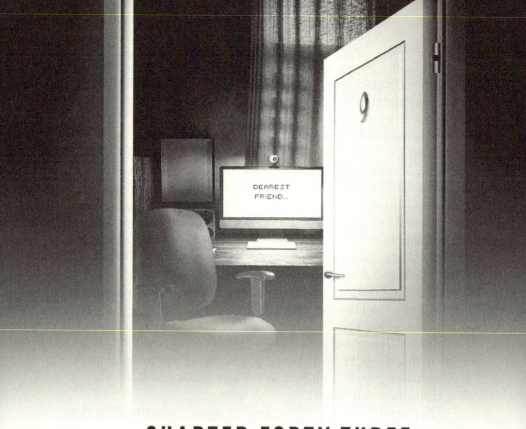

# CHAPTER FORTY-THREE

I'M EXTREMELY AWARE OF THE PASSING TIME AS I SPEND THE REST of the day and into the next trying to trace the lives of the three victims, putting together timelines of what happened.

Alyssa is able to gather some information as well and we meet up in one of the conference rooms of the precinct to piece it all together.

"What about Rachel?" she asks. "She's the only one who can tell us anything about what's leading up to this. What did she have to say?"

"Her parents haven't wanted her talking to anybody, but they were willing to give me a few minutes with her once they found out I was the one who saved her. I asked about the Shepherd, and she confirmed the same kind of story as we're finding with the others. Mysterious nameless, faceless person calling themselves the Shepherd coming into her life right when she was at her lowest point."

"They talked over a few weeks and this person encouraged her to make the decision that was right for her without thinking about anyone else because she's the only person who lives her life. She's the only one who has to be responsible for herself. When she made the decision that she wanted to kill herself, the Shepherd helped her choose drowning and the location. She said she felt really comforted and supported, and this person made her feel like she was completely in control. But she changed her mind when she hit the water."

"Thank God," Alyssa says. "So, she doesn't know who this Shepherd person is? Never got a name or met them in person?"

"No," I say, shaking my head. "They never met up. Rachel said they live in a different country and that's why they use videos. They said they wanted to be there with her, but couldn't be, so the video gave them a chance to do that. But one thing her parents mentioned to me that stood out is Rachel was out of touch with them for a few days before she went to that stream."

"Out of touch? Like she was missing?"

"Not so much missing," I clarify. "They just hadn't talked to her and didn't know where she was. But this was pretty normal for them—they go a few days without talking all the time. But Rachel herself admitted she went and stayed at a hotel to prepare herself."

"Prepare herself?" Alyssa raises a eyebrow.

"Apparently the Shepherd recommended she take some time to herself away from her usual environment as part of the full experience. She made some video diaries and talked to the Shepherd. Then it was her time and she went to the stream. She admits now that during that time she started questioning whether this was something she actually wanted to do, but because she'd already set the date and time, and was already prepared for the paid live stream, she felt a sense of… obligation."

The detective looks like she's going to be sick.

"Shit. Alright, well, according to Cora's roommate and her professors, she kept to her regular schedule right up until the end. There wasn't anything unusual about it. But Davi's family says he was missing for a week before he was found. Now, he wasn't a student and didn't have any connections to the campus, so that sets him apart from the others. But every other circumstance is just too similar to discount."

"We should reach out to all the hotels and motels within a fifty-mile or so radius of where he was found to see if he might have been staying there leading up to it," I offer. "The room might not have been in his name."

"I'll ask for security footage," she says. "We might be able to spot him."

"We need to hurry. If Angela's theory about her daughter is right, we could be getting close to the end of her time," I say.

Fortunately, it doesn't take as long as it might have to track down Davi's movements leading up to his death. Alyssa's canvass produced a hotel a couple of towns over that has footage of Davi checking in four days before his death. The manager is waiting in the lobby for me when I get there to see the footage.

Even though he said he was positive it was the same person, I'm nervous as I wait for him to cue up the video. If it's not actually Davi, we're back to the beginning.

"There," the manager says, pointing to the tall, thin young man coming into the lobby in the early afternoon days before his death. "It wasn't even check-in time yet, but we happened to have a room available. I checked him in myself. He wasn't very talkative, but I didn't get the impression there was anything wrong. It wasn't like he seemed upset or like he was trying to avoid talking to me. He just wasn't a chatty person."

"And the room wasn't in his name," I say.

"No. It was prepaid and he left cash at the desk for incidentals."

"You don't require a credit card at check-in?" I ask.

"I never have. It's one thing that sets my place apart, maybe not always for the best. But not everyone has a credit card. And hotels functioned just fine for a long time before there was such a thing as a credit card. So if the room is paid and they leave some cash at check-in, I'll let a person stay."

"Okay," I nod. "What about after he checked in? Did you hear anything from him? Did he order food, call down for housekeeping, anything?"

"He asked for extra towels and two days after he checked in, someone came to visit," the manager says.

"Do you have that on tape?" I ask.

"Sure."

My heart is beating faster as he moves the footage forward. If Davi had a visitor, I could be a step closer to seeing the Shepherd. Unfortunately, the video isn't as telling as I would hope. Rather than coming to the desk to ask about Davi's room, a figure comes into the lobby and heads directly for the elevator. It looks like a guy in his early twenties, the same age as Davi. He's wearing baggy pants and a sweatshirt with the hood pulled up.

"How do you know he was visiting Davi?" I ask.

"The doors have computerized systems in them that record every time someone opens it. His was the only door that opened within two hours of that person's arrival," the manager explains.

"Okay. Thank you for this. If you think of anything else, or find anything, please get in touch."

He agrees and I leave the hotel. I'm a bit deflated. I was hoping for more, but at least I'm getting closer to understanding the movements of the victims. It gives me some reassurance that Sydney is still alive and we have a chance to find her.

When I get back to my hotel, I'm shocked to see Dean standing in the lobby. He pulls me into a hug.

"What are you doing here?" I ask. "More importantly, what is Xavier not doing here?"

"He's here," Dean reassures me. "He's over at the aquarium having a conversation with the starfish. Remember, I told you we were going to be in the area. I know you said you didn't need us to stop by, but I figured it would be good to visit for a little bit anyway."

"Thank you," I say.

I hug him again, stepping back when Xavier comes up.

"I don't think calling it a chocolate chip starfish is a good idea. That implies a certain edible quality I'm sure he would prefer those who are easily swayed not to believe."

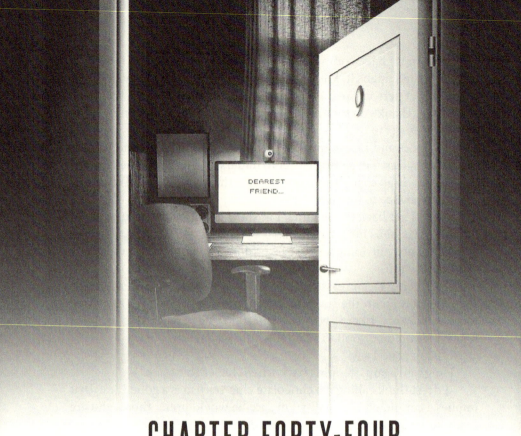

# CHAPTER FORTY-FOUR

THE BLANKET SETTLING AROUND MY SHOULDERS MAKES ME MORE aware of the cold in the moment before it warms me up. I reach up to take hold of the sides and tug it closer around me.

"Thank you," I say.

Xavier nods as he bundles up in his own blanket in the other chair on the hotel balcony.

"It's a nice view," he says.

I look over at him. "It's a parking lot."

"But the lines are so straight."

I laugh softly and scoot my chair closer to Xavier's. We look out over the parking lot for a few silent minutes. He doesn't ask me why I'm sitting on the balcony in the middle of the night, or what I'm thinking about. I can talk or I can stay quiet. Either way works for him.

"Have you ever thought about killing yourself?" I finally ask.

"No," he says. "But I've thought about not existing anymore."

"Are they different?" I ask.

"Life is precious, Emma. So valuable I'd never willingly take it away from myself. But also so valuable there are times when I thought it would be better to rid it of the burden of carrying me."

"You aren't a burden, Xavier."

"No one is."

I lean over to rest my head on his shoulder and stare up at the stars.

Warm, sunny weather coaxes me outside the next day and I sit on campus, still trying to immerse myself in Sydney's life. It doesn't make as much sense now as it did at the beginning. I realize now this isn't just about her. I'm sitting on a bench comparing messages and videos on my tablet when the shadow of someone stopping in front of me shades my screen. I look up and see James Underwood.

"Would it be alright if I sat with you for a second?" he asks.

I nod and gather papers and my bag from the bench beside me. "Sure."

He sits down. "I'm glad I ran into you. I was going to call you when I got to my office."

"Oh?"

"I've been doing extra group sessions and some open house sessions to help the students cope with what's happening. In the last few I've heard the same thing," he tells me. "The kids are talking about some person who is finding people online and guiding them through deciding to commit suicide and how."

I nod. "The Shepherd. No one seems to know who it is. But we have confirmed they've had contact with all of the victims, as well as Sydney. The question is how this person found each of them. Cora and Sydney are the closest linked. Rachel doesn't seem to have any connection to either one of them. No shared classes or activities—it doesn't look like they would have even crossed paths. And Davi wasn't even a student here. It's a matter of finding out how they were each chosen and why."

"I overheard a couple of them say they heard Cora changed her mind, but then changed it back when she heard about someone named M, who'd been through the same thing and ultimately killed himself. He wrote about how relieved and happy he was when he was coming close to it being over."

"How did they find that out?" I ask.

"I'm not sure."

"What can you tell me about the retreat that was held over spring break?" I ask.

"Not a lot."

"I thought you were the head of the small group department."

"I am, but each facilitator has a different approach for their individual groups, with different events and activities. I acknowledge that there are different beliefs and perceptions, and those influence how a person gives and receives therapy. I might disagree with the direction the facilitators take with their groups, but I can't outright reject it based solely on my own views, because that negates their beliefs and those of the patients, which diminishes therapeutic benefit."

"So, you disagreed with the retreat?" I ask.

He hesitates like he doesn't want to talk about this, but nods. "I take the approach that every person who contemplates committing suicide is responding in the moment and has a moment ahead of them when they would change their mind. There is never a time when ending your life is the right option. No matter what the situation."

This comes as a surprise. For some reason, I wasn't expecting him to make a statement that seems so intuitive, like it should be the general approach of the vast majority of people, particularly doctors and counselors tasked with helping people cope with the greatest challenges in their lives. Part of me was expecting some philosophical equivocation.

"That's not how the other facilitators see it?" I ask.

"It's not that they are pro-suicide," James explains. "They take what they refer to as an individualistic approach. Life is the sole territory and belonging of the individual, and so to them, it is not up to anyone else to determine what becomes of that life. The idea is to empower the individual to make their own decisions for their own body. Ideally, of course, drastic measures such as suicide would be avoided because of the empowerment of the patient—not because of a therapist specifically pressing against it.

"The official stance is that the doctor is to stay at an arm's length from the decision and they should not make their own personal views to be a part of the therapy, just as they wouldn't be for any other situation or condition. They are to work with the patient on their depression, anxiety, and other specified issues. They can help to provide clarity and a realistic view of specific situations and events in their life that might contribute to their feelings of wanting to kill themselves, and help them to visualize what their future might be like. But that's as far as it goes."

I can't believe what I'm hearing. I think about what Xavier said, about having moments in his life when he didn't want to exist, but would have never taken his own life. I understand exactly what he means. Now I wonder if these kids ever had the opportunity to.

I think about the person in the hotel footage visiting Davi. He was there for a reason. I can't help but wonder what he said and if there was anything he could have. If he'll carry guilt with him for the rest of his life, or if he can step back from it and know he had nothing to do with it.

"I have to get to a class," James says. "I teach psychology as well as work in the counseling center."

I nod. "Thank you for coming to talk to me."

"Absolutely. I don't know if it means anything, but I thought you should know."

He gets up and hurries toward the nearest academic building. I go back to reading through the messages on my screen, but I stop seconds later. His words reverberate through my mind and swirl around with Lila's and Sydney's.

I'm grabbing my phone to call Dean when it rings in my hand.

"Angela?" I say into it.

"Emma, it was used. Her card. Her card was used," Angela says frantically.

"Her bank card?" I ask. "Sydney's?"

"Yes. I asked that the bank not freeze her account, but flag it so that if it was used at all, we would get a notification. I just got a message that she used her card to book a hotel room."

Adrenaline spikes through me.

"Send me the information."

Half an hour later, I'm at the hotel where Sydney's bank card was used to secure a room. It's a conventional hotel that requires a credit card and an ID at check-in, meaning it was definitely Sydney who checked into the room. I explain the situation to the manager and she agrees to call up to the room.

"I'm sorry. No one is answering," she says after a few seconds of listening to the ringing.

"It's extremely important that I confirm her safety," I say. "I can get a detective here if that's what you need, but we're really racing against time here. Is there any way you can bring me up there? You've probably heard this before and it didn't mean anything, but I assure you I'm being very literal when I say this could be a matter of life or death."

She opens the top drawer of the desk and takes out the master key.

"Come on," she says.

"Thank you."

My heart is thundering in my chest as we dart up the stairs. The manager knocks, calling through it a couple of times before using the key to open it. I want to try to step in front of her just in case there's a scene inside she shouldn't see. But she steps in first and glances around. There's no reaction, and when I step in behind her I see the room is empty. It barely looks like it's been touched. She dips her head into the bathroom and shakes it.

"It's empty."

"Can I look around?" I ask.

"Sure. I'll be at the desk if you need anything."

She leaves and I call Dean.

"Is she there?" he asks.

"No. She was. She had to have been to check in. But there's no one in the room." I walk over to the edge of the bed. "Her tablet is here. It's on the bed."

"Is there anything on it?"

I swipe my finger across the screen and expect to see a password screen, but it opens right up. A message is already up on the screen.

"There's a message. *'Settle in. We'll meet soon to make your arrangements. I will call later with the details,'*" I read out.

"Settle in?" he asks. "Didn't she just book that room?"

"Yeah. Only a few hours ago. And it barely looks like she touched anything. There definitely wasn't any settling." I notice a pad of paper on the nightstand next to the phone. "There's a notepad here next to the phone. There are indentations on it like someone wrote something."

"The note did say the person would call with details," Dean points out.

"But why would they call the hotel phone?" I ask. "She has her cell with her. In fact, why would they call at all? They messaged the tablet, so why not just leave the details there?"

"Can you read the indentations?" he asks.

I look at the paper. This whole thing feels strange. There's nothing organic about the sequence of events or how the room is set up. But I'll play along. Picking up the pen beside the paper, I lightly scratch ink across the surface so it creates a reverse image of the words.

"There's an address," I say. "And a time. Forty minutes ago."

"I'll meet you there," he says.

"No. I need you to do something else for me. Go get my notes and check the timelines I've drawn for each of them. See if you can track communications with the Shepherd and with M according to those timelines, then look for comments on the forum that might correspond with any of them. Okay? I'll call you later."

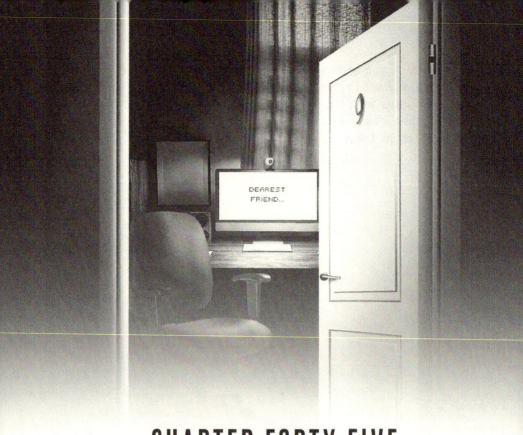

# CHAPTER FORTY-FIVE

The gravel is crunching under my feet too loudly, but there is nothing I can do about it. If someone is going to react to me being there, they are going to have enough warning anyway. The huge metal door, the only entrance, creaked when I opened that, too.

Follow the evidence. Everything points to her being here and being a danger to herself.

The tablet. The note. The perfectly secluded, defunct mail sorting building. It's all so plainly clear what is happening.

Which is why I don't trust it.

The creak of the door stops as I slide inside, trying to use as little space as necessary to get in and avoid any extra sound. The darkness inside was expected, but I was prepared. One eye was firmly shut for a few seconds outside, and when I open it and close the other, my vision improves.

I take a few seconds to survey the floor. It's mostly bare, but there are empty crates everywhere, most in various states of rot. It looks like the place was just shut down one day and they took what they could before locking the building up and walking away. It's creepy.

Slowly, I open my other eye and my vision adjusts quickly, allowing me to focus fully on the scene in front of me.

A table sits in a corner, one of those cheap megastore ones that can be put together in ten minutes and falls apart with a stiff breeze. A chair is beside it, turned out a bit like someone had been sitting there and got up quickly.

I take a tentative step forward and listen, waiting to hear the sound of someone walking around, someone waiting. I don't know why. That's not what the evidence is saying I will find.

When I hear nothing, I take a few more steps toward the table, my gun held low in both hands. I approach the table and examine the cluttered mess on top while flickering my eyes up and around to take in the surroundings. A hallway leads to what I assume is a loading dock room where trucks could pull in, and a stairway leads to a second floor just before it. A darkened doorway with a men's room sign on the wall beside it is the only other room on this floor. The door looks like it was torn off.

A book lies on the table, some schlocky detective novel with ancient crease marks along the spine. Xavier's voice pops into my mind, complaining about people leaving books open rather than using a proper bookmark, and how terrible the books look on a bookshelf afterward.

Beside the book is a pill bottle, the label ripped off. Remnants of pills, smashed up into fine blue powder, cover the cheap plywood surface.

A stack of messy, mud-caked clothes sits beside the blue-stained spot on the table. They look well-taken care of until recently. Pajama pants, a hoodie with the logo for Sugar Daddy candy in the center, socks, all piled up like the wearer just tossed them off when changing into other clothes.

A sound above me interrupts my thoughts and I freeze. It isn't footsteps, but something similar. The creak of wood. Could be rodents. Milling around upstairs, living in their own world where the decay and entropy of the building fostered the makings of a comfortable home. It could also just be the creaking of a building that's falling apart, perhaps even the reason it was abandoned in the first place.

Or.

Something shifts in the darkness of my peripheral vision. A flash of silver. Instinct takes over and I dive behind the table, knocking it over and rolling behind it.

Shots ring out, a deafening echo in the empty building filling all the available space with sound.

A bullet punctures the table and whizzes by my cheek, burying itself into the wall. Several others crater the wall where I was standing moments before. The sound is so loud, so explosive, that I don't need to call for help. Help arrives on its own.

I aim my gun in the direction of the sound and fire back, just as the metal door rips open and two figures burst inside. The bright purple of Detective Bakker's dress catches my attention. I open my mouth to shout out where I think the shooter is, and my eyes connect with Alyssa. The other officer with her raises his gun and fires into the dark stairway and for a moment, everything freezes.

Another shot. Alyssa's body jerks back violently and she spins before falling. Blood splatters the grey wall behind her and she crumples to the ground.

"Alyssa!" I cry out and stand, looking back at the darkness. Someone is running away, pounding feet echoing through the loading dock.

"Freeze!" the uniformed officer calls, chasing after the footsteps. Another gunshot rings out, but this one from his sidearm.

I run to Alyssa, pulling the walkie off my back and switching it on.

"Man down," I call into the mic, diving to my knees beside her. She's moving and moaning, which is a good sign, but I don't yet know where she's been hit. "Flood the building. Set up a perimeter. Get a bus. Go!"

Within seconds, three other officers are in and around the building, guns drawn. The officer who chased the gunman comes back, sweat pouring down his wide forehead as he holsters his gun. I roll Alyssa on her back and am elated to see her wincing in pain, a dark red spot expanding over her shoulder. She's alive.

"Alyssa, are you okay?"

"No, I just got shot," she grumbles.

"Detective," the officer standing behind me says, but my attention is on Alyssa.

"Just in your shoulder?" I ask. "Anywhere else?"

"No," she says, eyes clenching as she goes through a pain I know all too well. "Damn it!"

"Bus in route. ETA two minutes," the walkie on her hip says.

"Hear that? Two minutes. You're going to be okay."

"Uh-huh," she groans.

"Detective..."

"Son of a bitch ruined my new dress. Do you know how hard it is to find a dress this shade of purple that works for chases?"

I don't mention I don't think designers really consider the needs of a detective chasing an armed criminal when envisioning their creations. I just give her a small smile.

"Club soda," I tell her, the adrenaline still pumping in my system and making me want to get up and chase the suspect.

"Detective?"

"Yes?" I say, probably a bit more harshly than I intend.

"The suspect escaped," he says, "but they are hurt. There's blood on a doorframe. Fresh. It looks like they got caught on a piece of metal. They got out of the back and ran into the woods."

"Call for surveillance choppers," I say. "We'll find the bastard."

"We don't have those," the officer says.

I sigh.

"Do you have feet? They couldn't have gotten far," I say. "Find them."

Twenty minutes pass and the attacker has vanished. I'm sitting inside the ambulance as it trundles along the road, heading for the hospital. A nurse is applying pressure to the wound, and repeatedly reassuring Alyssa that she will be okay.

"I know," she says for the third time. "It's just my shoulder. I'll be fine."

"Just try to remain calm," the nurse says, his eyes on a monitor and his voice sounding nervous and confused.

"I *am* calm," Alyssa says. "You remain calm. I just need someone to take the bullet out of my shoulder."

In spite of everything, I can't help but try to hide a laugh. Alyssa is being a trooper and ignoring the searing pain as best she can, all while giving anyone who makes a fuss about it as much hell as she can.

"We will be at the hospital in just a couple of minutes," he says in what I assume is supposed to be a reassuring voice.

"Six," Alyssa says. "Even with your lights on, we are eight and a half miles from the hospital. If you get there in less than six minutes, the driver should be in NASCAR."

The nurse has no response to this, and Alyssa turns her attention to me.

"I'm sorry," I begin to say, wanting to express how terrible I feel about her being shot. She interrupts me almost immediately.

"Nuh-uh," she says. "No apologies. This is the job. I wasn't paying good enough attention and I got super lucky the shooter has bad aim."

"Still, I should have—"

"Should have nothing," she insists. "You did what you had to do to survive. I did what I did. I ended up shot. It's fine." She closes her eyes and winces as the ambulance rolls over a pothole and shakes the back violently enough that I have to hold onto the gurney to stay upright. She takes a long, deep breath and lets it out slowly before speaking again. "Any word on the shooter?"

"Nothing," I say, checking my phone to see if I have any texts from the other officers. "Blood on the doorway, like they scratched themselves rushing through it on a piece of metal, but otherwise, no trace. I think they got through the woods and into that subdivision on the other side of them. Probably had a car waiting."

Alyssa nods her head.

"Bastard," she says.

"Bastard," I agree.

Surprisingly, a smile stretches across her face and she rolls her head over to look directly at me.

"You know, I think I am going to get a new tattoo."

"You have others?"

"A few," she says. "But this one will be special. Going to put a circle around the wound and a little inscription. 'This scar came from working with Emma Griffin.'"

## CHAPTER FORTY-SIX

I FIND ANGELA RUNNING THROUGH THE EMERGENCY ROOM OF THE hospital and reach out to grab her shoulders and stop her. The look in her eyes is wild, tears making them red, her mouth open like she can't think of any words to say but is ready when they come.

"Where is she? Where is she?" she demands. Her eyes go to the blood on my shirt. "Oh, god."

"The detective working Sydney's case was shot in an ambush. She's in surgery to remove the bullet, but she's going to be fine."

Angela's knees buckle. "She got shot? Sydney shot someone? Why? Why would she do that? I don't understand."

I shake my head. "I don't think it was Sydney. This was the Shepherd."

"I don't... But Sydney checked into that hotel."

"She did," I nod. "But she wasn't there when I got there. There's a stairwell at the end of the hall that leads to an exit into the back parking lot. She could easily use that door and leave the hotel without being noticed or getting caught on camera. I believe she was following instructions meant to get me to that building."

"Why?" she asks.

"Because I'm getting too close to the truth," I say.

"What truth? Where's Sydney?"

Her voice is rising higher, her eyes bulging as the emotion threatens to consume her. I tighten my grip on her shoulders and meet her stare.

"Angela, I need you to trust me. That's all I can say right now. I need you to trust that I'm doing what needs to be done," I say.

She nods, but I doubt it's sincere. I can't really ask much more of her. It's difficult for a parent to truly extend trust in what amounts to a stranger when it comes to their missing child. A child who they know was wrapped up with the same people connected to two deaths and an attempted suicide.

It's a huge thing for me to ask her to trust me, but it's all I can offer right now.

I leave the hospital and get in the car with Dean. Since I rode in the ambulance, my car is still at the abandoned mail sorting facility turned crime scene.

"Are you doing okay?" he asks.

"I'm fine. And Alyssa's going to be okay, too. They have her in surgery, but the bullet didn't hit anything vital and she should be back in action after a couple of months of rehab and desk duty. Which I'm sure she is going to respond to just wonderfully."

"Sounds like you met a kindred spirit," he chuckles.

"Tell me what you found out. Were you able to talk to anybody who went to the retreat with Sydney?" I ask.

I had planned on handling those interviews, but after Alyssa was shot, I felt the need to stay with her. Having to give statements to the police and go through the initial stages of the investigation took even more time, and we don't have the luxury of approaching things casually.

"I had trouble getting anyone to tell me who was there because of privacy issues, but a little bit of swimming through the socials got me a couple of names," he tells me.

"Leave it to people to worry about privacy until it comes to posting," I say.

"Exactly. Now, obviously, there weren't any pictures of the retreat. I'm assuming things like that have a no-picture rule. But a few people made comments that sounded like they were planning on going to something that sounded very much like that retreat. And some others made posts in the days after the retreat saying straight out that they went. So, I message bombed all of them and got some responses.

"According to them, Sydney was definitely there the entire time, and seemed to be in great spirits. She was actively engaged in the activities and supportive of everyone who was there. I asked if anyone saw her going into the confessional, and only one said he did."

"Okay. And who were the facilitators running it? Mallory Kellan, I know."

"Yes. Gary Olsen and Crystal Majors."

"How about other staff? Did they mention anyone else who was working the retreat?"

"Not that they knew. It was held at a campground and they had their own staff, but they didn't really need a lot of people. They brought their own food and were mostly self-contained. There was a ranger and a camp host, but that's it. No one else from the college," Dean says.

"Perfect. And you got those timelines?" I ask.

"Yeah, but I don't know if I was reading the messages correctly. Some of the timing doesn't make any sense."

"No. I think you were reading them just fine," I say.

"Do you think the Shepherd told Sydney to make M up, or was it her idea?" Xavier asks from the back seat.

Dean's eyes snap to the rearview mirror and then back to me.

"What?" he asks. His eyes dart back and forth between us again. "What the hell?"

"M isn't real," I explain.

"And both of you figured that out?" he asks. He looks back at Xavier. "You weren't even investigating."

"I read the comments and messages," Xavier says. "The patterns couldn't be accidental. Not to mention he rose from the dead."

"What?" Dean snaps.

"You noticed it, too," I say. "You just said you don't think the timing was right. That's because you noticed the inconsistency. You just assumed it was a mistake. Or that you were thinking about it wrong. That's the thing about inconsistencies like that. They get overlooked. People don't want to admit they missed something or that they can't make the connections.

"It took me a while to notice it, but that's why I had you look over the messages. I wanted to see if you caught on. All of the interactions with M have the same kind of pattern, which makes sense if you are thinking of him as a person. He sounds like himself. But there are words and phrases that are repeated in various comments on Sydney's videos and in messages with other people. From Sydney."

"She made up an imaginary friend?" he asks. "Or did she think he was real?"

"Not exactly either," I say. "That's where him rising from the dead comes in. All three victims, as well as Sydney and Lila, the girl Van cheated on Sydney with, interacted with or heard stories about M. But the details about him shifted just slightly from person to person, and according to two of the people, he's dead. He killed himself after a courageous battle with depression ended with him taking control of his life by ending it. Cora mentioned it when talking to Shepherd. But Lila talks about him in the present tense."

"So did Sydney," Dean says. "In her videos, she thanks him and calls him her dearest friend and says he never judges her."

"Right. But she never mentions seeing him. Depending on who is watching the video, she could be talking about someone who she sees and speaks with regularly, or speaking about him in tribute and still talking to him in spirit. It's whatever they want to think according to their own experience with M.

"This isn't a psychotic break. This was intentional. There are no initial messages between the two or clues about when and how they met. The timing of the messages is always precise. She created M to use as a tool when she was talking to other people," I say.

"So, she's the one who has been encouraging people to kill themselves? Sydney is the Shepherd?" Dean asks.

"No," I shake my head. "There's someone else. And they manipulated Sydney into helping them. They recruited her. She is an example for the other people who fall into the Shepherd's grasp. She can then introduce them to M, who fits in with whatever story they need to hear to be more comfortable with their idea of killing themselves."

"Murder by proxy," Dean says.

"In a way. But the thing is, I don't think the Shepherd is trying to get people to kill themselves if they don't think they really want to," I reply. "Read that story about their sister. I think it's true. They probably changed her name and maybe even some of the details so it wouldn't be easy to trace, but I think they really did watch someone they love suffer with a horrible illness and find relief through assisted suicide."

"There's a difference between someone dying of a disease and someone with mental illness having a hard time," Dean says.

"Is there?" I ask. "My answer might not be the same as other people's. Remember what you said to me. Who's to say who is the villain and who is the hero? The Shepherd thinks they are offering support and love to a person who is making a decision about their life. They want to give them the non-judgmental support and guidance they likely aren't getting from anyone else."

"Are you saying you agree with her? That you think what they're doing is fine?" he presses.

"Absolutely not. They're manipulating vulnerable, hurting people to further their own agenda, then selling access to the aftermath. It's horrifying. And it means Sydney is in even more danger than I thought. I'd hoped with a friend as good as M, she had a chance of changing her mind. That she might have gotten wrapped up with the Shepherd, but was separating herself from it. Maybe she had even developed feelings for M and was willing to try things out. Now I know M isn't real. And her medication runs out tomorrow. She's been sustaining herself for this long, but I'm afraid, like Rachel said, her time has come. We need to find her. We figure out who did this to her from there."

# CHAPTER FORTY-SEVEN

"I NEED YOU TO THINK. WHERE WOULD SHE WANT TO BE? WHAT are her favorite places? Maybe somewhere she visited a lot when she was younger and really loved, or somewhere she always wanted to visit. Van said there were searches on her computer for different places where she wanted to go. We need to find where we think she would want to end her life."

Angela and Jasmine are sitting on the couch as I pace back and forth in front of them. They look at each other and start tossing out ideas. I have officers on speakerphone on direct order from Alyssa, ready to go to the locations or make calls to check on any lead. Sydney's medication ran out yesterday. We don't have any time left.

"One thing the Shepherd talked about to all of these people was choice. Over and over again, they talk about choice. And taking control over life and over the experience of their death. There's ritual and intention at every step of the process. I knew it wasn't actually Sydney at the abandoned building because she was told to be there and when. It wasn't what she wanted.

"Cora chose to jump from the building where she had the one class she was doing well in. Davi hanged himself in a clearing that wasn't far from the trailer where his grandmother used to live. During his vigil, his mother showed a picture of him having a picnic there with his grandmother when he was a little boy. Rachel went to the water because she didn't want to be in control. She wanted to give herself over to the water and die as close to the same time as she was born."

I stop. Blood rushes in my ears and for a second, it feels like my heart has stopped.

"Emma?" Dean asks. "Emma, what is it?"

"Angela, where did Sydney and Abigail spend the most time together?"

The color drains from her face. "Their favorite place was the treehouse in their backyard, but that was so many years ago. And the family doesn't own the house anymore."

"Call your husband. Get him over there. Now," I say.

Angela makes the call. She sounds tense and afraid as she explains to her husband what's going on, but there's also a shielded softness, like she misses him.

"He's going," she says.

"Tell him when he gets there, to video call us," I say.

The next twenty minutes stretches out into thin, untenable tension. I feel like I'm going to snap in two by the time Angela's phone rings again.

"The house looks abandoned," he reports. "I don't think anybody has been living here for years."

"See if the treehouse is still there," Angela says.

We watch as he walks through a sagging wooden gate and walks across an overgrown backyard.

"It's there," he says. "Sydney! Sydney are you up there?"

The image of an old, dilapidated treehouse appears on the screen. Slats of wood are missing from the sides and part of the platform seems to have cracked and fallen away.

There's no response, but that doesn't stop Wesley. He starts running and is soon at the bottom of a hanging rope ladder. It doesn't look stable, but he grabs onto it anyway and starts pulling himself up.

"Wesley, don't," Angela tells him. "You're going to fall."

"I don't care," he says.

The screen goes dark as he shoves the phone into his pocket and continues to climb. I don't need to see. The sound he makes when the creaking of the rope stops tells me everything I need to know.

"Thank you. I appreciate you calling me. Let me know if there's anything I can do."

I hang up the phone just as the door to the office opens and Dr. Villareal comes in. She smiles as she sits across from me.

"Agent Griffin. If we're going to keep meeting like this, we should just have coffee and go ahead and consider ourselves friends."

I give a single nod. "Maybe when all this is over. But I'm actually not here for social reasons. I wanted to be the one to tell you before you hear it on the news."

The smile fades from her face. She leans back in her chair and crosses her legs so the static-y fabric of her tights makes a rustling sound in the heavy silence between us.

"What's happening?" she asks.

"Sydney has been recovered. I'm sure you're aware that the medication she had available ran out yesterday."

"I hadn't really been paying attention, but it does make sense that the last refill was about a month ago. Where was she?" she asks.

"In the old treehouse where she used to play with her cousin when she was young. She was face up, looking at some glow-in-the-dark star stickers on the ceiling."

The therapist lets out a long breath, her head swinging back and forth as she stares at the carpet diagonally in front of her, lost in her thoughts.

"Orion," she mutters.

"I need to ask you a couple of questions. I know you can't say much, but I have to be honest, I'm really confused about this whole situation. I just don't understand what happened and I was hoping you'd be able to shed some light on some things so I can get a better grasp on them."

"Of course," she nods, her eyes lifting from the carpet to me. "What can I help with?"

"This time I'm going to have to ask you to be discreet. This is still an active investigation and I don't want some details to go out before we're ready."

"Absolutely."

"Thanks. First, we've been really looking into the other suicides and Rachel's attempted suicide. It was hard to see at first, but we found the links between all of them, and the only answer is that Sydney was responsible for it, through the persona she created called M. I thought there might have been another explanation, but now that we've found Sydney and we were able to read her note, I realize I'd gone off course. She was behind the suicides and the accounts," I say.

"I warned you she was close to a psychotic break," she says. "It was all a figment of her mind."

I nod. "I know. And it's horrifying to think of what must have been going through her head when she went into that treehouse. But what I'm not understanding is why she pretended she was missing before the others died. What did she get out of it? Or do you think she wasn't aware of it at all? That she was a different person when all that happened?"

"No," she says, shaking her head. "I don't think M was a delusion, and Sydney has never shown signs of dissociative personality disorder. These were intentional actions."

"But why?" I ask. "If she was suffering so much, why would she exploit other people's suffering? That's what I'm not understanding. Why did she intentionally go through the spectacle of disappearing, knowing her family and friends would worry about her, and work on encouraging people to kill themselves rather than just killing herself? It's like she wanted to take people with her."

"Encouraging people?" the doctor frowns. "That's how it's being interpreted?"

"One of the identities she was using to message people gave instructions for how to choose a method and talked them through coming to terms with doing it," I say.

"Come to terms with their choice," she parses. "That sounds like supporting someone for something they are going to do regardless. Showing compassion, not forcing them to do anything. I mean, I don't think we can say that there was anything malicious in Sydney's mind when she was doing those things."

"We talked about how successful Sydney was in school and her potential. Can't we say the same things about the other people? I know Cora wasn't a stellar student, but she was kind and creative. I've heard Davi had a huge family and was amazing at mechanical things. Rachel is studying to be a social worker, so she clearly wants to help people. I would think any of them would be worth saving," I say. "They might have been going through hard times, but Sydney dedicated so much of her time and energy to helping her peers cope with their mental health challenges and find ways to improve their lives. Why not these people? Why didn't she want to save them?"

"It isn't up to her to save anybody," she offers. "That's not why Sydney was in the peer counseling program, and it wasn't the goal of her working with them. That puts far too much power and control into her hands. These people were on their own path and were going to make a decision one way or the other. The question is whether it was the right choice. Some people look for angels to protect them and some just to comfort them. Maybe she was able to do both. And because she was already in contact with them, she felt responsible for seeing it through before it was her time. She promised not to abandon them, so she didn't."

I nod as I follow her lead in standing up. "I can't imagine how hard that must have been for her."

"Neither can I. In my career, it's hard not to only see the hurt. I spend a lot of time wishing there would never be a reason anyone would be in that position. I'm really sorry to rush you, but I have a session in a few minutes."

"Oh, no, I completely understand. Thank you for taking the time to talk to me."

"I hope I was of some help," she says. "For you and for Sydney."

"You were. You definitely cleared things up for me." I start toward the door. "It will be much easier for me to advocate for her now that you explained things."

"Advocate for her?" she frowns.

"When she's brought to trial. There are a lot of people, the victims' families included, who feel what she did was criminal, and there will be charges. Since I investigated the case, I'll likely be brought in to discuss it and they may ask me how I feel about what she did and what the potential consequences should be. I'll be much more comfortable speaking out for her to get medical treatment rather than just prison time. Unfortunately, I don't make those decisions and she still may end up getting a fairly harsh sentence."

"She's alive?"

I meet her eyes and nod. "Yes. They were able to stabilize her. She's still in the hospital, but should be released into custody within the next couple of days. Thank you again, doctor. You've been really helpful." I glance down at her outfit. "I really like that skirt. You always look so nice."

# CHAPTER FORTY-EIGHT

Later that evening I go to the hospital where Sydney is being treated. They have her sedated to help her body heal, so it will be a couple of days before she's able to talk to us about what happened. There aren't any other visitors on the floor, so the room is quiet and has been darkened for the night. There's still enough light to see her face and I look down at it for a few moments.

There's something surreal about looking at her now. I've seen plenty of pictures of her and I've heard her voice on the videos, but only saw her back when she was speaking. It almost feels like looking at a different person now that she is lying here, breathing softly, unaware of the world around her. Possibly even unaware that she's still alive.

I've been in that moment, the fragile, tentative place dangling somewhere between life and death, when there's the unanswered question of whether you've tipped to one side or the other. It seems like a moment that should be deeply spiritual, something mystical and awe-inducing. But it isn't.

That moment is vividly, gruesomely visceral. It is in those unsure seconds that you're forced to consider every single other moment of your life and wonder to yourself if they've been enough. You know they're not, but there's no way to fight it. There's nothing to do but to try to accept that there won't be any more chances, any more opportunities, any more moments. And yet, at the same time, wonder what will be if you do open your eyes. If anything will have changed.

That is a level of awareness that's excruciating. Awareness of the power and the failings of the body, the mind, and the basic reality of existence.

This isn't the first time Sydney has been in this moment, either. The thought of the doctor's report Angela gave me makes my throat ache. She tried to take her own life before, weeks ago, and her parents had no idea. It was typed up into her medical records and forgotten. This time she got closer. They were barely able to grab hold and drag her back.

Sydney won't be in it for much longer. They'll gradually ease the medication off and bring her out of the deep sleep. From there, she will have to learn how to move forward.

My phone buzzes in my pocket and I press it down against my thigh instinctively. I know the sound isn't actually going to disturb Sydney, but I still answer in a hushed tone.

"I'm coming. Just give me a second."

I pause at the doorway, then rush around the corner and into the small waiting room designed to give families a private space. I close the door carefully and wait. Several minutes pass without anything happening. The door doesn't open. There are no footsteps in the hallway. It's just me in the silence.

I become aware of the sound of my breath. My heartbeat gets louder in my ears. The longer I'm standing here alone in the room, the more the anxiety stings in the hairs on the back of my neck and beads sweat along my spine. Finally, I can't stand there anymore.

I come out of the waiting room and head back to Sydney's room. It's as quiet and still as it was when I left.

My phone buzzes in my pocket again, but I ignore it. I move through the hallway, looking in the rooms, checking behind the nurse's station. Ahead of me, I see the glow of the exit light above the stairwell and I move toward it, pushing through the door just as I hear a voice.

"Why didn't you choose me?"

It's Lila. The voice is coming from above me and I move quickly up the steps. As I turn the corner onto the landing two flights above, I see her. She's standing at the top of the next flight, her eyes focused up at someone above her. I try to get her attention, but she doesn't turn away.

"Why her? It could have been me. Why did you choose her?"

"You didn't have what it took, Lila. No one trusted you the way they trust Sydney. You don't really care about them. You only care about yourself." It's Dr. Villareal's voice rolling down the steps like a fog that's taken over Lila. "And I couldn't let that stand in my way."

"I did everything the same. I was exactly like her. I would have done anything you asked. Why did it have to be her?" Lila asks. "Why did you choose Sydney to help you?"

"Because she was needed. And she would make sure to do it right. Death is profitable when it's done right. But I couldn't put that in your hands. You are too selfish. You would have wanted it to be all about you." Slow footsteps echo down the hallway as the therapist descends toward Lila. "Fortunately for you, now it will be. Such a tragedy, losing two beautiful girls in the same day, just feet away from each other, both at their own hands. But it's what you both want. You remember that, don't you? You remember that feeling? It never left you, Lila. I'm just going to help you fulfill it."

I rush forward and grab Lila's waist, pulling her back away from the edge of the steps before Dr. Villareal can push her. I yank Lila away to safety just as a flicker of surprise—confusion—rage—sweeps over the doctor's face.

"You—" she sputters, but it's too late.

She stumbles, trying to right herself, but falls. Her body cracks as she tumbles down to eventually land at the concrete bottom of the steps, but she's alive. She'd managed to slow herself just enough to stop the plunge from being deadly.

Lila gasps as she stares down at her, then collapses in my arms. I lower her carefully to the floor and call Dean.

"Get doctors to the stairwell between the fifth and sixth floors. They'll need a stretcher. She was detoured, but I've got her. Sydney is fine."

I walk down the steps and crouch down beside the doctor as she groans in pain, writhing in her contorted position.

"How did you know?" she asks through gritted teeth.

"You weren't careful enough. You didn't realize how much the words you said would be parroted by the students who thought you were helping them. They trusted you, so they reflected you. And every time, they were leaving a trail. Of course, it wasn't just that. You do a good job of hiding, I'll give you that. Being able to declare yourself anonymous is helpful, especially when publishing papers and giving endowments. But I found you.

"It was smart to create distance between yourself and the small groups, but you seemed to forget that any kind of event like that retreat would require an upper administration sponsor. There was no way James Underwood would have anything to do with it, so it had to be you. That was where you got your claws into Sydney for good. You'd already been working on her for months as she posted those videos and poured her soul out to you.

"What gets me is you were actually paying attention to what was going on as well. In your own twisted way, you were trying to treat her. You said she was moving toward a psychotic break, and that was true, wasn't it?"

"Yes," she nearly spits at me.

"She has schizophrenia. It runs in her family. But she didn't know that. All she knew was that she couldn't seem to control her mind anymore. There were times when everything was fine, and then everything would change. She couldn't get through the door in the library. She went to that party and was completely out of control. She brought a stranger home to her apartment and the next day couldn't remember. She was drinking to subdue it, but that was only making it worse.

"She stopped seeing you because you recommended new medication, right? She didn't want to admit there was anything else going on, or that her thoughts were altered. But here's the thing. I've done a little research and I found out something interesting about that. People with schizophrenia often reject taking medication because they believe there's nothing wrong with them and it's the people around them trying to control or hurt them. Sydney was behaving in a completely predictable way, only no one realized it. No one paid enough attention to recognize it.

"And she took the moments of calm to the extreme. In one of her videos, she says she is afraid to look in the mirror sometimes because she doesn't know what she'll see, that she feels like a demon has formed inside her and is climbing her ribs, clawing its way up her throat, and will break her jaw in half to get out, and no one will stop it. That she won't be able to stop it. Then in that letter to her mother, she tells her that she knows that blue is her color. You dismissed it to Angela, but that's significant, isn't it?"

The sound of the gurneys is coming toward us and she tries to pull herself up as if she's going to be able to get away.

"You knew what that statement meant. That she understood what was happening to her sometimes and she wanted her mother to know, even if she was unrecognizable, that she was still in there," I say. "But you couldn't resist seeing only her pain. You talked to her about death and about releasing herself. And when she gave in, she lived. That's when she came under your control."

"You don't understand," she growls.

The doors open and the doctors rush in. I step back to get out of the way.

"Yes, I do. I knew as soon as I walked into that hotel room. You crafted that entire thing to appeal to me wanting to follow clues. You thought I wouldn't think past the breadcrumbs you left me. But you thought too hard. Sydney had no reason to go to a hotel after two weeks. She wouldn't just leave a message up on her tablet like that. And she had a cell phone, she wouldn't use the hotel phone. And it wasn't her choice. That's what you like to say, isn't it? It's all choice. But you made it look like the choice was made for her. She was given instructions on where to go and when. You could have been more creative."

The doctors get her on a board and hoist her onto the gurney.

"Oh, and one more thing." I step up to the side of the gurney and move a piece of her tattered tights aside to reveal a deep gash in her thigh. "This should probably be checked for infection. And a tetanus shot wouldn't be the worst idea. Metal in those places isn't the most sanitary." I look into her angry, pain-etched face. "You should have worn slacks."

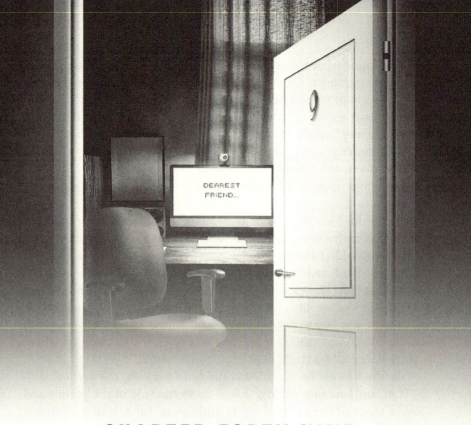

# CHAPTER FORTY-NINE

"**Y**OU LOOK LIKE YOU'RE FEELING MUCH BETTER."

Sydney nods. Her hair is brushed down glossy over her shoulders and there's more color in her face than there was the last several days.

"Jasmine came and did my makeup for me. But I am feeling better," she says.

"I'm glad."

"I want to thank you," she says. "You didn't give up on me. Even when you knew what I did."

"It doesn't matter. You were manipulated by someone you trusted. We all just want to understand what happened," I say.

She takes a breath and explains everything, from the moment she first started experiencing her new symptoms through the terror of feeling out of control, and the solace she found in the mysterious figure of the Shepherd.

"I thought I was being punished for what I'd done in the past. I was becoming a monster. Even when the doctor told me medication could help me, I didn't want to listen to her because I felt like that would only make things worse. Like it would take away the part of me that was still me, and I wouldn't be able to fight anymore.

"Hearing that I had a choice and that I didn't have to keep fighting was what I needed to hear. I wanted nothing more than to just feel like I was myself again. The more I thought about that, the more I missed my cousin. It's my fault she's dead and I wanted to be with her."

"It's not your fault," I tell her. "It's no one's fault but her father's. You didn't cause that."

"The first time I tried to kill myself, I was so angry when I woke up. I thought the monster inside me just wouldn't let go. That's when Dr. Villareal revealed who she actually was. I was upset, but she told me what I'd been through was amazing. It made me an angel. I'd survived my first journey so I could better lead others. I would still need to go, but I would choose a time and help as many others as I could before then."

"That was at the retreat," I say.

She nods. "She was in the confessional and I talked about what I'd gone through. She took that as me somehow intuitively knowing she was the person I'd been talking to all along. That's when she told me how valuable I was going to be. How much I was going to help. I felt like I'd been given a chance to redeem myself for the horrible things I'd caused. It was my chance to be worth something."

"When did the idea of streaming the suicides and selling the pictures come up?" I ask.

"She'd been connecting with people over video for a long time. She convinced them it was her way of being able to be there for them even though she couldn't physically be there. They wouldn't see her, but they knew she was watching, so it was reassuring. She found out about my videos and that I'd monetized them, and I think that's what got her thinking."

Sydney sighs and shakes her head, looking embarrassed and defeated. "I can't believe how much I let her fool me. I don't even know if anything she said was true."

"Some of it was," I tell her. "She actually did have a sister. And her sister really did have an assisted suicide. But it wasn't as smooth and clean as she made it out to be. Her sister suffered for a long time and wasn't able to find someone who would help her die. Eventually, the hospice nurse agreed to provide her with the medications to give herself an overdose. Dr. Villareal chose to make the story much prettier so it seemed peaceful and kind, but I can't help but think the real story might have been even more influential."

"I want to think she was really trying to help, at least at first," Sydney says.

"I believe she was. In her way. She just got lost somewhere along the line and got tangled up somewhere between really wanting to provide comfort and relief, and benefitting off of cultivating death."

"What's going to happen to me now?" Sydney asks.

"I don't know," I admit. "But I can promise you, I'm here. You can see my face. You can reach out and touch me if you want to." She takes hold of my hand and I smile at her. "You're going to be alright. Whatever happens, we'll deal with it then. For right now, all you need to think about is getting better."

When I leave Sydney's room, I go two floors up to the one where Dr. Villareal is handcuffed to a bed as her body tries to mend itself. I really want to think her mind is doing the same, but I know when I look at her that she doesn't need to heal. She did this because she wanted to. It was what she chose.

"Coming to taunt me again?" she asks when I step past the officer at the door and into the room.

"I didn't taunt you," I say. "I could have. I could have pointed out that you shouldn't have known about the Orion stickers on the treehouse. Or that you gave yourself away when you had Sydney start talking to Lila as M because no one in her life knew about her survived suicide attempt. No one but her therapist. It took her a while to figure that out, but she did. And I can't imagine how much that hurt. But I'm not going to bring any of that up."

"Why are you here?" she asks.

"I want to know why. You told me that people who are going to kill themselves are probably going to do it no matter what, and that Sydney wasn't encouraging them. She wasn't trying to force them to do it. So, why? What was the point?"

"To be there for them. To show them that even in their last moments, there is someone there to care for and value them," she replies. "That's the difference between peaceful choice and horror. The difference between Heaven's Gate and Jonestown. There should be someone there to give dignity and respect, and to handle the aftermath. To respect them."

"How can you talk about respecting life? You don't know what it means to cherish life or anyone living it," I say.

"Of course, I do. I love life. I cherish every second of it. It's beautiful and a gift, and that is exactly why I believe what I do. How can you say you are respecting and celebrating life when you resent every day of it? Choosing to let go is choosing to honor what it means to live," she says.

I shake my head. "No. There is nothing you will ever say to justify what you've done."

"You don't believe a person should have the right to end their suffering if they don't want to live any longer? That they should be forced to keep living even if they are in misery?"

"I can't give that question only one answer. And I am very glad I am not the one who has to make laws about it and start drawing lines and making determinations. But what I can tell you is that Rachel and Sydney are both glad to be alive. They are glad they still exist. And so am I."

I walk out of the room thinking of the months I spent fighting so hard against my therapist and how fiercely I thought I was defending myself. I didn't realize then how hard she fought back. And how glad I am that she did.

Sam, Dean, and Xavier are waiting for me when I leave the hospital. They've packed my hotel room and are ready to bring me home. I stand for a few moments in my husband's arms, holding Xavier's hand, feeling Dean's rested on my back. None of us say anything. We don't have to. I step back and let my shoulders drop, releasing the tension that they were holding.

"Let's go. Paul owes me a Game Night."

"Can I come?" Xavier asks.

"What game do you want to play?" I ask.

"Twister."

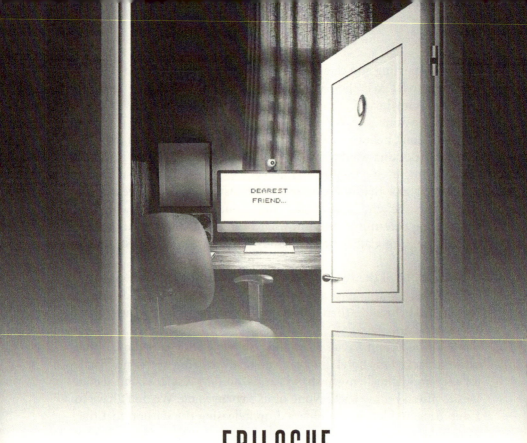

# EPILOGUE

My house smells like cinnamon rolls, coffee, and a late spring breeze coming through the window.

I heard from Angela this morning and found out Sydney was released from the hospital and decided to go to an in-patient treatment facility for a while to work through her trauma. She'll come out the other side stronger. I know she will. It doesn't mean she won't always deal with the challenges of her mental health, but she'll live, not suffer.

Sam comes in from his jog and leans down to kiss me on the top of the head.

"Is this why you couldn't join me for my jog?" he laughs as he passes through into the bathroom. "Because you needed to sit on the living room floor and eat cinnamon rolls while you read a magazine?"

"It's a newspaper," I say. "But yes."

"Newspaper?" he asks, coming back into the room and wiping his face on a towel. "Do they still make those?"

I make a face at him. "It's an article about Dr. Villareal. They're doing everything they can to tread lightly when talking about what she did."

"I guess they have to," he says. "It's not an easy topic to talk about."

"Especially when the person responsible thinks they were doing a kindness. Did I tell you she rolled herself in with Heaven's Gate? And essentially said at least she didn't cause another Jonestown? It seriously makes me feel physically ill."

"Jonestown. Wow. Reaching way back into the archives for that cult reference. But what's the other one?"

"Heaven's Gate?" I ask. He shrugs and I realize he doesn't know the story. "They thought of themselves as a religion and believed they were going to be taken to Heaven on a spaceship traveling in the Hale-Bopp comet. In order to get to it, though, they had to die, so they killed themselves. Only they did it in waves so that people were there to clean up and pose the bodies afterward. That's what she was referencing. That there should always be someone to handle the aftermath."

As I say it, I feel like a firework goes off in my brain. I drop my cinnamon roll to my plate and scramble to my feet to run to my office.

"What's going on?" Sam asks, following me.

"Someone to handle the aftermath," I repeat. I sit down in front of my computer and pull up the images of Salvador Marini's house after his death. "His fitness tracker. His dry cleaning. No mess. Someone was there."

"You already established that," Sam says.

"Yes, but they intended to be. They knew what was going to happen and they were there to clean up afterward. This was intentional, Sam. Remember Jonah's note in the ornament? *Find the Cleaners, find the truth*. Someone knew Marini was going to die." I draw in a shaky breath. "And maybe Marie, too."

# AUTHOR'S NOTE

Dear Reader,

Thank you for reading *The Girl in Apartment 9*. I hope this book answered some of the questions you had and all of your questions will be answered very soon as we wrap up this season of Emma Griffin books. Stay tuned, I appreciate your continued support with the Emma Griffin series!

If you can please continue to leave your reviews for these books, I would appreciate that enormously. Your reviews allow me to get the validation I need to keep going as an indie author. Just a moment of your time is all that is needed.

My promise to you is to always do my best to bring you thrilling adventures. I can't wait for you to read the Emma & Ava books I have in store for you!

Yours,

A.J. Rivers

P.S. If for some reason you didn't like this book or found typos or other errors, please let me know personally. I do my best to read and respond to every email at mailto:aj@riversthrillers.com

# ALSO BY
# A.J. RIVERS

### Emma Griffin FBI Mysteries by AJ Rivers

### Season One
*Book One—The Girl in Cabin 13\**
*Book Two—The Girl Who Vanished\**
*Book Three—The Girl in the Manor\**
*Book Four—The Girl Next Door\**
*Book Five—The Girl and the Deadly Express\**
*Book Six—The Girl and the Hunt\**
*Book Seven—The Girl and the Deadly End\**

### Season Two
*Book Eight—The Girl in Dangerous Waters\**
*Book Nine—The Girl and Secret Society\**
*Book Ten—The Girl and the Field of Bones\**
*Book Eleven—The Girl and the Black Christmas\**
*Book Twelve—The Girl and the Cursed Lake\**
*Book Thirteen—The Girl and The Unlucky 13\**
*Book Fourteen—The Girl and the Dragon's Island\**

### Season Three
*Book Fifteen—The Girl in the Woods*
*Book Sixteen —The Girl and the Midnight Murder*
*Book Seventeen— The Girl and the Silent Night*
*Book Eighteen — The Girl and the Last Sleepover*
*Book Nineteen — The Girl and the 7 Deadly Sins*
*Book Twenty — The Girl in Apartment 9*

### Other Standalone Novels
*Gone Woman*
*\* Also available in audio*

Made in the USA
Coppell, TX
03 June 2025

50266549R00152